D1927790

Sea Scope

Sea Scope

Debbie De Louise

Copyright (C) 2019 Debbie De Louise
Layout design and Copyright (C) 2019 Creativia
Published 2019 by Creativia
Edited by Brian Suderman
Cover art by Cover Mint
This book is a work of fiction. Names, characters, places, and incidents are the product of the author's imagination or are used fictitiously. Any resemblance to actual events, locales, or persons, living or dead, is purely coincidental.
All rights reserved. No part of this book may be reproduced or transmitted in any form or by any means, electronic or mechanical, including photocopying, recording, or by any information storage and retrieval system, without the author's permission.

Dedication

In memory of my parents, Florence and William Smiloff, who encouraged my love of reading and writing and in remembrance of John, the boy who gave me my first kiss.

Prologue

Sea Scope Inn, Twenty Years Ago

My brother Glen and I raced up the lighthouse steps. My ponytail swished wildly as my sneakers thumped against the spiraling iron. As usual, Glen pulled ahead and I slowed, my thighs aching. One hundred and sixty-seven steps later I joined him at the rail, hunched over and huffing. Smiling smugly, he stood arms crossed and relaxed.

"Beat you again, Sarah-slowpoke." He stuck out his tongue.

I straightened. "You little brat. I'll tell Mom."

Glen rolled his eyes and turned his back on me as he strolled along the edge of the gallery, peering over the guardrail.

Then he stopped.

"Hey, what's that?" he asked, leaning over the rail.

I hesitated. The last thing I wanted to do was look down. Glen, however, feared nothing.

"Get away from there, Glen. What did Dad tell us about standing too close to the guardrail?"

"You have to come see this, Sarah. There's a man down there," he said over his shoulder, pointing a chubby finger at the ground.

Despite my queasy stomach, I inched closer to the edge and followed his gaze to a man sleeping in the sandy grass. He lay face down and motionless, arms and legs spread-eagle, his plaid shirt ripped.

Chapter One

Long Island, present day

I was planning to leave even before I received my aunt's letter. The silence between Derek and I had grown too loud, too heavy. This invitation to visit my childhood home came at the perfect time.

I sucked in a cleansing breath and placed the letter on Derek's desk. He'd ask me about it eventually. Maybe.

I picked up the note and read again.

> *Dear Sarah,*
>
> *I hope you are well. I apologize for not being in touch for so long. I've been a bit under the weather but that is expected at my age. I plan to reopen the inn, and I wonder if you and your husband would like to spend some time there this summer? You can stay a week or two or the whole summer if you'd like. There will be three other guests. I'd rather not mention them by name, but you know them. I'm sure you will all enjoy becoming reacquainted.*
>
> *I'll call you sometime this week for your decision.*
>
> *Love, Aunt Julie*

Sea Scope Inn had once been a family business. It had belonged to my father and his sister, and to my grandparents before them. Aunt Julie managed it after Dad moved Mom, Glen, and me from South Carolina to New York in 1996 when I was ten. She closed the inn to the public that year but continued to live there while she worked at other bed and breakfasts along the coast from Charleston to Hilton Head.

Aunt Julie never married, although there were rumors she had plenty of opportunities. Why she'd chosen to invite me to Sea Scope now seemed strange, but I took it as a sign. Derek and I needed a break. Maybe going to South Carolina would help.

I put down the letter and went upstairs to what Derek termed "my garret," where I created sketches and artwork for the children's books I illustrated. Rosy, my red tabby, came out of hiding from behind one of my canvases. She was the inspiration for my current drawing for "Kit Kat the School Yard Cat," one of a series of books written by author Carolyn Grant, a good friend of mine.

I sat at the easel before my half-completed sketch of Kit Kat, a.k.a. Rosy, but I was inspired to draw something else. I grabbed my sketchpad and tore out a sheet. I laid down the sheet on the art table Derek had put together up here when we'd first moved in and began to pencil an outline of what I remembered of Sea Scope. As I drew, my mind filled in details. I recalled my mother telling me that my grandparents, whom I only vaguely remembered, had called the inn Sea Scope because of its view of the nearby lighthouse. Aunt Julie, an artist like me, had wanted to change the name to Seascape, but our father had insisted Sea Scope was a more suitable name, and so it remained.

The Sea Scope that spread itself across the page as I sketched was huge with several verandas and two floors wrapping around a house that commanded a lovely view of the sea. I recalled the sea gulls circling close to the top floor as Glen and I ran around playing hide and seek. As children with vivid imaginations, we also liked to concoct ghost stories and mysteries about the inn. Glen would scare me with talk of a murder upstairs in the Violet Room, the one I occupied next to his, that featured purple wallpaper and a lavender-crocheted blanket over its brass bed. He predicted that one of the guests would be smoking, even though all the guest rooms were non-smoking, and a fire would start and burn the place down. In yet another scenario, some robbers would break in and steal all the statues (there were a number of beautiful pieces of sculpture that graced both floors). Glen also imagined a time tunnel or a secret door behind the kitchen's pantry, but I laughed. My younger brother was too imaginative for his own good. How I missed him. A tear threatened to fall, as I continued to sketch. I wanted to add the two children skipping along the path in front of the house to the lighthouse, but I had to return to my work. The Kit Kat sketches were due to Apple Kids Books by the following day.

As I lay down the Sea Scope picture, the phone rang.

I thought it might be Derek, but he never called during the day unless it was an emergency.

"Hello?"

"Sarah. So nice to hear your voice," said Aunt Julie.

"Oh, hi. I just received your invitation."

"Wonderful. I hope you've been well. I'm looking forward to seeing you again. Are you and Derek able to make it?"

I paused. Aunt Julie didn't know we were no longer a couple, or at least headed for a breakup. "No. Derek won't be able to get off work. I'll be there, though. Thanks for inviting us, and I'm looking forward to seeing you again, too. How are you?"

It was my aunt's turn to pause. Through the line and hundreds of miles, I could see her, a tall woman who appeared even taller because of her fine posture. She'd taught me to practice walking by balancing books on my head.

"I'm well, but a little lonely. I'm so glad you're coming. I'm giving you your favorite room."

Aunt Julie, lonely? That was odd. When we lived at the inn, she always had people around her, and I knew she still taught painting and displayed and sold some of her portraits in the town's art gallery.

"Thank you." The Violet Room had always been my favorite, and I looked forward to the beautiful view of the sea from its windows. I could arrange to do some of my artwork there. One of the perks of my job was that I could do it anywhere.

"When would you like to come? I'm still preparing the inn for guests, but I'm telling everyone to arrive on the fifteenth. Is that good for you?"

"That's fine." Two weeks was more than enough time for me to pack up and go.

"Perfect. I'll see you then." She was about to hang up when I asked, "Aunt Julie, why did you decide to open Sea Scope this summer?"

My aunt was known for a sixth sense. I could almost believe she'd opened the inn because I needed a place to escape.

"I thought it was time, Sarah. Thank you for joining me. I look forward to having you back." Her reply was not what I expected. For some reason, I didn't believe it.

"Can you tell me something about the other guests?" I was curious about the people she'd invited to Sea Scope along with me.

"That would ruin the surprise. All I can say is that you'll be in good company. Now let me get back to work. I'm creating a portrait of Glen."

My heart sank at her words. The hurt was still raw. "I'll see you on the fifteenth, Aunt Julie."

"Wonderful. If you run into any problems with airline tickets, let me know. My friend, Karen, still works for United."

I couldn't remember Karen, but I thanked Aunt Julie again and said goodbye.

Rosy meowed at me, and I remembered I hadn't fed her. Derek would need to care for her while I was away. I was worried about how I would explain the trip to him, but I knew he wouldn't argue with me despite a few rehearsed protests. This was best for both of us, a way to prepare before the real split. In my heart, I hoped things would be different when I returned, but I didn't believe that absence made the heart grow fonder.

Chapter Two

By the time Derek came to bed, I was almost asleep. He slid in next to me as quietly as possible. It hadn't always been this way, our moving around one another like strangers. It seemed to have started two years ago with Glen's death, but it probably went back to the day he told me he wouldn't try any fertility treatments and we had to accept the fact we weren't going to be parents.

I kept my breathing steady as he turned away from me. We weren't that old. I had turned 30 back in the fall. Derek was 35. My parents had me at those same ages and Glen two years later, but they'd only been married a year before I was born. Dad's family thought he was a confirmed bachelor until Mom came along and swept Martin Brewster off his feet.

Derek began snoring. Up until two months ago, we were still making love occasionally but not with the fervor we had while trying to conceive. The doctors assured us we were both healthy. "Unexplained infertility" was the explanation that wasn't an explanation for our problem.

It was true I'd used birth control regularly until we decided to try for a family, but I hadn't taken a pill for three years. Glen's death made our situation more desperate, or at least I was desperate. The doctors said we could try in vitro, but Derek thought that was crazy. He knew our insurance wouldn't cover it and believed it was possible we could still get pregnant the old-fashioned way. Then he stopped making love to me.

I wondered if all the time he was putting into his classes and taking on extra workshops and intensives, attending teacher conferences and seminars, was his way of coping or whether he was seeing someone else. I hid my pain behind my paintings. Not the cute cat sketches, but a bunch of others I had hidden upstairs—paintings of us when we were happy—on our honeymoon riding a tandem bike, painting the rooms when we first moved into the house, lying on the beach at sunset with champagne glasses to celebrate our first anniversary. Memories that could've been in a diary but were composed on canvas instead. I'd never shown them to him, and as I respected the privacy of his office, he never set foot into my art studio unless invited.

There were a set of other paintings, too. I started them after Glen died. They were paintings of my brother and me as kids at Sea Scope inside, around, and on top of the lighthouse. There was only one of Glen as an adult the last time he'd visited me before leaving for California and his death. In the darkness of the bedroom with Derek snoring beside me, I pictured it. Glen shared many of my features in a male version. He was fair and wore his hair shoulder length. I'd always been after him to cut it, but I had to admit it looked good on him. The only fault in his face was a scar on his cheek. He'd gotten it in a college bar fight when he told someone about his father's suicide and they called his dad a coward for shooting himself and not even leaving a note of explanation.

I pushed these thoughts aside and tried to sleep. If Glen was around, I could confide in him about Derek, something I couldn't do with Mom or Carolyn even though I knew they both suspected we were having difficulty in our marriage. Glen had a special way of listening, and that's probably why he became a psychologist. I laughed to myself at the thought of him in his leather jacket riding his motorcycle around L.A. In his office, he provided a safe ear to drug addicts, those struggling with their sexuality, wannabe movie stars, and pregnant teens. He'd sit there with his hands cupped together, give them a deep appraising glance, and make them feel, during an hour on his couch, that they were still worth something, still had something to live for, unlike his own father.

I wasn't surprised when I finally fell asleep and dreamed of Glen and me at Sea Scope. There was no calendar in my dream, but I knew what day it was. I'd dreamt about it for years until Glen suggested I see his psychology professor who also had his own practice. I had two visits before I quit. Talking about the dream did nothing to eradicate it because it wasn't a dream. It was the memory of what happened that summer nearly twenty years ago. The day my brother and I found Michael's body under the lighthouse.

My consciousness took over, and the scene began to fade. I woke with a start. I was sweating and had thrown the blankets off. My stomach also felt queasy.

Derek stretched beside me but didn't wake. I glanced at the alarm clock. Two a.m. I didn't want to go back to sleep. I was afraid of having another dream. I lay in bed trying not to think of anything and then decided to go up to my garret and draw, hoping it would relax me.

Chapter Three

Sea Scope, Two weeks later

Julie Brewster had just finished a phone call with her niece Sarah. She was pleased the young woman was coming and wasn't surprised she was bringing along a friend instead of her husband, but Julie didn't like too many strangers at Sea Scope. It reminded her of what happened nearly twenty years ago when that college boy, Michael, was found dead by the lighthouse and her brother moved his family away. A year later, Martin killed himself. She squeezed her violet eyes shut a moment and then opened them wide. No time for tears or regrets. Life was for the living. Survival of the fittest and all that. She was a Brewster, descendant of a fisherman who built Sea Scope and brought his new bride through the doors. Jeremiah and Josephine Brewster made their home into a bed and breakfast to serve many of the town's tourists. They raised Julie and Martin there and taught them the hospitality trade. Josephine, a wonderful cook, taught Julie to bake muffins and other breakfast fare in the cozy kitchen where their guests joined them in the morning. Martin helped sweep the porch and the upstairs veranda, and he and Julie assisted their mother changing beds.

When their parents retired and moved to an assisted living complex in Florida, it was natural that Julie and Martin took over the family business. Julie had already earned a degree in hotel management, but Martin chose not to attend college and went into the construction field instead. After he married Jennifer, a social worker he met while working on a building project at the Beaufort clinic where she was employed, the couple moved into the suite of rooms at the top of the inn. The children arrived soon afterwards, and Jennifer left her job. Martin contributed his construction work, and Jennifer helped with the inn's bookkeeping. When they moved away to Long Island where Jennifer grew up, Julie closed the inn to the public and took jobs at nearby resorts. Without a husband and children to provide for, she managed her money well and continued to live at Sea Scope. Last year, on her sixty-ninth birthday, she decided to retire. She knew reopening Sea Scope would be a good source of retirement income, but the old fear returned. She thought it might be a good test to invite a few people she knew to stay there first.

Julie sat at the vanity in her bedroom, the room known as the inn's Gold Room. The walls were wallpapered in cream and gold. The bed featured a yellow and white bedspread and sheets. It had always been her favorite. Only the art studio directly above could compete for her affections. Like her niece, she also enjoyed painting, but her renditions weren't of cute little animals for children's books. She liked to capture portraits of people and had a collection of many faces that composed her portfolio of over forty years.

Looking at her own face as she brushed out her long auburn hair, Julie was happy with her reflection. She knew she could pass for someone in her fifties. The only wrinkles marring her skin were a few laugh lines around her mouth and eyes. She'd had a good life, a full one, and despite her family's unasked questions about marriage, she'd had many lovers and never regretted avoiding matrimony.

Julie's violet eyes, that men said reminded them of Elizabeth Taylor's and which they thought complimenting would get them a fast ticket into her bed, twinkled as she applied mascara. Everything was going to be fine. If things went well, she would ask Sarah to join her at Sea Scope and help her run the inn. She had a feeling her niece was having marriage problems. If that was the case, Sarah might be open to moving back to South Carolina. If not, maybe she could convince

Derek to relocate there with her and apply for a teaching position at the local university.

Julie still had her robe on when she went downstairs. At Sea Scope alone, she didn't bother baking muffins and breakfast treats. She'd grab fruit from the bowl on the table and put on a pot of tea. Even when one of her lovers stayed over, she rarely made a big deal over breakfast. Usually, she'd talk him into getting up and making eggs for them.

As she chose an apple from the wrought-iron fruit basket, she heard a noise at the front door. There was a small mailbox on the porch, but usually she picked up the mail from the inn's P.O. box in town. She liked to take a daily walk there. It helped to keep her figure trim.

As she was about to check the sound, Alabaster came meowing into the kitchen looking for his breakfast. Alabaster, or Al, for short, was a black cat she'd adopted to keep her company five years ago. She'd named him for the white, stone-like material as a joke and thought it funny that he often hung out by the inn's statues that were composed of the same substance.

"Hi, Al. I was just going to check the mailbox before feeding you."

The cat followed, tail held high as Julie walked out to the porch. The postal box stood to the side beyond the rockers and patio swing. It was a long white box that needed a touch up. She made a note to repaint it when she had time.

As Al circled her legs emitting short cries that signaled his hunger, Julie checked for mail. There was one letter inside the box. It wasn't in an envelope and bore no stamp. Someone had dropped it off. She figured it was an advertisement, but when she unfolded the paper, she saw that it was a note written in childish handwriting. Each letter had been marked with a different crayon. As one sensitive to color, she realized that the hues composed a rainbow missive.

She took the paper and sat in one of the high back rockers she had covered with padding with her mother years ago and had replaced one lonely spring when she was between boyfriends.

Al continued to beg for his breakfast.

"One minute, boy. Let me read this."

Julie had forgotten her reading glasses inside. She didn't like wearing them because they aged her face. She squinted at the words, the light crayoned letters making them difficult to read.

> *"Do you really think you should reopen the inn? How many more deaths do you want on your head?"*
>
> *Your nephew, Glen*

She gasped. Al sensed her dismay and stopped crying, his body alert to danger; the fur on his back starting to rise.

She was tempted to tear up the paper but reconsidered. Should she go to the police? They were never helpful in the past, and this was obviously a prank. Glen was dead, buried in the family cemetery nearly two years ago.

She decided to ignore the note but brought it inside with her and placed it in a drawer in her bedroom.

Even though her morning was now ruined, she went back downstairs, fed Al, and ate her apple. In two days, Sea Scope would open its doors to guests. She wouldn't change her plans. Neither Sarah nor anyone else need know about the note. Everything was going to be fine.

Chapter Four

Long Island

I didn't expect Derek, at the last minute, to change his mind about accompanying me to Sea Scope. He was actually pleased that Carolyn was taking his place.

"You two girls will have a great time cavorting around Cape Bretton. Maybe you'll both pick up Southern guys," he teased.

I didn't find his comment funny. "I'm only going because Aunt Julie invited me. The place doesn't hold the fondest memories."

He looked up from his coffee cup as we sat at the kitchen table. "I think it's time you exorcised those demons, Sarah."

I didn't honor that with a reply.

"Does your mother know you're going?"

That was a difficult question. I had intentionally avoided calling her since I received the invitation. I had an aversion to lying, and yet my mother wouldn't take the news well. I couldn't risk her having another breakdown. She was on the edge, and only the numbing effects of alcohol and an assortment of pills her psychiatrist prescribed kept her from falling off the precipice. Glen's death had her hospitalized for two months.

"No. I haven't spoken with her."

"You're probably better off not saying anything." Even Derek was aware of the danger of mentioning Sea Scope to my mother.

I finished my coffee and rinsed the empty mug in the sink. I was still feeling a bit queasy after the dream/memory from the night before. However, I feared there was another reason for my nausea. It started when I missed my second period last week. It would be ironic that, after all our arguments about fertility treatments, I would end up pregnant naturally. It was rotten timing and not something I wanted to share with Derek before I left. I couldn't even be happy about it because of the uncertain nature of our marriage at this point.

On the day we were departing, Carolyn arrived later than the time we had agreed to meet. She was always several minutes late, so I wasn't worried. We had allowed ourselves a full two days to get to Sea Scope with a stopover wherever we both got too tired to continue driving. I would've been happy to fly, but Carolyn hated planes.

Derek's summer intensive workshop didn't start until ten, so he was there to see us off. He had helped me pack my car and made sure my cell phone was charged and that I had first aid and highway emergency kits. He'd also filled the gas tank the night before, something I'd almost forgotten about in my haste to pack.

"Call me when you get there," he said as we stood outside, the warm July breeze weaving through his dark hair and fanning back my bangs.

He reached out and smoothed them into place with his fingertips. "You take care, Sarah."

For a moment, I saw the old warmth and wanted to postpone my plans. I could stay here and woo my husband back, tell him about the baby if my suspicions were correct, and make everything between us right again. Then Carolyn pulled up in her red sports car, and I realized it was too late. I was glad we'd agreed to use my slower but sturdier Camry for the drive.

Derek helped Carolyn move her bags into the small space that was left next to mine in the trunk.

"Why do you ladies pack so much? Doesn't your aunt have a washer and dryer down there?"

Carolyn smiled. I couldn't see her eyes through her dark sunglasses. She tapped Derek on the arm. "We aren't only bringing clothes. We need accessories, makeup, and other girl stuff."

I noted the bright blue scarf she was wearing, one of the accessories she mentioned. I had a thought about Isadora Duncan and then cleared it from my mind.

"Well, you take care of my wife. Don't drive more than two or three hours without taking a break and switching drivers."

He came back and stood at my side. "Have fun, ladies." Although he addressed both of us, he was looking at me. I had another urge to call the whole trip quits, but Carolyn had closed the stuffed trunk and taken a seat on the passenger side to wait for me to join her.

"Thanks," I said. I wanted to add that I'd miss him, but his lips were on mine cutting off my words. It was a brief kiss, shortened because Carolyn was watching us, but I felt something in it I hadn't felt in a long time.

"I'll call you when we stop for the night," I said, a little breathless from the kiss.

"Even before if you want. My classes end at two today. I'll check my cell afterwards. Have a good trip and say "hi" to your aunt for me."

I nodded as I got behind the wheel. I considered keeping my visit short. There was no reason I had to stay long. Maybe Carolyn would also want to leave after a week or two. I wondered how her boyfriend Jack had taken the news of her trip.

Derek stood in the driveway waving to me as I pulled away from the house. I also saw Rosy in the front window. Derek had promised to take good care of her while I was gone, but I knew I'd miss her company rolled up on the side of my pillow at night or stretching out by my canvas as I worked upstairs in the garret.

"Aren't you excited?" Carolyn asked and then answered the question herself before I could reply. "I am. I've never been to South Carolina, and the only lighthouse I've ever seen was the one at Montauk Point when my parents took me out East as a kid."

"Don't expect much," I said. "The area is pretty, and I suppose the lighthouse is nice, but if you've seen one, you've seen them all." That wasn't exactly true. The Bretton Island Lighthouse was an attraction that brought many tourists to Cape Bretton, but my memory was tainted by what occurred there. It was the last place I looked forward to visiting.

Carolyn seemed to read my mind. "Sorry. I remember what you told me about what happened at the lighthouse, and I know that must cloud its view for you. Maybe seeing it as an adult will help you get over the experience."

She echoed Derek's comment about exorcizing my demons. As I picked up the main road to enter the highway, I wondered if that was possible. Was Aunt Julie trying to do that same thing by reopening the inn?

The beginning of our drive went well. We still faced a bottleneck of traffic crossing the bridges and passing through the endless toll booths, but Carolyn kept up a steady stream of conversation and questions to pass our time.

"You have to prepare me, Sarah. What is your aunt like? Who else will be staying there with us? Why did your aunt decide to open the inn now?"

I kept my eyes on the crowded road as we inched along and tried to answer. "My aunt is a strong woman. You met my mother. Aunt Julie is the exact opposite of her."

"Was your dad like your aunt?"

The sun was in my eyes, and I wish I'd had the sense to bring sunglasses like Carolyn. I lowered the visor to help shield the glare, but my eyes were still tearing. I knew part of the reason was my response to that question. "I thought Dad was strong, but I guess as a kid, you have a different view of the adults in your life."

"Sorry. I forgot he died when you were eleven."

Carolyn knew all about Dad's suicide the year after we moved to Long Island. I changed the subject to answer the earlier questions she'd thrown at me. "Aunt Julie didn't tell me who else is staying at Sea Scope. I know she invited a few people she said I knew but hadn't seen since I moved away. The place isn't officially open yet. She mentioned that this is a trial run before the grand opening this fall. She retired last year, so she needs income to supplement her pension."

"She worked at other resorts in the area, right?"

I nodded but kept my eyes ahead on the road. "Yes, but she never stayed anywhere for long because she liked to be in charge, and the only place she was ever able to totally do that was at Sea Scope."

"She sounds a bit domineering to me."

"Not really. I think the best word to describe her is confident. She prefers to guide people rather than lead them. She'll be seventy next week. She's my dad's older sister. He would've been sixty-five."

"I think I'll like her. You said she also paints."

I had a quick memory of sitting beside Glen in the oak-paneled drawing room while Aunt Julie sketched us. That drawing still hangs in my garret. "She's a portrait painter," I clarified. "I wish I had the skill to paint people."

"You do a great job with cats."

I was about to thank her, but we'd exited the bridge, and I was looking for an EZ pass lane to pay the toll.

"It's that one on the right," Carolyn motioned, waving her hand.

"Don't do that," I cautioned, following her direction.

"Sorry. You can play backseat driver when it's my turn to take over."

The red bar lifted, and we passed through the lane. I stayed right to catch the exit south. Derek and Rosy were already miles away.

We made a stop after three hours as Derek suggested. The rest stop we chose had a McDonald's and, although it was a little early for lunch, we decided to eat. We also needed to stretch our legs and use the bathrooms that, thankfully, were clean. The temperature was rising close to mid-day, and it would only get hotter as we headed south.

"I could use a cold drink," Carolyn said reading my mind as we walked into the restaurant.

"Me, too. I think I'll get a shake."

There was a long line at the counter. Women and men in t-shirts and shorts, some traveling with their children, were stopping as we did for food and rest.

"Good thing we didn't wait. Imagine this line at noon," Carolyn commented.

Ahead of us, a young blonde woman stood next to two sandy-haired children, a boy and a girl about eight and ten.

There was something about the mother that reminded me of mine all those years ago. Other than a weekend in Charleston and a family trip to Disney World when I was six and Glen was four, we had never traveled much while we lived in Cape Bretton except around Bretton Island and Beaufort, one of our neighboring towns.

I watched the little girl, a head above her brother, ask him what he wanted to order. She was acting like a server. She even held a small pad of paper in her hand. It was likely she'd been using it to draw while on their drive, as I used to do as a child.

The boy had a box of crayons. "I'll write my order," he told his sister. She handed him the pad.

"What are you having?" Carolyn asked from beside me.

I still had my eyes on the children. "A cheeseburger and small fries with a vanilla shake. What about you?"

"I'm a Big Mac girl, and I never pass up the shakes. I'll take the chocolate."

The little boy handed the pad back to the girl with his crayoned list. As much as I always loved to draw, Glen used to taunt me by hiding my crayons. He often left notes written in crayon around Sea Scope with clues to where he'd hidden them. He enjoyed the game. During our last summer there, he'd started leaving Aunt Julie his crayon clues after hiding silverware, a book, or piece of jewelry. She'd never gotten too upset over it, but our mother punished him once when he played the trick on her by hiding her favorite sweater. He'd never attempted it with Dad, but I think our father would've found it funny.

The woman was placing her family's order. She read from the scribbled paper her daughter handed her.

The heat hit me like a sudden blast, and I felt faint.

"You okay, Sarah? You look pale. Don't worry. We're next. The food will do you good, and then I'll take the wheel."

I smiled. "That prospect doesn't make me feel better."

She laughed. "I know I'm a bit heavy on the pedal, but I'll wait until we've finished eating before racing us off."

"Thanks so much."

The kids walked with their mother out of the restaurant holding their Happy Meals and sodas and squabbling over the toys.

We were next at the counter. Carolyn insisted on paying for us both with the proviso that I would pay for dinner.

There were a few benches outside, but most people were eating in their cars or saving the food for another stop. The benches had umbrellas, and I welcomed the shade as I took a seat across from my friend.

Carolyn took her Big Mac out of the brown bag and unwrapped it. "I'm starved." She put a straw in her shake and sipped it down with a bite of burger.

I ate a piece of my cheeseburger and two fries and then drank my shake.

"Not hungry, Sarah? If you eat at that rate, we'll need three days to get to Sea Scope."

I paused. I was naturally a slow eater, but my stomach was starting its waves again. I hoped I wasn't going to throw up this time.

"Please, Carolyn. I'm not feeling well."

"I don't mean to rush you. Take your time. You can wrap that up. I brought a cooler. It should stay good a few hours in that, although I'm not sure how tasty a cold burger will be. At least we can salvage your drink."

I took a deep breath. "It's okay. I'll get something later." I got up, still a bit shaky, and tossed everything into a nearby garbage can.

Carolyn lowered her sunglasses and looked at me with concern. "What's wrong? I have Tylenol and Tums on me, and the medical kit is in the car."

"Thanks, but I don't need anything. I'm feeling better now." I took another deep breath, but the smell of Carolyn's burger lingered in the air, and I felt my stomach rise again. I stepped away toward the parking lot.

"Maybe I need to walk around a bit. You finish your lunch. I'll be right back."

The stopover area wasn't scenic, but it felt good to stretch my legs. It also helped clear my mind of the images of the family so similar to mine. I wondered about the father. Was he waiting in the car for his wife and kids to bring him back food, or were they traveling alone while he had to remain at work like Derek? The last scenario was that the woman was a single mother, divorced, widowed, or never married.

My cell phone buzzed from my purse. I forgot I'd turned it on when we'd gotten to the rest stop. Carolyn and I both had chargers with us, so we didn't have to worry about losing battery power. It still made more sense to keep the phone off while it wasn't being used.

I looked down at the display hoping there was a message from Derek, even though I knew he was still in class. I blinked a few times as I read the text. The sun was bright, causing glare on the screen. I moved into the shade of the ladies' room that I'd used earlier halfway around the spot where I'd left Carolyn.

It wasn't Derek. Nor was it an advertiser. The sender listed indicated it was Glen Brewster, my dead brother. What type of sick joke was this? I still had Glen's cell programmed into my contacts. I'd never thought to delete it, or maybe I subconsciously felt deleting it would make his death real. That's how he would explain it to me if I were one of his patients.

"Why are you going to Sea Scope, Silly Sarah?" read the black words against the white screen. I recognized the childhood nickname Glen called me.

I wanted to delete the message and pretend I'd never received it, but I couldn't bring myself to do it. Should I tell Carolyn? Share it with Aunt Julie? More importantly, who was using Glen's phone? After Glen's accident in California, his body was transported back to Long Island. Because Mother and I couldn't bring ourselves to sort through his belongings, Aunt Julie had flown to California and gone through the items in his apartment. As far as I knew, the cell phone had never turned up. When Glen's motorcycle overturned on an L.A. highway, it may have flown from his jacket or been pocketed by someone at the scene. Mom said she called the company and had the service cancelled, but I wasn't sure she did. She suffered her second breakdown a short time later.

"Sarah, are you all right?" Carolyn sprinted over to me. "I finished eating and thought I'd catch up with you." She glanced at the phone in my hand.

"Did you get a message?"

I cleared the screen. "No. I was just checking. I'm turning it off again. We should get back on the road."

I wondered if Carolyn knew I was lying. I cycled down the phone and turned in the direction of the parking lot.

Carolyn followed without a word.

Chapter Five

Sea Scope

Julie Brewster wasn't surprised her first guest arrived a day early. Wanda Wilson still lived in Cape Bretton and was one of her best friends despite the fact the woman was young enough to be her daughter. In fact, there were times Julie thought of Wanda as the child she'd never had. She knew Wanda reciprocated the feeling because Wanda's parents, traditional Southern Blacks, had evicted her from their home when she became pregnant at sixteen by a married white man.

There was a period, before the tragic lighthouse incident, when Wanda and her daughter, Wendy, lived at Sea Scope. Wanda couldn't afford to pay for room and board but made it up by accepting a job as the inn's housekeeper. The young woman worked hard keeping the rooms clean, checking in guests, and helping Julie cook and serve breakfast. Julie recognized in Wanda the toughness that was part of her own personality and rewarded her with glowing recommendations for positions in Hilton Head resorts when Sea Scope closed. Julie and Wanda ended up working together again briefly at one resort. She was a comfort to Julie when her brother took his life and again when her nephew Glen was killed in a motorcycle accident. However, Wanda and Julie drifted apart the last two years after Wendy had divorced and moved back home. Julie was looking forward to catching up with Wanda and that's why she was eager to include her old housekeeper as one of the inn's first guests upon its reopening. She also knew Sarah would be pleased to see Wanda again.

Julie was in the living room dusting and rearranging the furniture when the bell rang. Most visitors to Sea Scope used the brass door knocker in the shape of a ship's anchor, but the bell was useful because it was easier to hear from the upstairs rooms. Julie had it installed after the inn closed and she was living alone in the house.

Opening the door, she smiled. "I had a feeling you'd come early. So good to see you, Wanda."

The woman on the doorstep, in her late forties, retained a youthful appearance. Her ebony-colored skin bore no wrinkles, and her large, dark eyes were lit with energy. She rested her hand on a rolling suitcase that featured a floral tapestry design. As soon as she saw Julie, she let go of her bag and threw her arms around her. "I've missed you, Julie. I'm here to help you prepare for the big event."

Julie chuckled. She held Wanda at arm's length. The woman was tall even wearing flats under her ankle-length skirt. Despite the eighty-degree heat, she wore a light traveling coat over her sleeveless blouse.

"Don't you think about helping me. You were invited as a guest, and I would hardly call this a big event, although it's very special to me. The actual opening, as I explained when I called you, will be in the fall. You might consider this the cocktail party before the wedding reception."

Wanda grinned, her snow-white teeth standing out in contrast to her dark face. "It's still exciting, my dear. Now will you please let me in, so I can check your arrangements? I peeked in the backyard and saw that your garden is in full bloom. You'll need flowers in every room. I also brought recipes for the guests."

Julie took a step back to allow her friend to enter. "Most of the rooms are still closed off, Wanda. We're only having four guests including you. Think of this as a vacation. I'm so glad you could get the time off to make it, although I know you can only stay two weeks."

Wanda entered pulling her suitcase behind her.

"Let me take that." Julie put her hand out, but Wanda waved it away. "I can handle this fine. Have you placed me in my old room?"

"Of course." Julie knew Wanda would be partial to the peach-colored room on the second floor. Like the Gold Room, it was a cheerful place that took best advantage of the light on that side of the inn. The Peach Room was actually a small suite with a connecting door. While Wanda and Wendy had slept in the main room, the second room had been converted into a playroom for Wendy when she was young. Wanda always welcomed Sarah and Glen in there, especially on rainy days, so her daughter could have playmates. Sarah and Glen didn't have an official playroom at the inn; instead, they considered all of Sea Scope their own private playground. After they'd moved away, the place became silent. At night, alone in the empty house, Julie imagined she still heard tiny footsteps stamping up and down the stairs and echoes of giggles that were long gone.

The thump of Wanda's suitcase across the hall tiles as she rolled it toward the stairs drew Julie from her reverie. "Are you sure you can manage?"

"I'm fine. I'll take my stuff upstairs and then meet you in the living room, and we can catch up a bit."

"I'm looking forward to that. I'll make iced tea. I picked up your favorite Jasmine Spice from the tea shop in town."

"Sounds lovely, dear."

They decided to sit on the porch to talk while sipping their drinks. Julie had also brought out fruit and a few muffins.

"I apologize I didn't bake these," she said as she placed a basket on the table between their rockers, a tray holding the iced tea carafe, two small glasses, and the fruit bowl.

Wanda smiled as she picked a handful of red and green grapes. "No worries. I'm watching my diet, anyway. I brought along recipes for healthful and low-calorie baked goods. They were a great success in Hilton Head."

"I'm sure they'll be delicious, unlike those commercial diet cakes." Julie made a face as she poured the tea into the glasses and then sat next to her friend. "Not that you need to worry about your weight. You don't look a pound more than when you worked here twenty years ago."

Wanda bit into the grapes and swallowed them down with a gulp of tea. "It was much easier in those days. I was always running after Wendy, but ever since I hit forty, it takes daily workouts to keep trim." She wiped her mouth with a napkin from the tray. Julie noticed she'd removed the traces of grape on her lips without smudging her bright red lipstick.

"So, tell me what this is all about, dear?" Wanda had taken another gulp of tea and directed her eyes on her host.

Julie drank a lingering sip of tea to postpone her reply. Lowering the glass, she said, "I already told you, Wanda. I'm retired, and I need another source of income. This place is way too big for me. There's no reason why I shouldn't take advantage of it and open it to guests again."

Before Wanda could comment, there was a noise from behind them, and Al scooted on to the patio. Waving his tail high, he approached the rockers. His golden eyes scanned the women, and he let out a low "meow."

"Al," Wanda exclaimed as the cat came to rub against her ankles, his head lifting the hem of her skirt to caress them. "How did you get out here?"

Julie laughed, a bit relieved that Al made his appearance before Wanda could say anything negative about her plans. "I installed a cat door a few months ago because he was constantly crying to go in and out every few minutes. He never goes very far, but he loves the porch. He finds a sunny spot and sunbathes."

Wanda scratched the cat's head. "Good to see you, old boy." Wanda was an animal lover, even though she didn't have any herself. When she'd stayed at the inn, she'd asked Julie why she didn't keep pets there. She thought a dog at the inn would be an asset for protection as well as company for the younger guests, but Julie was always afraid of people's allergies. It was only after the inn closed that Julie got a cat and installed an alarm system in the house. She paid a monthly fee for keeping it monitored by the Cape Bretton police, but she was embarrassed to admit she hardly used it. Now that she was opening it to guests, she would start setting the alarm after ten p.m. After the menacing note she'd received a few weeks ago, she had even started using it while she was home alone.

"I understand your idea about supplementing your pension, Julie," Wanda said as Al left her and went over to his mistress. "There might be better ways. You could sell this place and move into a smaller house. You're very talented with art. If you promoted your work more, you could make a nice income."

Julie shook her head as she put her hand down to pat Al. "I've spent my life in the hospitality industry. My parents opened the inn. It's a family tradition I'd like to maintain. I can't let old shadows stop me."

"Your parents and your brother are gone. You don't have any children. There's no one to pass the inn down to."

Al suddenly raced away in pursuit of a wren he eyed in a bush. Julie watched as the bird flew off, and the cat gave up his chase. "I'd like to leave it to Sarah."

Wanda put down her glass and gazed back at Julie. "Is she one of the guests that are joining us tomorrow? Is that your plan? If so, I can tell you it's not a good idea. Sarah hasn't been back here in twenty years. The poor girl experienced the fright of finding Michael's body. She was old enough to remember that day and young enough never to forget it." Her voice rose from the gentle southern tone she usually used to one that Julie seldom heard.

"Calm down, Wanda. I'm not forcing this upon her. I don't plan to be dying anytime soon, although I'm turning seventy next week. However, when my time comes, I've put her in my will for inheriting Sea Scope. What she does with it is up to her. The reason I invited her this summer is because I haven't seen her since Glen's funeral, and I thought it would be a nice change for her to visit here. We have a lot to catch up on that can't be done over the phone or online. I was hoping her husband would accompany her, but she's bringing along an author friend instead. It doesn't matter. I'm planning to try my best to help her create new memories that will wipe out the old ones."

Wanda put down her glass and stood up, pushing back the rocker. "Do you really think that's possible? I doubt it, but I'll help if I can. I'm going to gather flowers to arrange in the guest rooms. Will you join me?"

Chapter Six

On the Road to Sea Scope

Carolyn insisted on driving the rest of the way before we stopped for the night. She said she was concerned about how pale I looked and didn't mind taking over the wheel.

"I hope you're not coming down with something, Sarah," she said when we got back in my car, and I handed her the keys.

"I'm fine, really. I can drive when you're tired." I wasn't too sure of my words. Although the nausea had subsided, I was still in shock over the weird message I'd received on my phone. It lay closed in my purse. I wasn't even bothering to plug it into the car charger.

We made better time with Carolyn at the wheel, but she adjusted her speed in consideration of my stomach and to help us avoid a ticket or accident.

"I really don't mind driving long distances," she said from beside me when we were back on the highway. "It's planes I can't stand. I hate the feeling of not being in control. When you fly, your fate is in the pilot's hands."

I was tempted to repeat the argument about there being more road accidents than plane crashes, but I was relieved to sit back in the passenger seat. While I didn't love flying, I wasn't that wild about driving either, particularly at night. Thankfully, except for a few rest stops,

Carolyn continued driving through the dark until she pulled us over at a motel somewhere in North Carolina.

"This should work for the night. I hope it's clean," she said.

We'd brought overnight bags for our stop on the way to Sea Scope. We took them from the back seat after Carolyn parked the car.

The lobby of the Econo Lodge was plain and efficient looking. There was a young man at the check-in desk.

Before I could approach him, Carolyn cut in front of me and dug her credit card out of her wallet. She'd already arranged to pay for our overnight stay since we were using my car and gas, and she was getting free board at the inn.

"Good evening," she said to the check-in clerk. "We need a room with two beds, please. Just for tonight."

The man looked young, most likely a college student working part-time. His reddish hair was straight and neat. It hung to his ears. "Good evening, ladies," he greeted. "Our doubles have twin beds. Check out is ten a.m."

"We'll be leaving earlier," Carolyn told him. She slipped her credit card on to the counter. "Can we pay now and leave our keys in the morning?"

The man nodded. "That's fine. If you use the Cable TV or phone, there will be an additional charge added to the card."

"No problem."

I stood next to Carolyn as the transaction was completed, and she took the printed receipt and two room key cards from the clerk. She handed me one. It said "105."

"Head down the hall to the right," the clerk directed us with a finger pointed toward the lobby. "Have a nice stay. We don't have a restaurant, but you can grab something at the Dunkin' Donuts across the street for breakfast."

"Thanks," we said in unison.

As we toted our bags down the hall, Carolyn remarked in a whisper, "It's pretty quiet here. I don't think they get many guests. That's not a good sign."

"It's Thursday night, Carolyn. I'm sure more people will check in tomorrow for the weekend."

The floorboards creaked under the thin carpet as we located our room. It was halfway down the hall, an identical beige door to its neighbor.

As Carolyn inserted the key card and waited for the green light, something I never had patience with, a woman about my mother's age and twice her weight came down the hall pushing a trolley full of bedding and towels.

"Good evening, ladies," she smiled. "If you need anything during your stay, call room service."

"Thank you," Carolyn said as she managed to line up the card in the slot and simultaneously push the door open.

The lady passed, and I followed Carolyn into the room. It was sparse but clean with twin beds covered by plain, mud-colored bedspreads. The walls were the same dark cream beige as the hall and lobby. We placed our bags on the single chair by the door. Carolyn pulled aside the brown drapes and stood before the window looking out. "Parking lot view, of course." She reclosed the drapes and turned to me. "I'll take this one if you don't mind." She brought her case over and placed it on the bed closest to the window.

"Sure," I told her as I sat on the bed by the door. The phone stood on the nightstand between us along with a plastic card listing the motel's phone directory and a small Bible.

"I'm going to freshen up and check out the bathroom, Sarah. Why don't you give Derek a call? You promised to do that when we stopped." She opened her overnight bag and removed a large Ziploc of toiletries and her pajamas.

"Thanks for reminding me," I said as she took her bag and opened the door across from our beds.

Although I'd planned to call Derek, my mind was still on the crazy text I'd received. My heart began to race as I turned on my cell phone. Would there be another message from the person who was playing such a mean prank? How did they get Glen's phone, and how did he or she know the nickname my brother had called me as a child?

An electronic beep signaled my cell was awake and a message had been received while it was turned off. My heart was still beating fast. I was almost afraid to glance at the screen. As I'd ridden next to Carolyn the past eight hours, I'd had time to think about the message and what I should do about it. I'd considered calling the number to see who would answer, but even with Carolyn running the shower water, I was afraid to do that. A text would be easier. I could reply to the one that was sent and ask who was sending it and why they were pretending to be Glen. My other option was to ignore it and wait for the prankster to send something else. If the message I'd received was from Glen's phone, that decision had already been made.

I turned on the lamp by the bed and glanced at the screen. It wasn't from Glen's impersonator. It was from Derek.

Sarah, please don't forget to call. I'm thinking of you.

My heart was still racing but now for another reason. Maybe going away to give us breathing space had been a good idea after all.

I clicked the call icon next to Derek's name.

He answered on the first ring. "Sarah, I've been waiting for your call. Is everything okay? Where are you?"

"Hi, Derek. I'm fine. We're in North Carolina at an Econo Lodge." I glanced down at the motel phone. "Room 105." I added the room's direct line. "We'll only be here overnight. Carolyn wants to make an early start after breakfast tomorrow."

Derek sighed. He sounded tired and possibly lonely. "I heated up the leftovers you had in the fridge. They were good. Rosy wanted some. I didn't think she'd like pasta, but you never know with cats." He laughed, but he didn't sound happy. "Please call me again tomorrow before you get back on the road. Make sure you have enough gas to finish the drive. I love you."

My heart melted. He hadn't said those words to me in months. "I love you, too, Derek. Carolyn's eager for us to continue our trip right after breakfast, so it might be easier for me to call from Sea Scope. I promise I'll do that as soon as we arrive. Goodnight, honey."

"I'll be counting the hours."

The phone signaled, "end call," as Carolyn came out of the bathroom in plaid pajamas, her hair tied into a toweled turban on her head.

"I heard that. How sweet. He misses you already."

"Aren't you going to call Jack?"

"She walked over to her bed, lowered the towel, and began to scrunch up her long hair. "I told you we don't have that type of relationship. He calls me or not."

"Your turn, Sarah. She looked toward the bathroom door that she'd left open. "It's clean in there by the way. Not spotless, but no bugs as far as I can tell."

"Well, that's a relief," I said grabbing my night items and heading for the bugless bathroom.

When I'd finished my night-time routine and joined Carolyn, she was sitting up in bed with her reading glasses riding the bridge of her nose as she jotted in a notebook.

"What are you doing?" I asked, slipping into the bed next to hers. "Did you get inspiration for the Kit Kat books from our drive?"

She paused and looked over at me. "No, but I should be working on the next book. Actually, I'm writing in my diary. I try to add to it each night before I go to sleep. It helps me wind down."

"Hmmm. I used to have a diary when I was young. I didn't have time to keep it up as I grew older." That wasn't exactly the truth. I'd started writing a diary while I was at Sea Scope. It wasn't a typical diary because, even at that young age, I'd enjoyed drawing. All my entries included artwork—not doodles but sketches. The accompanying text was usually brief. *I was on the beach with Glen and we found a horseshoe crab (with a drawing of the crab, of course). Aunt Julie and I baked breakfast for the guests this morning (illustrated with the muffins we'd made). Mom took us shopping at the Dock shops (a row of stores arranged in a line across the page). Dad took us fishing. (a copy of the fish*

I caught that made Glen jealous). The entries ended after the incident at the lighthouse. In all the commotion that day, after I got back to my room, I didn't realize my diary was missing. When I did, I thought Glen was playing a prank on me, but there was no crayon note around indicating that was the case. I expected to find it when we packed to move, but it never appeared. I could've started another one, but I took it as a sign that our time at Sea Scope was over.

"When are you going to break the news to Derek?"

I jumped out of my reverie. The question from Carolyn came out of the blue. She'd put down her notebook and glasses and was giving me that direct gaze that meant she expected an answer. It reminded me a bit of Aunt Julie when she'd found me with my hand in her cookie jar.

"What news, Carolyn?"

"Don't beat around the bush with me, Sarah. After knowing you these last three years, I can tell when you're keeping a secret. It's also very obvious you're expecting even though you're not showing yet."

Oh, God. If it was obvious to her, my aunt would know as soon as I walked through the door. "I don't want to tell anyone right away. I've only missed two periods. I haven't even had it confirmed, but I've been feeling nauseous and there are a few other signs." I thought of my sore breasts and the way my body felt different.

"We could pick up a pregnancy test at a drugstore on our drive tomorrow. If it's positive, and I'm sure it will be, you should see a doctor. Your aunt must have one. Is your family doctor still around?"

"Who knows? I haven't been back to Sea Scope in twenty years." I thought of Dr. Henderson, who Glen teased and called Dr. Hen behind his back. He would be close to seventy because he'd been around my aunt's age when he'd treated us for all our childhood ailments. "I told you I'd rather not say anything to anyone yet. Please keep this to yourself, Carolyn."

"But when do you intend to tell Derek?" she asked again.

I sighed and looked away from her gaze. "I think I told you how things have been strained between us. That was my deciding factor in accepting my aunt's invitation. I wanted to give us space. I was afraid."

I paused. "I didn't want to be one of those women who get pregnant to save their marriage. I know a baby doesn't do that."

"Oh, Sarah." Carolyn's voice took on a soothing quality as if she were comforting a child who'd scraped her knee. "Everything will be okay. You two have been trying to conceive for years. Derek will be ecstatic. I saw the way he looked at you and kissed you when he saw you off. He loves you. All couples go through these periods. Believe me, I've had enough experience with men."

"You've never been married, Carolyn. It's a whole different ball-game. I know he loves me, and I love him, but there's been something not right between us lately. I even feared he was seeing someone else." I looked back at her. She was still staring at me, but her hazel eyes had warmed.

"I think your imagination is playing tricks on you. Was there any evidence?"

"No, but he's been spending a lot of time at school and going to education conferences and even taking overnight trips. We don't talk as much as we used to, at least not about anything important. We haven't even made love since the night I probably conceived two months ago."

Carolyn was silent a moment. When she replied, it was in the same soft voice. "Honey, maybe you shouldn't have gone on this trip. Is there any chance you can get Derek to join you? It'll be like a second honeymoon. You guys need to reconnect. A change of atmosphere would help. I can only stay for two weeks. That'll be the perfect time for you to convince Derek to come. I don't care about his classes. He can find someone else to teach them." Her voice began to rise. "Your marriage is more important. For gosh sake's you're having his baby. He has a right to know. It could change things, open up his eyes a bit. I think he's already regretting letting you go."

"Do you really think so?" I already had that feeling myself but needed it confirmed by an outside party.

"Yes, definitely. Now let's try to get some rest. I set my travel alarm for six. We'll get up, grab breakfast across the street, and then hit the road. I'll start off driving and then you can take over when I get tired."

Carolyn was so much like my aunt when it came to making sensible plans. I was the one who had a hard time deciding between the right or left paths.

"You're not going to tell anyone, are you?"

Carolyn put her book aside on the nightstand between us and turned off the lamp. "I'm very good at keeping secrets, Sarah. Goodnight."

Chapter Seven

Sea Scope

Julie woke with a start. Light rain was drumming against her window, but that's not what woke her. A melody drifted from downstairs, a sad song that brought a memory along with the scent of grits and eggs. Then she remembered her first guest had arrived a day early and was most likely taking on the task of making breakfast.

She got out of bed, donned her robe and slippers, and followed the humming and aroma to the kitchen.

Wanda was dressed and standing at the stove cooking, her long dark braid bobbing to the music. Without turning around, she said, "Mornin,' Julie."

"I thought I told you I would prepare something for us for breakfast today." Julie hadn't planned anything fancy. She wasn't used to cooking for guests anymore.

Wanda looked over her shoulder. "I couldn't help it. I like to begin my day early, and a good breakfast is the best way to start. Have a seat. This is almost ready. I expected you would be up soon."

Julie bristled at the thought of being served, but she did as Wanda asked. There were two plates, glasses, and mugs on the table along with a pitcher of orange juice. She poured herself a drink as she glanced at the clock and saw it was almost 9:00. She hadn't wanted to sleep so late. Sarah and her friend, as well as another guest, would be arriving today.

"Coffee is on and so is hot water if you prefer tea," Wanda said turning off the stove and scooping scrambled eggs and grits onto a plate that she brought to the table and placed in front of Julie before she served herself.

"I'll get coffee. This is strange, your serving me."

"Like old times." Wanda's smile lit up the dim kitchen. Julie had to remember to change the lightbulbs. On gloomy days, the effect was depressing. The rain was growing heavier. Unlike the gentle spring rains that touched Cape Bretton almost daily, dripping off the hanging moss on the trees that flanked the front walk, it looked as though Sea Scope was in for a drenching.

"Listen to that rain." Wanda had gotten up again and brought toast, jam, and butter to the table. She knew where everything was. Julie had always been very organized, and she hadn't varied where she kept any of the silverware or kitchen utensils.

"I hope the rain doesn't delay your guests."

Julie was worried about that. "The other guest arriving today isn't coming as far as Sarah and her friend."

Wanda pursed her lips, her expression questioning. "When are you going to reveal who the other guests are, Julie? I tried to pry it out from you yesterday without any luck."

Julie laughed as she took a forkful of the tasty eggs and grits and swallowed it down with orange juice. "You'll know soon enough, Wanda."

"Why are you being so secretive?"

They were interrupted by a tapping at the door. At first, Julie thought it was the rain being driven against the wood by the wind, but Wanda said, "Speak of the devil. I think someone's already here."

Julie jumped up from her seat. Surely it couldn't be Sarah and her friend. She didn't expect them until the evening. "I'll get it. You wait here, Wanda."

Wanda raised her eyebrows but made no comment as Julie rushed from the table.

As Julie went to answer the door, she wondered why the visitor hadn't used the bell. Maybe it was broken again. She'd need to have it checked. Although she prided herself as being pretty handy around the house, it always helped that she usually had a man on hand to assist her. Currently between lovers, she was finding it increasingly hard to manage alone.

The knock sounded again as she reached the door. She resisted the urge to check the peephole and opened it to the tall man standing there dripping wet.

Even if he'd shown up uninvited, she would've recognized him immediately because of the physical similarity to his father.

"Russell. Come in. You're soaked." The rain had darkened and flattened his sandy curls against his head. Deep blue eyes greeted her, and she suddenly remembered she was still in her robe.

"Hello, Ma'am. So sorry I'm early. Traffic was light coming out of Savannah. I guess people are staying off the roads in this weather." He came through the door, water from his long trench coat spattering on the tiles of the entryway.

"Let me get you a towel. Do you want to change your clothes? Your room is ready. I've given you what used to be the Lighthouse Room. I don't know if you remember it from when you visited with your father. It faces the lighthouse and has nautical décor."

Russell glanced down at his suitcase. "I actually do remember it, and I think you're right. I should change."

As he picked up his case and headed for the staircase, Wanda came from the kitchen. She stopped short, and her eyes widened at the sight of the visitor. "My goodness, Russell, you're the spitting image of your father. If you were a bit older, I would've mistaken you for Bartholomew."

"You're right, Wanda, this is Bart's son, Russell, all grown up," Julie said.

Wanda smiled. "How are you Russell? Is your father joining us here, too? Do you remember me?"

Russell tipped his head in greeting. "Of course I remember you, Wanda. You always treated me to sweets when I visited." He winked. "I would shake your hand, but I don't want to get water all over you. I was about to go change. Dad is fine, but, as I told Julie, he's away with Lydia in Europe on their honeymoon."

"Lydia? I didn't realize Bart had married."

"Yes." Russell glanced over at Julie. "It was nice of you to send them a wedding gift. Dad was very appreciative."

"It was the least I could do since I couldn't attend." The truth was she hadn't felt right about accepting the invitation. She'd been surprised to receive the lace-edged card to the grand event in Savannah. It had brought back memories of her relationship with Bart, a man ten years her junior whose wild affection for her she couldn't return. Feeling happy he'd found someone but knowing it might hurt him to see her again, she'd ripped up the paper. Her gift to the couple and Russell's invitation to Sea Scope were small attempts at making amends to Bartholomew Donovan and his son.

"I'll be right back, ladies," Russell said, rolling the suitcase upstairs.

As he disappeared out of sight, Wanda called to him, "There's breakfast in the kitchen. I can heat it up for you when you come down." She turned to Julie, her face suddenly serious, "Why in the world did you invite him, and why did you give him Michael's room?"

Chapter Eight

On the Road to Sea Scope

Instead of stopping for breakfast at Dunkin' Donuts the next morning, Carolyn suggested we head to the diner next door.

"I need something a bit more substantial and healthier than fast food before I start driving, and you need good nutrition for that baby."

We were already in the car having dropped off our keys at the front desk with the morning motel clerk, an older woman who thanked us and told us to come again the next time we were in the area.

"Before we hit the diner, we need to make a quick stop in the Walgreens next door," Carolyn added. "It's better you confirm what we both already know as soon as possible."

I sighed. It was an overcast day but that would probably make driving easier without the glare from the sun obstructing the view. I wondered what the weather would be like in Cape Bretton. As a child there, I recalled the heat and humidity with rains that came often but intermittently during the summer. However, the weather never bothered me much. When you're a kid, temperatures don't affect you the same as they do when you're older. "I don't know, Carolyn. I'm not sure I want to take the test."

She was already pulling the car into a spot near the drugstore. "Why not?" She looked over at me. Because of the cloudiness, she wasn't wearing her sunglasses, and I could see the question in her eyes. "Are you afraid?"

"I am a bit scared," I admitted.

She reached over and patted my arm. "Honey, I know how much you've wanted this for so long. I'll buy the test for you and then you can try it after we eat at the diner. It won't take very long." She paused and made her final appeal. "At least do it for me. I'm dying to know if I'm right. I'm already picturing being his or her godmother, for Pete's sake."

I laughed, and it relieved the stress. "Okay. Go get it, but I'll pay you back for it. Would you like me to come with you and select one?"

She smiled. "I don't think they offer many choices, and I'm picking up the cost. It was my idea, after all, and you did agree to pay for breakfast."

I waited in the car while she went into the store. She was back within five minutes, as if she knew the exact aisle where the home pregnancy tests were found. I wondered if she'd ever used one. She was secretive about her past lovers, but she'd told me once about someone special with whom she came very close to walking down the aisle with until she discovered he was already married.

Returning with the Walgreen's bag discretely containing the box, she handed it to me.

"Thanks," I said as she restarted the car. "I think."

Carolyn dug into her sunny-side up eggs and hash browns as she sat across from me in the diner booth. I had ordered the same thing but was moving the fork around pretending to eat.

"What's wrong, Sarah? Are you having morning sickness again?"

I laid down my fork in the mush I'd created from the hash browns. "No. It's nerves."

"About the test?"

"That and going back to Sea Scope today. I'm looking forward to seeing my aunt, but I have no idea who else she's invited. I'm also not sure I should've left Derek." My third and unspoken reason was that

I was still thinking about the strange text message. I hadn't received another one when I checked my phone that morning, but I planned to find out who was behind it. I wasn't sure what to do yet. Carolyn's insistence on confirming my pregnancy was at least partially taking my mind off that.

"We're a bit too far to turn around. I think you'll feel a lot better after you take the test. You want to do that now and then come back and finish your plate, or maybe you want to order something else? You really need to eat."

"Yes, Mother."

She smiled. "What do you want to do?"

I had placed the Walgreen's bag in my purse and brought it with me into the diner. "I might as well get this over with." I stood up. "I'll be back in a few minutes."

Carolyn gave me a thumbs-up sign. "I almost want to go with you, but I think I'll stay and finish my meal. Don't keep me in suspense, though. I'll be waiting."

I was thankful the ladies' room was empty. The diner itself would normally be busier, but it was Saturday morning and regular commuters were still in bed. Most of the taken tables were occupied by seniors. As I made my way to the restrooms, I passed an older woman sitting with two friends and overheard her talking about her grandchildren. It made me consider my mission and what I was about to discover. If I was indeed pregnant, it wouldn't only mean that Derek and I would be parents but that my mother, a widow who now only had one child, would be a grandmother for the first time. My aunt, never married, would become a great aunt. It was, however, painful to think that Glen would've also been an uncle.

After following the instructions on the HPT, I waited for the results. I sat in the stall trying not to stare at the stick. I was accustomed to doing this and the numerous disappointments that had followed, but I'd never seriously believed I was expecting until now.

I was amazed that it didn't take long for the thin line to appear and then darken to show that the test was indeed positive. I wasn't sure if I felt like crying or jumping for joy. The emotions that welled up in me threw me for a loop. I didn't realize it would hit me that hard. I'd been avoiding the confirmation that, in my heart, I'd wanted so badly.

Wrapping the stick in toilet paper, I slipped it back in my purse. I didn't want to throw it out. Maybe I'd save it to show Derek. I wouldn't need to show it to Carolyn. She'd know as soon as she saw my face.

I tried to keep a neutral expression as I went back to join her at the table. Both our plates had been cleared, and she was sitting there drumming her nails against the counter. It looked as if she had bitten a few of them. I realized she had been as nervous as I was awaiting the news.

"You'd make a terrible poker player," she said as I sat across from her again avoiding her gaze.

"What happened to my food?"

"They're bringing a new plate. Don't avoid the issue. What's the verdict? No, wait, I see a smile peeking out the corners of your mouth. It's positive, isn't it?"

"Would you like to see the stick?" I pretended to open my purse.

"I believe you, Sarah. I would hug you right now and make a commotion, but those ladies over there might report us to the manager, and I really want you to eat before we get on the road again."

I glanced in the direction she was looking. The grandmother and her friends were staring in our direction. "When did old ladies start bothering you, Carolyn?"

"When I realized I was getting close to their age." She grinned.

The waitress arrived with my new plate before I could argue with Carolyn that she was a year younger than I was, and I'd already crossed the big 3-0 threshold of no return for women.

"Would either of you like anything else?" The waitress looked at me and then at Carolyn.

"No, thank you. I'd like to pay now while my friend finishes. We have to get back to our travels soon."

The woman nodded and tore a sheet from the pad she kept in her apron pocket. Taking a pen from the same place, she jotted down our totals and passed it to Carolyn.

"I thought I was paying," I said as Carolyn fished in her bag and took out her Visa handing it to the lady with the check.

"Consider this a congratulations breakfast. Now eat up, so we can hit the road and share the great news with your Aunt Julie."

Heading south from the diner, the clouds thickened as if we were driving toward rain. Ironically, now that I had proof of my impending motherhood, I found it hard to believe.

"So, when are you going to tell Derek?" Carolyn asked as we took the exit on to the highway.

"I was considering tonight when I let him know I've arrived safely at Sea Scope, but I think that might not work. I'd rather tell him in person. It's not something you say over the phone."

Carolyn laughed. "Are you kidding, Sarah? You know what I think?" She didn't wait for my reply but answered her own question. "I think we should pull over right now, and you make that call. Derek will be so ecstatic that he'll find someone to take over his all-important summer intensive classes and get his butt down to South Carolina."

While part of me really wanted that, I was hesitant. "I don't know, Carolyn. It's early on a Saturday morning. Derek likes to sleep late on the weekend when he's not teaching. I usually get up hours before him and work in the studio. I hate to wake him. This can wait until tonight."

"I disagree." Carolyn was firm. "Derek probably can't even sleep without you. He's most likely awake and waiting to hear from you. It'll be a wonderful surprise."

I knew there was no arguing with her. My cell phone was charging in the car's cigarette lighter. I removed it and turned it on. The screen read, "8:30." "Okay. You win. He might be up already, but he won't be expecting my call this early. I might even scare him. He's a bit worried about us being on the road."

"The worry will be replaced with joy. Believe me." Carolyn was already pulling over to what I now saw was another rest stop. "I'm going to use the bathroom to give you privacy while you make your call." She undid her seatbelt, turned to me, and patted my arm again. "Good luck, Mommy."

I watched her walk into the McDonald's and then looked down at my phone. My fingers were shaky as I tapped the contacts list and brought up Derek's name. There were two phone numbers listed; his cell and our home number. Since it was early, Derek might have his cell phone off. I decided to call the home line. I pressed it and put the device to my ear, listening as the ringing started on the other end. I suddenly realized I was holding my breath. I released it and continued to wait for a reply. After several rings, I considered hanging up. He probably was still asleep. As I was about to press the "end call" button, there was an answer.

"Hello," said a young female voice tentatively.

Oh, my God! I ended the call in shock. Tears welled up inside. I'd been right these last few weeks. Derek's sweetness at my departure was actually guilt. He had already moved his lover into our home.

By the time Carolyn got back to the car fifteen minutes later, I was sobbing into a wad of wet, pocket-sized tissues, the only ones I had on hand.

"Sarah," she gasped when she saw me. "Honey, what's wrong?" She got in the car and handed me the napkins she'd gotten with the two muffins she'd purchased in the store. "Use these, for God's sake. I can go in and get more. I thought I'd pick something up for our ride, but tell me what happened? Why are you crying? Did you speak to him? What did he say?"

I took the napkins, ignoring their roughness as I blotted my eyes and blew my nose. "I didn't talk to him," I explained, my words breaking like my heart. "Someone else picked up."

As realization hit, her eyes widened. "Oh, no. Was it a woman?"

I sniffled and looked down at my lap. I'd wadded up the soaking tissues. "Yes. It's what I thought. He's having an affair with one of his students."

"Sarah." Carolyn reached out and rubbed my arm. "Don't jump to conclusions. Call back. I'll do it if you want. There's got to be another explanation."

"No." I fought to compose myself. "I've had a feeling about this for a while now. It's a common thing. Professor cheats on wife with young student. It's my fault." I choked again. "I was so obsessed about having a child. I should've believed Derek that we didn't need fertility treatments. I shouldn't have let it build a wall between us."

"Stop blaming yourself, Sarah. If he's cheating, and that's a big "if" right now, it's his own decision. He's the one responsible, not you. But let's say you're right—and I'm not convinced about that—once he learns you're expecting, that will change things. I'm sure he's not in love with this girl who picked up the phone."

I took a breath and tried to calm myself. "I can't think of an explanation for a young woman answering our house phone at 8:30 a.m. on a Saturday. Can you?"

Carolyn looked away, and I knew the answer. "Okay, Sarah. If you don't want to call back now, we'll wait. He's expecting you to call from your aunt's house tonight. You'll ask him then before you mention the baby. There's no way he can tell that you called, right? You don't have caller ID or anything?"

I kneaded the wads in my lap like Rosy occasionally did the quilt I kept on the bed. "No. I didn't say anything, so the woman would probably tell him it was a wrong number."

"Even so, he might think it was you. He might worry and try to call."

I hadn't considered that. "I was going to turn the phone off again."

"Don't." Carolyn took the phone and placed it in the charger. "Let's get back on the road. You ready?"

I tossed the wet tissues into the small trash area between our seats. "I guess so." My heart was heavy. A part of me wanted to tell her to turn around and take me home, but I wouldn't be able to face walking through the door, smelling my husband's lover's lingering perfume, possibly finding her entwined with Derek in our bed. I feared our conversation. He was as bad a liar as I was, but men are always better at hiding the truth than women, in my opinion. I glanced out the window at the darkening skies as Carolyn maneuvered back on to the highway. We were both silent as we headed into the storm.

From the notes of Michael Gamboski

Drawing of the ancient lighthouse at Alexandria (Wikipedia)
The study of lighthouses is known as "Pharology," named after the famed lighthouse of Alexandria. Pharos of Alexandria, the first known lighthouse, was built in Egypt between 300 and 250 BC and stood 450 feet high.

Chapter Nine

Sea Scope: Twenty years ago

Sarah was excited. Today was the Fourth of July, and she and Glen would be allowed to stay up late and attend the fireworks display by the lighthouse along with Wendy, Ms. Wilson's daughter. Even better, Russell, Mr. Donovan's son, would be joining them. He'd arrived with his father that morning, and they were staying through the weekend. It was always more fun when Russell came for overnight visits. Sarah's mother said Russell made a nice companion for Glen, but Sarah considered him more of her friend because they were closer in age. He was twelve, two years older than she was, and already attended Cape Bretton Middle School. She loved talking to him about lighthouses and the town's history. His father had written several local history books, and Russ was able to quote facts that Sarah would never learn in school.

She jumped out of bed and dressed quickly. It was only seven, but she never slept late even when school was closed. There was so much to do at Sea Scope. She enjoyed watching new guests arrive, helping Ms. Wilson prepare breakfast, and playing hide and seek throughout the inn with her brother. They always had to be careful not to disturb guests or they would be punished by their father or aunt.

After pulling on a t-shirt and jeans and slipping into sneakers, Sarah started to leave the room when a piece of folded paper fell across her path. She picked it up and opened it, immediately recognizing one of Glen's crayon clues. This one read:

You can find me in the room with the view of the lighthouse.

Sarah tapped on her brother's door with the message clutched in her hand. "Glen, let me in. I found your note. Mom's going to be mad at you if she sees this." Sarah knew their mother didn't want them to interrupt Mr. Gamboski, the student from Cape Bretton University, who was spending time at the inn working on his thesis about lighthouses. Michael encouraged the children to call him by his first name. With dark straight hair and owl-shaped glasses framing a youthful, round face, he looked like a kid himself.

Glen answered the door on the third knock. "Quiet, Sarah." He was still in nautical pajamas, a finger to his lips. "I'm in the middle of an experiment." Her brother was a science nut. He liked nothing more than playing with the kits their father bought for him at the Exploratorium store in the Cape Bretton mall. He also collected additional sets from the science museum they visited once a week during the summer. The museum was within walking distance of the beach and close to the candy shop with its renowned salt-water taffy. It was also near the ice cream parlor with the best scoops in South Carolina, as Aunt Julie often claimed. They usually brought a backpack containing their bathing suits, towels, and sunscreen, so they could go on the beach after visiting the museum. Their mother said they could swim as long as a lifeguard was on duty. When they tired of the water, they could sit on the sand and watch the sea gulls swoop around or observe the other beachgoers. Before heading back to the inn, they would pick up a box of taffy to share and an ice cream cone each that they'd lick on their way home. The clothes they'd worn to the museum would be stuffed in their backpacks. Glen would have his wrapped around a new science kit. He wanted to hide it from their mother who said he made too much of a mess with the materials, but their dad encouraged his interest and even gave him extra money with his allowance to cover his museum visits and purchases from its gift shop.

Sarah stepped into her brother's room. Her eyes immediately noticed the large green spot by the bed that looked like goo. A glass beaker stood next to it filled with the same stuff.

"Oh, no. Glen, what are you doing? Mom will kill you."

Her brother put on his guilty expression and answered in that whiny voice she hated. "I made slime. Wanna feel it?" He stuck his hand in the goo and began bringing it to her.

She backed away. "Gross. Don't touch me with that stuff. Where did you get the ingredients to make it?" Sarah knew most science kits didn't contain all the items needed for their experiments. The extra things were usually found in the kitchen or bathroom. Their mother would have a fit if she discovered Glen had used the alcohol, baking soda, or bleach from the inn's laundry room.

"I brought stuff in my room last night. I only took a little of everything. Mom won't notice it missing."

"Maybe not, but Ms. Wilson will. She keeps track of everything here, and she'll know if something is low. She's alerted Mom to your stealing in the past."

"It's not stealing. It's borrowing." His voice was rising into a whine again.

"Borrowing means that you return what you took," Sarah explained. "I don't see you giving any of that back, and who would want it now?" She stared at the beaker that looked like it contained watery puke.

Glen still had the slime on his hands, but he knew better than to stick it on Sarah. Once, he'd stuck gum in her hair, and Dad punished him for a week by having him mop all the floors at the inn.

"You better wash your hands and clean that up," Sarah said in her big sister voice as she looked back down at the slime. "I want to find Russ and Wendy and go to the beach. The sun is starting to come out. Remember, tonight we'll all be seeing the fireworks. If Mom finds out what you did with your crayon clue or that goop, she may keep you home with her." Their mother never attended fireworks. She said loud noises bothered her. The truth was that she was deaf in her left ear, so Aunt Julie said she was afraid of losing hearing in the right.

That got through to Glen. He took the beaker into his bathroom, one of the few at the inn that was connected to a bedroom. She figured her parents had given him that one on purpose. When he came out after running the water for a good five minutes, his hands were clean, and he held a wet sponge. He got down on his knees and scrubbed up the green blotch.

"Good," Sarah commented as he stood up. "Let's go downstairs but put something on first."

Glen went to the bureau next to his bed and took out a pair of shorts and a t-shirt with a lighthouse print on it similar to the one Sarah wore. "Turn around."

Sarah laughed. She'd seen her younger brother naked before, but she respected his privacy and did as he asked.

"Okay. I'm done," he said a few minutes later.

She turned around. "You need to get rid of this." She handed him the paper with his crayoned message. "You don't have any other copies around, do you?" It wasn't unusual for him to leave a bunch of identical clues throughout the inn.

"Well…" The guilty look crossed his face again.

"You're asking for trouble. You better retrieve those."

"Why can't we just go to the beach? No one plays my game much anymore, anyway." He pouted.

She loved her younger brother, but she hated when he acted like a baby.

"You can leave them if you want, but don't blame me for what happens. I know how you love the fireworks."

"Can you help me get rid of them then? I'll tell you where I hid them."

Sarah glanced at the Barbie watch her mother had given her for her tenth birthday. It was nearly 8:30.

"Ms. Wilson will be expecting us at breakfast soon. We'd better hurry." On weekends, breakfast at the inn was served from 9 to 10 a.m. each morning. During the week, it was served earlier between 7 and 8 a.m.

She and Glen scurried down the hall trying to be quiet. Even though their mother was partially deaf, Aunt Julie and Ms. Wilson made up for it with their cat-like hearing.

The children decided to split up to cover different areas. Glen had already filled Sarah in on where he'd placed the other notes. While their family had rooms on the east side of the inn, most of the guests stayed in the West Wing and a few slept downstairs. There was also a Honeymoon Suite at the end of the West Wing. Glen directed her back to the East Wing to retrieve the notes he'd left by their parents' and Aunt Julie's rooms. He assigned himself Michael's and the Donovans' rooms. They agreed to meet in the dining hall for breakfast when they were done collecting and throwing out the notes.

"One last thing, Glen," Sarah whispered. "What did you leave in the Lighthouse Room? Do you think Michael will find it?"

Glen donned his mischievous smile. "That's the idea of the game."

"Don't tell me it's that slimy goo?"

"I wouldn't do that, Sarah. Do you think I should get rid of it?"

"You'd have to go in his room."

"I would knock first."

Sarah considered. "You might wake him and, even if he's up, he could be taking a shower, dressing, or working on that big report he's doing for school."

"Then I'll wait until he leaves the room. I'll do the others first."

"Be careful."

Glen nodded and slipped away in the other direction.

As she passed her and Glens' rooms, Sarah saw notes sticking under the two doors across the hall, the Gold Room that Aunt Julie occupied and the Garden Room that was their parents'. She tiptoed toward the doors, knelt down, and began to gather the notes.

She'd already pocketed the one by Aunt Julie's door when the one next to it opened. Her mother stood in the doorway in a robe, her short blonde hair unbrushed. "Good morning, Sarah. What are you doing out in the hall? Where's Glen?" She glanced down at the paper by her foot and picked it up. "Don't tell me he's at it again with these stupid crayon notes." She rolled the paper into a ball and handed it to Sarah without reading it. "Go throw this away and tell Glen that if he doesn't behave today, he's not going to the fireworks."

"I've already told him that, Mom. Is Dad up?"

"He's been up for hours. He said he was going for his morning jog around the lighthouse, but he should be back in time for breakfast. I'll be down in a few minutes. Why don't you give Ms. Wilson a hand in the kitchen?"

"Sure. I'll do that." Sarah left her mother and headed downstairs. In her rush, she almost collided with the statue next to the stairway. It was one of a dozen or so scattered around the inn that her grandparents collected and that Aunt Julie proudly displayed. Glen had broken one once, but luckily their father had found a sculptor who could repair it. All of them were nautical in theme. The one by the stairs was a mermaid etched in marble, her fish tail intricately carved.

Sarah still had Glen's crumpled note in her hand. She took the matching paper and tossed both of them in the trash bin discretely hidden downstairs behind a potted plant. As she walked toward the dining area, she smelled the aroma of coffee brewing and eggs frying. She also heard Ms. Wilson humming a southern tune. Wendy's mother sang in the church choir. She had a lovely, lilting voice that her daughter inherited.

When Sarah entered the adjoining kitchen, Ms. Wilson called to her. "Good morning, young lady. You're the first one up."

"No. I'm not. Mom's getting dressed, and Glen's on his way. Dad went to the lighthouse, but he should be back soon."

"Then you're in time to help me set the table." Ms. Wilson took a stack of plates from the shelf above the stove and placed them on the counter. "Can you reach these? Be careful, only take a few at a time."

Sarah was used to helping in the kitchen. "Where's Wendy?" she asked, picking up the plates.

"She's outside in the garden gathering flowers for the guest tables. She'll be in soon. Do you think you can handle a hot dish, too?"

"Yes, Ma'am." Sarah enjoyed being helpful. After placing the dishes around the dining tables, she went back into the kitchen for the plate of fried eggs that Ms. Wilson handed her with a pot holder while she carried out the hash browns. They went back one last time for the jug of fresh orange juice and the coffee pot.

"There," Ms. Wilson said, looking over the table when they were done. "All ready for our guests. Now let me fetch Wendy. She might need a hand with the flowers."

Right after Ms. Wilson went outside, Aunt Julie and Glen came into the dining room. "Hi, Sarah," she greeted. "Look who I caught sneaking around the West Wing." She held two of Glen's notes in her hands. "I was straightening out the unoccupied rooms in case we have guests checking in for the Fourth. Although we don't have reservations, we might get drop-ins."

"Please, Aunt Julie," Glen began again in his whiny voice, "Don't tell Mom or Dad. I really want to see the fireworks tonight."

Aunt Julie crumpled the papers into a ball. "I'll get rid of these, but you're still being punished. I have chores you can help me with later. I also need to know what you left in Mr. Gamboski's room."

Glen took a minute to answer. "It was a seashell that I picked up at the beach last week. It's very pretty. I even cleaned off the sand. I think he'll like it."

"That's not the point." Aunt Julie's voice had grown stern, but they both knew she had a soft side. "You shouldn't be going into guest rooms. I've warned you about that many times."

"But Michael isn't really a guest. He's a friend." Sarah knew Glen admired Michael and even looked up to him like he would an older brother.

"Just because Mr. Gamboski is with us all summer, doesn't mean you shouldn't treat him like our other guests. I'll get the shell when he's out of his room. Where exactly did you leave it?"

"On his bureau. He has cool stuff up there and lots of library books he took out to help with that big paper he's writing."

"That's called a thesis," Aunt Julie explained. "It's a report that college students write. It takes a lot of time and research."

"I don't think the shell would bother him."

Aunt Julie sighed. "I'm sure it won't either, Glen, but it's the idea that you put it there without asking."

"But that's part of the game, Aunt Julie."

She sighed louder. "I don't have time for this. I'm getting rid of these notes and will do something about the seashell later. Be prepared to work for me this afternoon, young man."

As she was about to leave, Michael arrived. He surveyed the room through the thick lenses of his glasses. "Would you all be talking about this, by any chance?" He held out a pearly, cone-shaped seashell.

Glen looked embarrassed. "I'm sorry, Michael. I put it there. It was for the crayon clue game. I won't do it again. I know I shouldn't go in people's rooms without asking."

A crooked smile touched the corners of Michael's mouth. He came over and ruffled Glen's hair. "Don't worry about it, pal. In fact, I think I'd like to keep it as a paperweight for all my notes." He turned to Aunt Julie. "No harm done, but your aunt's right that you need to ask permission before entering a room. I'm sure you wouldn't want anyone hiding things in yours while you're sleeping."

Glen looked over at Sarah. "My sister barges in on me all the time."

"I do not," said Sarah. "I always knock. You're the one who walks in on me all the time."

"Children," Aunt Julie raised her voice. "Quiet down and sit at the table. I'll be right back. I want to see what's keeping everyone." She left before Sarah could explain that their father was out, Wanda was in the garden with Wendy, and their mother was taking her usual long time putting herself together to face the day.

Chapter Ten

Cape Bretton, South Carolina: Present day

On the last leg of our trip to Sea Scope, the skies let loose and heavy rain descended on us. We'd made several stops before crossing into South Carolina, and I'd taken over the driving the last hour despite Carolyn's assurance she could handle it. I could tell by her drooping eyelids that she was nearing her exhaustion point, and we were still many miles from the inn. Neither of us had brought up Derek or the baby again. We'd driven mostly in silence and only spoken briefly about general topics when we'd had lunch and an early dinner at two of the rest stops.

I knew Carolyn was giving me time to think, and I'd come to a few decisions along the way. I wouldn't spend the whole summer at Sea Scope. I would return to Long Island with Carolyn after my aunt's birthday and attempt to salvage my marriage. I wouldn't beg Derek or throw the news of the baby in his face, but I'd confront him in a non-threatening way and ask exactly how deep his feelings were for the student with whom he was having an affair. If it was just a fling, I would forgive him and take responsibility for my part in what led him to seek a lover. If, however, it turned out that he fancied he was in love with this girl, I'd have to accept it and go on with my life. My aunt was a great role model, an independent woman who, while enjoying men, had no difficulty surviving without a husband. Mother, on the other hand, fell apart after my father died. To be honest, she'd never been strong to begin with. At eleven, I had been faced with raising my brother while my mother sunk deeper into the bottle. Although caring for a newborn was much different than overseeing a nine-year-old boy who was mature for his age, it was a wonder both we grew up normal without seeking the solace of drugs or committing any crimes. Glen's alcoholism didn't start until college, and he considered it social drinking even after he graduated with his psychology degree.

"How far is it now, Sarah?" Carolyn asked from beside me. "Are you sure you don't want me to drive? It's pretty nasty out now, and it's getting dark. I know you don't like driving at night."

"I'm fine. You relax. You've been driving all day. We'll be there soon." I was no longer looking forward to arriving at Sea Scope. I would call Derek, as I'd promised, but I'd keep the conversation short just to let him know I'd arrived safely. The serious discussion would be done in person when I returned. Even though my mind had mostly focused on the female voice that answered at my house, I also thought about the text message I'd received the previous day. I still hadn't had the opportunity to investigate it, but I meant to do that once I was alone in my room at the inn. Aunt Julie said she was giving me the Violet Room again. She would likely place Carolyn next door in what used to be Glen's room. I wondered who else had been invited to Sea Scope for this preview opening and if they were already there.

When we crossed the bridge to Bretton Island, Carolyn exclaimed, "I wish my first view of Cape Bretton wasn't in the pouring rain. It still looks lovely. I can see the lighthouse in the distance."

I'd noticed it, too, but tried to ignore the emotions that welled up in me at its sight. We followed the one-lane road to Sea Scope next to dripping Spanish moss. The road wasn't well lit. I had to concentrate to find the turns that led to the inn, relying on my memory more than the car's GPS instructions which were often inaccurate.

"It's coming up," I notified Carolyn as we took another twisting turn, the wipers furiously swishing against the windshield in a futile attempt to clear it of the downpour.

"Thank God," she said. "Be careful, Sarah. I can hardly see the road."

The tires felt like they were rolling in mud as I accelerated so the car could crest the hill up to the inn. I finally came to a stop a few feet from Sea Scope's door next to two cars, one I recognized as my aunt's Honda. I wondered who the green Fordbelonged to.

"This is it," I told Carolyn who was already gathering her purse and overnight bag. "I think we can make it inside without using an umbrella if we run for cover under the porch."

Carolyn looked ahead at the house. It was not as large as I remembered, but things always appear bigger to children. I could tell, even in the dark, that it needed upkeep. The bushes out front were overgrown and, although I couldn't see the back garden, I assumed it also needed tending.

"It's absolutely beautiful," Carolyn said with her hand on the car door. "I love these types of Victorian sea homes. It looks like the houses I saw when I visited Cape May years ago. The view of the water and lighthouse must be amazing in good weather. I can't wait to see the inside."

"I'm glad you approve. It looks a little unkempt to me and not as large as I remember, but it still exudes that Southern charm of which my aunt and father were proud. C'mon, let's make a run for it. It looks like one of the other guests is already here. No need to drag along our suitcases. The overnight bags we used in the motel should be fine. We can get the other stuff tomorrow."

Carolyn nodded, throwing open the passenger door to the onslaught of rain. I ran up the porch steps behind her. When I got there, I tapped the anchor doorknocker even though I saw there was now also a bell.

"Welcome to Sea Scope," I said, taking a deep breath as I waited for an answer.

From the notes of Michael Gamboski

Boston Lighthouse, circa 1716 (Wikipedia)
The first lighthouse built in America was Boston Lighthouse in 1716 on Little Brewster Island. It was destroyed during the American Revolutionary War and rebuilt in 1783.

Chapter Eleven

Sea Scope, Twenty years ago

Right after Michael came to breakfast, Martin Brewster came through the parlor door. He had his gray sweatpants on and a Bretton Island t-shirt that was dripping with sweat. Sea Scope didn't have air conditioning, but ceiling fans kept it tolerable during the Southern summers.

"It must be close to ninety already," he said, wiping his dark hair back from his face.

"How was the lighthouse?" Aunt Julie asked.

"It's all set for tonight. We should go there early to get the best view." Every year Cape Bretton's town committee held a fireworks show on Bretton Island. The best location was practically right on Sea Scope's front lawn by the lighthouse.

"I hope it isn't too noisy," Jennifer Brewster said, entering the kitchen. Her hair still looked unbrushed, and her green-flowered peasant blouse clashed with capri-length orange pants. Sarah was secretly glad she hadn't inherited her mother's fashion sense. Her love of art and color had come directly from her aunt.

"Put in ear plugs like you usually do, and you'll be fine," her husband told her.

Wanda came back with Wendy and, as they entered the kitchen, Mr. Donovan and Russell finally showed up.

Julie and Glen were excited to see the other two children. Aunt Julie had already promised that Russell could sleep over with Glen the whole weekend and, not to make Sarah jealous, Wendy could stay with her until Sunday.

When everyone was seated, talk continued about the evening's events. Everyone was looking forward to them except Sarah and Glen's mother. Sarah noticed Bart Donovan showing Michael a book. She figured it was one of the books Mr. Donovan had written about lighthouses and made a note to ask Russell about it when they went to the beach after breakfast.

Glen and Russell had big appetites and wiped their plates clean to the delight of Ms. Wilson, but Sarah was too eager to get outside. She mushed the hashed browns and eggs together and drank a quick sip of orange juice.

"What's wrong, Sarah?" her mother asked. She hadn't eaten much herself but had drunk several mimosas that Ms. Wilson had added to the table for the adults.

"I can't wait to get down to the beach. Can all of us go?" She looked at Wendy next to her with her napkin in her lap and her long braids pushed back, and Glen who was talking to Russell about his science experiment.

"After you help Ms. Wilson clean up."

As people began to leave the table, Sarah and Wendy stacked the dirty plates and brought them to the sink where they helped Ms. Wilson wash them. The boys continued talking.

"Shouldn't they be helping, too?" Sarah asked.

"Don't worry. I'll give them chores later," Aunt Julie said, wiping a few dishes. "Your brother owes me an hour's work today, so don't let him stay at the beach too long. I want him to pay up before we leave for the show."

When the dishes were done and Sarah and Wendy had also wiped down the tablecloth, Sarah beckoned her brother and Russell to get their beach stuff so they could leave. The children went upstairs to their rooms and then met outside on the porch with their backpacks.

Russell and Glen wore their swim trunks and a t-shirt. Sarah and Wendy both had one-piece bathing suits under tank tops and shorts. The girls were the same age and about the same height and weight. Russell, the oldest, was also the tallest while Glen, the youngest, was the shortest.

"Is the science museum open today?" Glen asked as they began their walk toward the beach.

"I doubt it," Sarah replied. "It's a holiday. The shops may be open, though. We can get candy and ice cream after we swim."

"I want to go up to the top of the lighthouse," Russell said. "My dad showed me photos of lighthouses all over the country. I'd like to compare them to yours. I even brought along my camera to take pictures."

The four of them were walking in two rows, the girls in front and the boys behind. Sarah looked back at Russell. She was amazed at how much he looked like his father with his deep blue eyes and sandy curls. She'd never seen Russell's mother. Sarah was told she'd died shortly after Russell was born. It must've been hard on Russell, but he was always happy. "Is that the book your dad was showing Michael this morning?" she asked.

His face lit up. "Yep. It's an amazing book. I'll show it to you if you'd like, Sarah." He sounded so proud of his father.

"That would be cool. Thank you, Russ." Sarah loved talking to Russell about lighthouses and the history of Cape Bretton that his father had been recording for years. Most people knew that Cape Bretton had been named for a marine killed in action during World War I but not that the young man's father had the lighthouse built in his memory.

"Does the book have anything about science in it?" Glen asked.

Russell shook his head. "No. Sorry."

Glen pouted. "Then show it to Sarah. I'm not interested in history."

"How come?"

"It's dumb. That's all."

The lighthouse was on their right and straight ahead were the small group of stores known as the dock shops and the changing rooms for the beach. The science museum was set back by itself.

"History isn't dumb," Russell told Glen. "It's very important to know about our past and the people who lived before us."

Sarah could tell Glen was ignoring him. He'd already spotted his favorite place. "Can we check to see if it's open?"

"It's Fourth of July, Glen, but go ahead. We'll meet you over there."

Glen took off like a bullet, and Sarah found herself walking between Wendy and Russell. She could see their shadows in front of her—Wendy's moving with her swinging braids; Russell's looming over both of them, a tall shadow of his father.

Sarah could imagine Wendy felt like a third wheel when she and Russell began talking about lighthouses on their way toward the museum. She felt sorry for Wendy, but the girl was rather shy and wasn't much of a talker. Sarah felt she had less in common with her than with Mr. Donovan's son even though Wendy practically lived at the inn, while Russell only came by with his father. Lately, the two of them had been visiting more often, and she was happy about that.

It turned out the museum was open but only for limited hours. Glen insisted on going in, even though he and Sarah didn't have much money because their father hadn't yet paid them their weekly allowance.

"Don't worry," the man at the check-in desk said when Glen explained. He knew them as regular customers and waved them inside.

"We don't have much time," Sarah reminded her brother. "Aunt Julie wants us home early, so you can do chores before the fireworks show."

"The museum's only open until noon today," Glen pointed out. "If you and the others want to do something else while I look around, that's fine with me."

"I think we should stay together," Sarah said. "Mom always tells us to do that."

"I agree," Russell added, walking over to a display of fossils in the first room they entered. "See, Glen, science does involve history. These are thousands of years old. Read the tags."

Glen joined him. "That looks like stuff we pick up on the beach. I'd rather be in the lab or the space room."

"Even those areas are related to history," Russell said. Glen walked past him into the next room. Wendy followed behind without saying a word. Sarah was alone with Russell for a few minutes as he continued to look at the fossil display.

"You'd better be careful when you sleep in Glen's room tonight," she said, walking around a glass case that contained a crab-like object. "He made slime this morning. I had him clean it off his floor, but he's always doing messy experiments. I wouldn't be surprised if you found something creepy in your bed." She knew that Aunt Julie had a few cots in the house for when the children slept over. She planned to move two of them into Glen and Sarah's rooms before they went into town at 9 p.m.

Russell flashed her a smile, and her heart started to flutter. Sarah had never had a boyfriend before, although a few of the boys in her fifth-grade class had a crush on her. She was turning eleven in a few months and was curious as to how it would be to kiss a boy. When Russell smiled at her like that, she had an urge to find out, but she turned away instead. One of her girlfriends at school, Carmen, who looked a bit like Wendy, told her that it was best you played hard to get with boys. She told Sarah she'd already kissed Jordan Palmer, one of the cutest boys in their class but not half as handsome as Russell.

"Don't worry, Sarah," Russell said, following her to the next exhibit. "I can handle your little brother."

A sudden noise from the laboratory section of the museum startled them. Sarah ran to find Glen. Russell raced along with her into the next room.

"Glen, what have you done?" Sarah was horrified. A table, over which a sign hung reading, "Do Not Touch," had toppled onto the floor spilling its contents.

"I didn't mean to knock it down," Glen whined. "I got too close, and it fell over."

"Is that what happened?" Sarah asked Wendy.

Wendy's eyes were so wide the whites showed around the dark pupils. "I didn't really see, Sarah."

"It doesn't matter," Russell said as a museum guard entered the room. "We're all in trouble now."

The guard looked at the four of them huddled together and then down at the floor. Broken glass from the beakers was scattered across the area and a variety of liquids mingled in a large, muddy puddle on the tan tile. "I'll get someone to clean that up. Don't go near the glass, kids. Did any of you get hurt when it fell?"

Sarah sighed with relief. The guard wasn't blaming anyone but was concerned with their safety. They all shook their heads, thankful their parents weren't being notified or charged with the museum's loss.

As the guard spoke into his phone requesting a janitor, Glen said, "I think we should go to the beach now."

Chapter Twelve

Sea Scope: Present day

The door creaked open, another sign of Sea Scope's age. I exhaled the breath I didn't realize I was holding as my aunt answered. She hadn't changed much, but it had only been two years since I saw her last at Glen's funeral. For a woman on the verge of seventy, she looked years younger. Her red hair flowed around her face but was becoming on her, unlike the shorter styles older women usually wore. It didn't have a touch of gray or white. I supposed she frequently colored her hair or had it done at the beauty parlor. She smiled at me and made the long trip worthwhile.

"Sarah. Come in. I can't believe it's still pouring out there. And you must be Carolyn." She held the door wide as we entered.

A flash of memory hit me as I stepped into the entryway. It suddenly felt like yesterday that Glen and I raced through these halls, glided down the staircase bannister, and made jokes about the guests.

Aunt Julie embraced me. Not one for showing emotion, I was surprised by the strength of her hug. "It's so good to have you back, Sarah." I noted her use of the word "back" instead of "here," implying I was moving in and not just visiting for the summer.

After a moment, she let me go and turned to Carolyn. She extended her hand. "It's so nice to meet you, Carolyn, or would you prefer I call you Ms. Grant?"

"Carolyn is fine." She shook my aunt's hand. "It's also a pleasure to meet you, Ms. Brewster. Thank you for inviting me. Your house is beautiful."

A slight pink entered my aunt's cheeks. "If I call you Carolyn, you must call me Julie, and I'll give you the grand tour tomorrow. For now, you must be tired from traveling. I assume you left your bags in the car, and I don't blame you. We'll fetch them in the morning."

"Are any other guests here?" I asked as we followed her into the living room.

"Everyone except your mother. I'm picking her up at the airport tomorrow. Her flight was delayed."

"Mom?" I was shocked. The last time I'd spoken to my mother she'd mentioned nothing about coming to Sea Scope. If I'd known, we could've driven down together. Why the secrecy?

"Jennifer was a little hesitant about coming," my aunt continued. "I didn't actually ask her until a few days ago when I sent her the airline ticket. I figured she wouldn't refuse knowing I'd spent the money. I told her not to say anything to you. At that point, I thought you were still coming with Derek. When you called and explained that you were driving down with a friend, I knew I'd made the right decision. Jennifer wouldn't have made your ride comfortable." She raised her eyebrows, and I understood what she meant.

"Have a seat, both of you. I'll put on tea unless you'd like coffee. It's a little late for that."

Carolyn and I sat next to one another on the tapestry-covered couch. A black cat entered the room and came purring and rubbed against my ankle.

"Oh, there's Al," Aunt Julie said, and I remembered she'd talked about having a cat at the inn. "I see he likes you."

"Isn't it bad luck for a black cat to cross one's path?" Carolyn asked. I knew she was partial to dogs, although she didn't currently have any pets.

My aunt laughed. "That's a crazy superstition. In parts of the world, such as England and Japan, people believe black cats bring good luck."

"Can you at least give us a hint as to who else is here?" I asked changing the subject. "I assume they're already in their rooms?"

My aunt nodded, an amused look in her eyes. "It is nearly ten p.m., but you'll meet them soon, although you already know them. Let me go put on the tea, and we can spend a few minutes chatting. As I told you, I've given you the Violet Room again, and Carolyn will be right next door." She didn't add "in Glen's room," and I was thankful for that.

After she left us, Carolyn said, "Your aunt likes surprises. I hope the weather is better tomorrow. I'd love to see the lighthouse up close."

"I'm sure that will be part of the grand tour," I told her, leaning down and petting Al who was still circling my legs.

"I'd be glad to show you the lighthouse, Ma'am," came a voice from the stairway. I blinked as a tall man entered the room, and Al scooted away. Bart Donovan. No, it was his son Russell twenty years older.

"Good to see you again, Sarah," he said. "I believe Julie said your name was Carolyn." His deep blue eyes looked toward my friend.

"Yes." Her voice sounded strange as she answered him. She stuttered. In all the time I'd known her, I'd never heard her sound flustered, but Russ had grown into a handsome man, and I also found myself reacting to his attractive grin.

"Pleased to meet you." He came to the couch and held out his hand. Carolyn stood and shook it. She looked as though she were in shock, unusual for her because nothing short of major disasters cracked her composure. He then turned to me. I got up and extended my hand, as well. Instead of shaking it, he kissed it and then embraced me and gave me another light kiss on the cheek. A jolt of memory hit me.

"Welcome back to Sea Scope, Sarah Brewster. I must say you've grown into a beautiful woman." I felt a blush heat my face as I acknowledged that he had also used the word "back" when referring to my visit. He'd also called me by my maiden name.

"It's Sarah Collins now," I corrected.

"My apologies. Mr. Collins is a lucky man."

I felt a need to explain my husband's absence. "Derek's a professor. He's teaching a summer class at the university where we live on Long Island."

As we looked into one another's eyes, a familiar voice said, "My word. We're all together again." I turned to see Ms. Wilson carrying in a tray of cookies. "Your aunt's getting the tea, but she asked me to bring these. It's so good to see you, Sarah." At least she hadn't said "back," too.

"Ms. Wilson." I left Russell and walked over to her. "You look like you haven't aged a day."

A bit of color rose in her cheeks, lightening them. "I'm middle-aged now. I was a kid, not much older than Russell and your brother, when I worked here."

She'd been even closer in age to Michael. I remembered us celebrating his twenty-first birthday when he'd stayed with us. Ms. Wilson must've been twenty-six at the time.

She laid the tray on my aunt's oval table that was decorated with a vase of fresh flowers. Ms. Wilson always loved to place floral arrangements around the inn and in the guest rooms. The table was polished to gleaming. I assumed she'd given my aunt a hand sprucing up the place as soon as she'd arrived.

"Help yourselves." She glanced over at Carolyn and Russ. "Please stop calling me 'Ms. Wilson.' It makes me feel old. My name is Wanda."

My aunt returned at that moment carrying another tray with tea. I noticed it held five mugs. She must've anticipated the others joining us.

Setting the tray down next to the cookie platter, she smiled. "I'm so glad you've all met one another or re-met as the case may be." She looked in my direction.

"I haven't met Sarah's friend," Wanda said.

Carolyn, still standing, walked over to her. "I'm Carolyn Grant."

Wanda shook her hand. "Wanda Wilson. I worked here twenty years ago when Julie and Martin ran the inn.

"How is your daughter?" I interrupted. "Is Wendy visiting with us, also?"

She shook her head. "I'm afraid not. I know she would've loved to see everyone again, but she hasn't been up to socializing much since she went through a divorce a few years ago. She told me to send her regards, but she preferred to stay home."

"I'm sorry to hear about her divorce."

Wanda nodded. "Yes, but sometimes it's for the best. They hadn't been married long, and there were no children involved."

Her words caused my stomach to knot as I remembered my situation and how I had to call Derek when I got to my room.

"It's very interesting," Russell said taking a seat on the other side of Carolyn, "Everyone except Sarah's friend here was around that summer."

I sat back down in the spot I'd previously occupied while Wanda and my aunt took the two armchairs across from us.

"That's true," Aunt Julie confirmed. "I hope you'll all have a much more pleasant stay this time."

I understood her meaning. She, Wanda, Russell, and I, as well as my mother who would be arriving the next day, were at the inn that fateful July before it closed. Was that a coincidence, or were we part of an intentional guest list my aunt had prepared?

From the notes of Michael Gamboski

Lighthouse illustration (Creative Commons, OpenClipart Vectors)

A lighthouse is a tower, building, or other type of structure designed to emit light from a system of lamps and lenses, and to serve as a navigational aid for maritime pilots at sea or on inland waterways. Lighthouses mark dangerous coastlines, hazardous shoals, reefs, and safe entries to harbors, and can assist in aerial navigation. Once widely used, the number of operational lighthouses has declined due to the expense of maintenance and use of electronic navigational systems. (Wikipedia)

Chapter Thirteen

Sea Scope: Twenty years ago

After the incident in the museum, the rest of the morning passed uneventfully as the children enjoyed swimming under the watchful eye of the lifeguard, a man around Michael's age. He wasn't on duty alone. A blonde girl in a bikini sat next to him on the lookout station drinking through a straw in a tall plastic cup.

"Hi Adam. Hi Sandy," Glen waved at them. He, Sarah, and Wendy knew them well. Russell hadn't been to the beach with them that summer until now.

Adam waved back as he picked up a can of Budweiser and took a sip. Sarah had started learning about alcohol in school the past year and wondered if the lifeguard drank as much as her mother, although her mother wasn't a beer drinker. She recalled the bottles of scotch and gin that she'd once seen sealed behind the doors of her mother's armoire, hidden by her long dresses and the evening gowns she'd never worn.

The children spent a few hours swimming, walking along the sand searching for seashells, and enjoying the warm sun on their bodies as they built sandcastles. Sarah was never any good at it, but Glen and Russell, working together, had built one that stood tall and didn't sink down into the sand. Glen had found the most seashells and put a bunch in his backpack. Sarah made him promise not to hide them in any guest rooms.

Russell and Wendy had gone ahead to the ice cream shop while Sarah and Glen were gathering up their stuff. Glen turned to her suddenly when she mentioned his latest crayon clue caper. "I forgot to mention that something strange happened when I got the paper from under Michael's door," he said.

She paused, shaking out the beach blanket that was full of sand from when the four of them had lain on it. "What did you see?" she asked her brother, prepared for one of his dramatic stories. She always humored him when he talked about ghosts and other sightings at the inn.

"It wasn't what I saw. It was what I heard." He spoke in a whisper even though no one was around except the seagulls swooping down on the sand and the young lifeguards who were deep in conversation with one another and not listening to them.

"Okay. What did you hear? Do you mind helping me fold this while you tell me?" She threw the end of the blanket toward him. He grabbed it as he replied. "There were these strange sounds coming from inside Michael's room. They scared me a little."

Sarah pulled her ends together. "Maybe there was a monster in there," she teased. "I wonder how Michael slept through the whole thing."

Glen brought the other end of the blanket up to meet Sarah's side. "It wasn't a noise a monster would make."

Sarah took the folded blanket and stuffed it inside her backpack. "What did it sound like? Could Michael have been snoring?"

"No." Glen shook his head. "It sounded more like those weird noises that come from some of the guest rooms late at night when I sneak around the hall. I hear it a lot from the honeymoon room."

Sarah raised her eyebrows. Aunt Julie had spoken to her last month about what she called "the birds and the bees" even though it had to do with men and women. She said she thought Sarah was old enough to know these things and that her mother was wrong in wanting to wait until Sarah turned fifteen.

After explaining to her about menstrual periods, something Sarah was not looking forward to starting, Aunt Julie had described what couples did behind closed doors to make babies and show their love for one another. Sarah had thought the facts were a bit gross, but Aunt Julie had laughed and said, "You won't feel that way in a few years, honey, believe me. Now don't tell your mother we had this talk. She might be upset with me. If she ever does come around to speaking about it, pretend it's the first time you've been told." Then she'd winked at Sarah and made her feel like she was in on a special secret.

"You deserved getting spooked," Sarah told her brother returning to the present. "Maybe it'll teach you a lesson to stop snooping near people's doors. Now let's go catch up with the others and have ice cream." As she raced Glen toward the Scoopery and their two friends, she was curious about what he'd said. Michael was staying at the inn alone and, as far as she knew, he'd never brought a girlfriend to visit, not even at his birthday party the week before.

Chapter Fourteen

Sea Scope: Present day

We spent an hour chatting and briefly reacquainting ourselves over tea and cookies. The discussion about Michael and the summer of 1996 took a back seat as my aunt led the conversation to her plans for the grand opening of the inn that fall.

"How come you're waiting until fall?" Carolyn asked. "Isn't summer the busy season here?"

"That may be true, but autumn is beautiful in Cape Bretton, and there are many weekenders. Besides, I'm not totally prepared yet."

Wanda, quiet up until then, gave my aunt a strange look and said, "I imagine you aren't prepared yet because you aren't ready to run this place yourself."

It was then that I let out a yawn I'd been trying to stifle for the last twenty minutes. It gave Aunt Julie an opportunity to wrap up the evening and avoid replying to Wanda's comment.

"It's getting late, and Sarah sounds tired. Why don't we all get some sleep and continue to catch up on things at breakfast. I have to leave early to pick up Jennifer. Her flight is arriving at nine, but I don't want to be late since it's a bit of a drive out to Charleston. Would you all mind coming down to breakfast around seven? I know that's early for a weekend morning. If you'd rather sleep in, I can make us all a lunch or brunch when I return."

Russell was the first to reply. "It doesn't matter to me. I get up early to write, anyway."

"You're an author?" I noticed Carolyn had gradually slid closer to him since we'd arrived.

He smiled and turned her way. "Didn't Sarah fill you in about my father's books? She loved my showing them to her when we were young. I guess I followed in his footsteps, although I write fiction. I base all my books in South Carolina. My current one is taking place in Cape Bretton, but I'm changing some facts and calling it by another name."

"How interesting," Carolyn declared. "I'm an author, too. I write children's books. Sarah is my illustrator."

"Sounds like we have something in common." He winked at her, and I could see Carolyn was enjoying the attention. She seemed upset, though, when Wanda asked Russell, "What type of book are you writing about this town?"

He paused and looked across at her. "I write mysteries, Wanda."

"I see. Can you share your plot with us, or is that bad luck before it's published?"

Carolyn brought Russ's attention back to her by saying, "Maybe Russell can share that with us tomorrow. I think Julie's right that it's time we head to our rooms and get some rest. I've been traveling all day, and my eyes are about to close."

"Of course." Wanda pursed her lips in the old way that I remembered when she had more to say but was keeping it to herself. "I'll help clean up while you all go upstairs."

As she and Aunt Julie began gathering up the mugs, trays, and other garbage, my aunt said, "I appreciate that, Wanda. You've been so helpful, even though I consider you a guest. I don't expect you to do this the rest of your stay."

"We're all guests," I said, "but that doesn't mean we can't each give you a hand, Aunt Julie. I'll be happy to cook and clean while I'm here."

"That's up to you. I'll welcome the help, but I want you to enjoy yourselves. If there's anything about your room or the inn that you feel should be changed, please let me know. Although I want everyone to consider this a vacation, it's also a test run for when I officially reopen the place to the public."

I'd already noticed the repairs that needed to be done outside but hadn't looked too closely at the interior.

As Carolyn and I headed for the stairs, Russell was right behind us. "Do you ladies need your luggage taken out of your car tonight?"

I could still hear the rain battering against the windows. "It's pouring out, Russ, and we have everything we need in our overnight bags but thank you for asking."

He smiled. "I don't mind going out in the rain for you, but if you don't need anything, I'll get your cases in the morning."

At the corridor upstairs, I beckoned Carolyn to turn right. Russell was already headed left to the West Wing. He'd told me Aunt Julie had given him Michael's old room because she felt the view of the lighthouse would inspire his writing.

"Why didn't your aunt put us all on the same side of the inn?" Carolyn asked, and I knew she was disappointed Russell's room wasn't near ours.

"I think she was trying to put us in our old rooms. She figured the two of us would want to be nearby, so she gave you my brother's room which is right next door to mine."

"Does that mean I'll be in a little boy's room?"

I laughed. We were standing outside the Violet Room. "No. My aunt redecorated both rooms after we moved and added queen beds to them. We used to sleep on twins."

"Do you want me to come in with you for a few minutes?" I could tell Carolyn was thinking I might need support when I called Derek.

"You can come in to see it, and I'll show you yours, but I'd like to get to sleep as soon as possible." The truth was I wanted time alone to think before I phoned home.

Carolyn nodded as I opened the door. "We don't get keys?"

"The rooms are never locked," I explained. "Even when we stayed here, guests were free to lock them from the inside for privacy, but there were no keys like you would have in a hotel, at least not ones my aunt gave to guests. She was able to unlock any of the rooms in case of an emergency."

"Strange," Carolyn said, stepping into the Violet Room. "I've never stayed at a bed and breakfast, so maybe that's how they work."

"I guess." Flipping up the switch by the door, I turned on the light and then laid my overnight bag on the neatly made bed.

"This is a lovely room," Carolyn said. "The purple is beautiful." She walked around checking the view from the window that I knew looked out on the water but featured only a partial view of the lighthouse.

"Oh, wow! A window seat. I always wanted one of these when I was young." She sat on the edge turning toward the bookcase in the corner. "Were those your books?"

I walked over to her and glanced at the spines of the books on the shelves that looked recently polished. Not a speck of dust covered any of the books even though they'd sat there for twenty years. A few were art books but most were young adult novels—*Jane of Green Acres*, *Little Women*, and *The Wizard of Oz*. I'd been a voracious reader as a child.

"That was my reading spot," I explained. "Glen was jealous he didn't have one, but he only read science books, and he used his book shelves for all his science kits."

"But I thought you said your aunt redecorated these rooms?"

"I meant she changed the beds, and I think she repainted Glen's walls. He used to have them plastered with posters of the planets, the periodic table, and other science charts. We'll see if it's still decorated that way. Maybe Aunt Julie wants me to go through my books and Glen's items before she does anything with them."

As we started to go, Carolyn suddenly said, "Wait. What's that by your pillow? Did your aunt leave you a note?"

I followed her gaze to the folded piece of paper on the bed. My hands shook as I took it, memory of the crayon notes flooding back.

"What does it say?" Carolyn peeked over my shoulder as I unfolded it.

I read it quickly and folded it back up. "It's nothing."

"Sarah." Her voice was insistent. "Why are you hiding it from me? What's going on?"

I knew she wouldn't give up until I told her everything, so I filled her in on Glen and his favorite game as well as the text message I'd received during the trip.

As I spoke, Carolyn's expression became serious. "Why didn't you tell me this earlier? Someone is pretending to be your dead brother. You need to find out who and why."

"I was thinking of redialing the number or sending another text and watching for the reply. What do you think?" It felt good to confide in a friend.

"I would say ignore it, but now that you've gotten a physical note, it's obvious someone here is responsible. Please let me see it."

I passed it to her, and she read the short, crayoned message aloud. "Send Mother home."

"What does that mean? Your mother isn't even here yet."

I shrugged. "I wish I knew, Carolyn. I can't even understand how Aunt Julie persuaded Mom to come. She hasn't set foot in this place for twenty years. She never speaks about it and always shuts me up when I try. I'm also unconvinced she's recovered from the breakdown she had after Glen's death. It's almost cruel of my aunt to bring her back here."

"Not only cruel, maybe dangerous."

"You think these notes are threats, not a sick joke someone is playing."

She passed the paper back to me. "I wouldn't throw this away, Sarah. I'm not sure there are fingerprints on it, but if something more substantial happens, you may want to call the police."

"I'd need to show it to Aunt Julie first."

Carolyn looked at me. "How do you know she's not the one doing it? She has the most access to your room, and it's possible she even has Glen's phone. You said she went through his things in his apartment in California."

"That doesn't make sense. Why would she leave a note telling me to send my mother home when she was the one who invited her here?"

"I know that's strange, but it's still a possibility. Otherwise, it has to be either Wanda or Russell. I can't see it being Russell."

The way she said his name confirmed she was attracted to my old friend. "Why do I get the sense you like Russ?"

I'd never seen Carolyn blush before, but her cheeks reddened at my words. "I have to admit he's quite handsome, and we have something in common. I hope this trickster doesn't cut my visit short because I'd like to spend time with him. I checked his hand, and I see he's not wearing a wedding ring."

"Don't get your hopes up, Carolyn. Even if he's single, he might be seeing someone, and he's just here to work on his book. You also have to consider Jack."

She laughed. "I told you, Jack and I aren't serious. And what about Derek? You're still planning to call him, aren't you?"

I sighed. "Yes. I want to do it alone, though. Please understand."

"Of course, but what are you going to do about the note and the text?"

"Nothing right now. I'll keep the note, as you suggested. I might talk to Aunt Julie about it tomorrow if I get a chance. Mom will be coming, and I can't do it in front of her."

Carolyn picked up the overnight bag she'd left on the chair by the door and put her hand on the knob. "I understand. I think I can manage settling into my room myself, but I'm locking the door behind me. If you need anything, knock or call me on my cell. I'll have it on. It has a full charge."

"Okay," I promised. "I wasn't planning to lock my door, but I guess I should in light of this." I looked back at the note, folded it up, and put it in the bedside drawer.

"Goodnight then," Carolyn said, opening the door to leave, "and good luck with Derek. Keep an open mind when you talk to him."

"That's what I intend to do, but I'm only checking in. I'll tell him I decided to come back sooner, so it gives him notice to get his girlfriend out of our house."

"I wouldn't do him that favor. I'm still not sure he has anyone staying there, but if he does, it's better to surprise him. As much as I'd hate for you to catch them in the act, it might be the best option." She walked back to me and gave me a hug. "Remember, I'm here for you no matter what."

I felt tears gather behind my eyes but tried to keep them from falling. "Thank you, Carolyn. That means a lot, and I agree with you."

From the Notes of Michael Gamboski

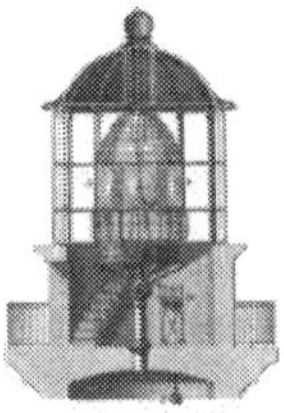

Lantern Room with Fresnel lens (Wikimedia Commons)

The Lantern Room is the glass-enclosed room found at the top of the lighthouse that holds the lighting system. The Watch Room is the room below the Lantern Room where the keeper stored fuel and stood watch. The Gallery is the platform, walkway, or balcony found outside the Watch and Lantern Rooms. Keepers used the gallery to clean the outside windows of the Lantern Room.

Chapter Fifteen

Sea Scope: Twenty years ago

When she got up, Sarah was surprised to find her mother sitting outside on the porch and the kitchen empty. Ms. Wilson always woke early even on the weekends, and her aunt was never far behind. However, it was a rare thing for her mother to rise before ten a.m. on any day of the week.

The house was silent when she'd made her way downstairs not even bothering to disturb Glen. There weren't many guests here yet, but several were expected the following week for the Fourth of July holiday. Currently, there was only Michael. He had checked in last weekend and said he was taking a summer class that involved independent study which meant he didn't have to attend school, but he said it was more work than going to classes. Sarah seriously doubted that, and Glen wanted to know if you could take independent study in third grade.

Sarah joined her mother on the porch. She was relieved to see that this was what her father termed one of his wife's "sober days." She wasn't quite sure of the definition of that word; but, on those days, her mother looked prettier and younger, her eyes clear and not red, and her voice gentler.

"Good morning, Sarah." She smiled when she saw her daughter. "It's a beautiful day. Dad is out jogging early again, and I didn't want to waste time in bed. Did you know your aunt has the most unusual birds nesting in that tree over there?" She pointed in the direction of one of the Oaks that graced the walk up to the inn.

Sarah nodded. "I think Glen can name them for you." She remembered her brother spending the whole spring bird watching before school, his handy Audubon guide stuffed into his backpack.

Jennifer Brewster chuckled. "I bet he could. Come sit here next to me, Sarah. We don't get much time to talk together with the inn always so busy."

Sarah took the rocker next to her mother. "Where is everyone this morning, Mom?"

Her mother tossed back her honey blonde hair that she usually wore up in a bun. Sarah recalled her father saying it was spun gold compared to Sarah and Glen's copper locks. "Ms. Wilson and your aunt went into town to shop for decorations for the birthday party tonight. You remember, it's Mr. Gamboski's birthday."

"He lets us call him Michael," Sarah corrected, "and, yes, I remember the party. Aunt Julie told me it was going to be a surprise." Although her aunt didn't celebrate all the birthdays of the inn's guests, she'd mentioned to Sarah that this was a particularly special birthday like Sarah had celebrated in October when she'd turned ten. Sarah knew Michael was going to be twenty-one, but she didn't understand why that was a special birthday because it wasn't an even number like ten, twenty, or thirty. They'd never even celebrated their mother's birthday when she turned forty that past May, but that could've been because she'd spent it in bed on one of her "non-sober days" and Dad had apologized to everyone that his wife wasn't feeling well and that she wanted to spend her day alone.

"Is there anything you'd like to talk about, Sarah?" Her mother's question brought her back to the present.

"Why is twenty-one a special birthday, Mom?"

"In certain states, twenty-one is considered the legal age to do more grown-up things, Sarah. It signals the beginning of adulthood."

"I thought that was puberty." Sarah nearly bit her tongue after having let that slip remembering her aunt had made her promise not to mention anything about the "birds and bees" talk she'd given Sarah last month. Thankfully, her mother was in such a good mood she didn't question Sarah's knowledge of the term.

"That's different, Sarah."

"So what things can people do when they are twenty-one that they can't do at twenty?"

"It's not what they can do; it's what they're permitted to do by law."

Sarah didn't understand. "If you mean driving, you can get a driver's permit in South Carolina at fifteen and can vote at eighteen." She remembered those facts from school.

"Yes, that's true, Sarah. If you're under twenty-one, however, you can't get into certain places particularly those that serve alcoholic beverages. The laws vary in different states, though."

Sarah digested that. "Does that mean Michael can drink scotch and gin like you now?"

She watched her mother wince, and her gray eyes darken. "I think it's time to go in, Sarah. Your aunt and Ms. Wilson should be back soon. Maybe you can help me sweep the kitchen."

Chapter Sixteen

Sea Scope: Present day

After Carolyn left, I locked the door behind me. I took the note from the bedside table and looked at it again. What my friend contended about possible suspects was true. I couldn't see Russ being the culprit either, so it had to be Wanda, but why? Should I confront her? Should I speak to my aunt first?

Still not having a firm plan, I put the note away and picked up my cell phone. It was almost eleven. I couldn't postpone the call to Derek any longer. As I located him on my contact list, I wondered if he would be in bed with his young lover when I called. The thought made me almost put away the phone. He'd told me he would wait for my call no matter how late it came. I was afraid to call the house line again, so I tapped Derek's cell number and held my breath.

He answered quicker than expected. "Sarah." He breathed heavily, but I didn't hear anyone in the background. "I was so worried. I checked the weather, and I saw there was a bad rainstorm down there. Is everything okay?"

I couldn't believe how concerned he sounded, how my heart raced hearing his voice. I tried to keep my own under control. "I'm fine. I'm in my old room here. We were all talking downstairs a while. It's been twenty years since I've seen most of the other guests."

Derek let out a breath. "I'm so relieved. I feel terrible that I wasn't able to come with you."

Yeah, right. I never realized he was such a good liar, but I found myself matching him by saying, "I told you that's okay. I understand you're teaching the summer intensive."

"It's over in two weeks. I was thinking of driving down there. It'll be in time for our anniversary."

Why was he telling me that? Did he think he'd have enough of his girlfriend by then, or would he back out at the last minute with an excuse? I pondered whether I should mention that I was returning with Carolyn by that time, but I remembered her suggestion to surprise him. "That might be nice. Look, Derek, it's late and I'm tired from the drive. I'm about to go to sleep."

"I'll let you go then, Sarah. I'll call you tomorrow. I love you. I miss you."

I wondered if he heard the coldness of my tone when I told him I loved and missed him, too. I ended the call before he did, the tears I'd held in check suddenly flowing. Carolyn advised me to keep an open mind, and I wanted with all my heart to believe that the father of my child wasn't cheating on me and really wanted to join me at my aunt's when his class was over. However, the logical part of me said it would be naive to trust in Derek's honesty and his false promises.

I dried my eyes with a tissue and picked up my phone again. I had one last thing to do before bed. I needed to call the person pretending to be Glen. If it was really Wanda, I'd only be calling over to the West Wing. I was disappointed but not surprised when the call went immediately to voicemail. I should've expected that, as well as my reaction when I heard Glen asking me to leave a message and he would get back to me. My heart did a somersault at the sound of his voice. Glen would never get back to me because he was dead. I hung up and texted a reply to the message I'd received earlier. "Who are you? What do you want?" Before I hit 'send,' I added, "If you don't reply, I'm contacting the police."

After I checked that the message was delivered but not yet read, I put the phone back in its charger and changed for bed, my mind filled with so many questions.

I tossed and turned for a half hour before getting up to check the phone again. I saw that my text still hadn't been read.

I knew that it wasn't the strange bed that kept me from sleep but my mind refusing to wind down. I had an idea that concentrating on something other than my situation would help, so I turned on the light and went to the bookshelf. I told myself it wouldn't matter if I read a children's story, as long as it distracted me from my problems. As I searched, I suddenly noticed a book tucked the wrong way among the neatly lined shelves. I pulled it out to find the diary I'd lost when I was ten. Bringing it to bed, I wondered how I'd feel reading it after all this time. I opened the cover to reveal a penciled sketch of Sea Scope that I didn't recall drawing. Throughout the diary was my doodled artwork along with my descriptions of the people and events from 1996.

Instead of reading through the first few entries, I decided to choose a random date. I flipped through the pages until my hand rested on one toward the back of the book, the entry dated June 29th. I recalled that was the day we'd all celebrated Michael's birthday. I propped up the pillow behind me and leaned against it as I began to read my account of the party.

From the notes of Michael Gamboski

One of Michigan's 124 lighthouses (Pixabay.com)

There are lighthouses in 31 states. States without lighthouses include Arizona, Colorado, Iowa, Kansas, Montana, and Nevada. The state with the most lighthouses is Michigan (124).

Chapter Seventeen

Sea Scope: Twenty years ago

Wanda let Sarah and Glen help decorate Michael's birthday cake after it had cooled. Since Glen wasn't very good at frosting and often ended up making a mess, Sarah was chosen to use the butter knife to spread the white icing over the chocolate cake. She had a hard time resisting licking the buttercream topping, but Wanda stood watching, her eyes passing on a secret warning. Glen's job was to place the small lighthouses and boats Aunt Julie had found in a craft store in a circle around the top. Ms. Wilson had already written 'Happy Birthday Michael' in light blue icing in the center and added the 2 and 1 numeral candles behind the greeting.

Sarah's father was blowing up balloons while their mother was hanging the inflated ones around the patio because the party was taking place outside in the warm summer night. Aunt Julie had found string lights in the attic and citronella lamps to keep away the mosquitoes.

Everyone was excited as they waited for the guest of honor to appear. He'd left after dinner, as usual, to work at the lighthouse. He always brought his notebook, library books, pens, and a camera with him stuffed into a satchel that Sarah considered a grown-up version of a school backpack. He spent about two hours each night at the lighthouse, wrapping up around eight. Occasionally, he let her and Glen tag along and help him with his research. He hadn't asked them that night, and they were glad because they wanted to help prepare for the party.

Once everything was in place, Ms. Wilson offered to be the lookout to alert them when she saw Michael approach. She stood by one of the oak trees at the end of the drive, a thin silhouette in a floral dress that Sarah had never seen her wear before.

It was hard for Sarah to stay quiet but even more difficult for her brother. Their mother kept putting a finger to her lips and telling them to settle down. Wendy didn't need to be reminded because she was naturally soft-spoken. She'd stacked all of Michael's gifts on a table in the corner as her mother had instructed and stood in silence guarding the pile. Even the children had given Michael presents. Sarah had contributed a writing pad; Glen a paperweight from the science museum; and Wendy a batch of cookies she and her mother baked along with the cake. Sarah didn't know what was in the large package decorated with lighthouses or the medium sized one with boats. She only knew her father was giving Michael a gift card to the bookstore and that Aunt Julie hinted that she'd found a perfect shirt she thought Michael would love. Sarah had also seen a small, unwrapped white box tucked behind a plant on the gift table. She didn't think it was one of Michael's gifts, but she wondered why it was there.

When Michael hadn't returned to the inn by nine, Sarah's father proposed he go to the lighthouse and see what was keeping him. Even though school had let out for the summer and Sarah, Glen, and Wendy could stay up late, everyone was eager to get the party underway.

Sarah watched as her father joined Ms. Wilson at the end of the walk who, having tired of standing, had propped herself against the tree. Sarah could barely make out their figures in the growing darkness. Aunt Julie hesitated to switch on the outdoor lights because she was afraid it would ruin the surprise.

Even though Sarah couldn't see them, she caught their words that drifted back through the night.

She heard her father say, "I can get him. I don't mind."

"That's silly," Ms. Wilson replied. "It's late and growing dark. You go back and wait with the others."

"We can go together."

"Ms. Brewster may need me."

"Everything is ready. She just needed someone to wait for Michael, but he's already an hour late."

Sarah wondered why their voices were rising. Were they arguing? Then she watched as Ms. Wilson crossed her arms and leaned back against the tree as her father turned and began walking in the direction of the lighthouse. He'd gotten his way with Ms. Wilson as he usually did in disagreements with her mother.

It felt like forever but was probably no more than twenty minutes or so before the two men ambled up the path. Side by side, they were about the same height, but Sarah's dad was stockier than lanky Michael. Although he was old enough to be his father, Mr. Brewster was in great shape. At forty-five, he could easily pass as Michael's older brother.

Ms. Wilson, who was still standing by the oak, stepped in front of them. She took Michael's hand, and led him to the patio where Aunt Julie switched on the lights at that exact moment and everyone stood up and yelled, "Surprise! Happy Birthday, Michael!"

Sarah couldn't be sure from his expression if he was truly surprised, but as soon as the announcement was made, Ms. Wilson threw her arms around him. Before letting him go, she whispered in his ear, but the words couldn't be heard over the chattering of the crowd. Sarah's mother was next. She gave him a brief hug after which Mr. Brewster shook his hand and patted him on the back. Glen, Sarah, and Wendy gathered around him chanting, "Happy birthday to you, Happy birthday to you," but Aunt Julie told them to save their singing for the cake. She gave Michael a quick kiss on the cheek and led him to a seat.

"I don't know what to say," Michael replied. "You're all so kind. Thank you." In the lights hanging from the porch rafters, Sarah saw he was blushing.

"It wasn't my idea, Mike," Sarah's dad said. I would've taken you out to a bar since you're now old enough to go." He glanced over at the children. "Blame my sister. She always likes an excuse for a party."

Aunt Julie tapped him on his arm. "I didn't hear you complain too much, Martin."

"Ouch," Sarah's father said in reaction to the light punch.

"Why doesn't Michael open his gifts now?" Ms. Wilson suggested.

"That's a great idea," Sarah's mother said. Sarah noticed she had stepped away from the group who were gathered around Michael and was eyeing the unopened champagne bottle on the table by the other drinks.

Aunt Julie said, "Since Wendy did such a good job putting out the gifts, maybe Sarah and Glen can help bring them to you, Michael. Sarah, can you bring over the first gift, please?"

Sarah and Glen took turns bringing the wrapped packages to Michael to open. The medium-sized gift was the nautical shirt that Aunt Julie had mentioned. It was light blue to match Michael's eyes, with short sleeves, a button-down collar, and a lighthouse on the left breast pocket. After Michael said how much he liked it, Sarah's father handed him the envelope with the bookstore gift card. Michael had already opened the gifts from Sarah, Glen, and Wendy, so there was only the large gift remaining. Sarah brought it over, wondering what it could be.

"I think I'll need help opening this," Michael said.

"Maybe you should read the card first," Aunt Julie suggested.

Sarah noticed that Ms. Wilson had edged closer to Michael's chair.

Michael slipped open the envelope. Sarah caught a glimpse of the card inside. It featured a picture of a lighthouse in the setting sun. Sarah considered she would love to paint like that if her aunt could teach her, but Aunt Julie only painted people.

"Thank you, Wanda," Michael said closing the card. Sarah wondered why he hadn't read it aloud, but he was already tearing open the gift's silver wrapping. Sarah helped him by undoing the tape on the other side. Ms. Wilson looked on with a nervous expression as if she wasn't quite sure what Michael would think of her present.

When the wrapping was removed, Sarah could see from the photo on the box that it was a stand for his camera.

As Michael lifted it out, Ms. Wilson said, "I thought you could use a tripod for all those photographs you're taking."

"That's very thoughtful of you," Michael said, and Ms. Wilson pursed her lips. She didn't look happy about how he'd received her gift.

"Now let's have cake," Aunt Julie said.

"I have a bit of a headache," Sarah's mother said coming out from the shadows. "Please excuse me, Michael. I think I should go to bed." As she walked to the patio door, Ms. Wilson followed. "I think I'll join you. Sorry I can't clean up, Ms. Brewster. I'm very tired. Enjoy your night, Michael." She looked toward her daughter. "You can stay if you want, Wendy." The girl nodded and moved next to Sarah.

"More cake for us," Glen whispered as Aunt Julie lit the candles and lowered the lights.

It was the three children and Sarah's aunt and father who remained as Michael blew out the 2 and1 numeral candles and the one for good luck that Aunt Julie had added.

They sang as Michael closed his eyes and, in one breath, blew out all the candles.

Sarah's father patted him on the back. "Good job. I hope you get your wish."

Aunt Julie then asked Sarah and Wendy to help her cut slices of the cake to serve on the happy birthday plates decorated with lighthouses. Sarah's father popped open the champagne bottle but asked Glen to pour lemonade for the three kids.

"Can't I have a taste of that?" Glen asked as his father passed Michael the first glass of the sparkling liquid.

"You know you're too young, Glen," he said, as his son pouted and grabbed one of the larger slices of cake.

Aunt Julie declined the champagne and joined the children in drinking lemonade. Sarah's father proposed a toast to Michael on his twenty-first birthday, and everyone clinked glasses.

As the party wound down, Wendy offered to help Aunt Julie clean up. Sarah and Glen went back inside, and Michael and their father remained talking on the porch.

Upstairs, Sarah noticed the light was on under her parents' door and realized her mother was still awake.

"Do you think we should check on Mom to see if she's okay?" Sarah asked her brother.

"You can if you want. I'm going to bed."

Sarah noticed Glen was holding a folded-up napkin. "What's that? Don't tell me you sneaked out another slice of cake."

He grinned.

"Aunt Julie will be mad if you get crumbs all over your floor."

"I'll clean them up. I promise." He opened his door. "Goodnight, Sarah."

Sarah waited until he was inside and then walked across the hall to tap on her parents' door. It took a few minutes, but then her mother called her to come in.

Sarah stepped into what was known as the Garden Room, her mother's favorite because it looked over the back garden. The shades were drawn, so the room was dark. Her mother sat on the bed, an empty bottle at her feet, wadded up tissues next to her. Even in the shadows, she could see her mother's eyes were red, a combination of drinking and crying.

"Are you okay, Mom?" Sarah asked in a low voice.

"I'm fine. Now you go to bed. It's late."

Sarah didn't want to upset her mother more by disobeying her, so she turned to go. As she had her hand on the door, her mother called to her, "Goodnight, honey. Thank you for helping with the party. I'm sorry I'm such a party pooper."

"That's okay, Mom. I know you get bad headaches." What Sarah knew was that the headaches usually followed not preceded her mother's drinking bouts.

On the way back to her room, Sarah thought she saw Ms. Wilson going downstairs in her robe. She figured she was headed outside to get Wendy and finish helping Aunt Julie clean up. It had been an interesting party, but Sarah didn't think a happy one.

Chapter Eighteen

Sea Scope: Present day

I looked up from the diary. Along with my comments, there'd been several sketches scattered among the pages—a drawing of Michael's cake, the birthday card featuring the lighthouse, mother sitting in the Garden Room with the empty bottle on the floor and the tissues at her side. I saw the talent in the budding artist, although the sketch of my mother wasn't very accurate. Aunt Julie was the portrait artist in the family.

I was beginning to feel tired enough to sleep. I put the diary back on the bookshelf hoping to read more during my stay. Besides bringing back childhood memories, it might lend a clue as to what was presently going on at Sea Scope.

I'd turned off the light and gotten under the covers when I heard a noise outside the door. It was a soft scratching. Then I remembered the cat. Did he roam the halls at night or sleep with my aunt? I slid my bare feet into slippers and opened the door. There were no lights on in the hall, but I could still make out the dark shape of the cat as he stood watching me from bright, glowing green eyes.

"We meet again, Al," I said leaning down to pet his head, but he was off in a flash. I was about to close my door, when I heard another sound. A shuffling noise came from the room across from mine, what used to be my parents' room. As far as I knew, the room was unoccupied because my mother hadn't yet arrived. Before I could check it out, someone whispered my name. I jumped.

It was Russell in pajamas. "Sorry to scare you, Sarah. I couldn't sleep and was thinking of going downstairs for a nightcap. It looks like you haven't had any luck in the snoozing department either. Want to join me?"

I was conscious of my thin nightgown. I hesitated.

"If we're lucky, Wanda may still have a few of those delicious cookies left." His grin put me at ease.

"I don't want any cookies, but I'll come along. A nice glass of milk might help me get to sleep."

Russell let me go ahead of him down the stairs. The house was quiet on the lower level. I assumed everyone upstairs was asleep except for whoever was in the room across the hall. I hoped it was my imagination and that the noise I'd heard had only been part of the creaks and groans of the old house.

To Russell's delight, a few cookies were still covered on a plate on the kitchen table. He went to the refrigerator and poured us both a glass of milk. "I feel like a kid having cookies and milk before bed," he said sitting across from me.

"Thanks for pouring my milk." I took a sip.

"You sure you don't want to share the cookies?"

I looked into his blue eyes. Maybe it was the late hour or my memory of our childhood friendship, but I found myself blurting out my concerns of the last days. "Russ, odd things have been happening since I arrived at Sea Scope and even while I was on my way."

He raised an eyebrow as he bit into a cookie. "You know I was always a good listener. Tell me what's up, Sarah."

I took a breath and relayed all the incidents to him starting with the text message and ending with the noise in the Garden Room.

"Hmm." He considered. "Sounds mysterious and like someone is playing a cruel joke on you. You should tell your aunt about it." He paused. "By the way, I'm very sorry my dad and I didn't come to Glen's funeral. We were away at the time. When we got back and heard the news, we sent your mom and Aunt Julie condolence cards. I considered Glen a younger brother back then because I didn't have one."

I felt a lump gather in my throat. "I don't know who's behind this. Carolyn believes it's Wanda, but I have no idea why she would do it."

He finished his cookie. "Let's go upstairs when you're done with your milk. I want to take a look at that phone and the note."

Russ accompanied me back to my room and then went across the hall and opened the Garden Room beckoning me to come inside with him. He switched on the lights and looked around. It was empty and a little musty, although I noticed the window was open a crack to let in the warm night air. There was also a fresh arrangement of flowers next to the bed.

"No one appears to be here," he said after checking the closed doors of the bathroom and wardrobe.

I glanced in his direction. The room was familiar, the same queen-sized brass bed with the rose-covered quilt and light pink walls. My mother had loved this room, seeing it as her private oasis while my father hardly visited it except to sleep.

Russell opened the armoire. I half expected to see my mother's hidden stash of liquor inside, but it was empty.

"Maybe your aunt was putting the final touches on this room for your mother tomorrow," he suggested as we both left the room.

I didn't believe that explanation, but I nodded as if I was considering it.

"Let's go see what's happening in your room then, shall we?"

I nodded again still feeling anxious.

As I stepped through the door with Russ behind me, something brushed against my leg. I stifled a scream as I jumped.

"It's only the cat," Russ said as Al scooted down the hall. "You must've closed him in when you left."

"No. He was down the hall when I closed the door." I distinctly recalled seeing Al head toward my aunt's room.

Russell followed me inside. "Show me your phone and the note."

I went to the bedside table to disconnect my phone that I'd left charging there and to retrieve the crayoned message from the drawer underneath. The charging cable hung limply against the bed, and the drawer was empty.

"They're gone," I exclaimed panic causing my voice to rise.

"Are you sure, Sarah? Maybe you left your phone elsewhere. Look around."

"I had it charging right there." I indicated the loose wire. "I'm also sure I left the note in that drawer."

Russell picked up the phone cord and went around me to check the drawer. When he looked back at me, his face was serious. "This isn't good, Sarah. Do you have a tracking app on your phone?"

"I do, but I think I shut it down."

"If you didn't, there might be a way to find it." His eyes met mine. "Does your husband have the app on his? Maybe you can call him and see if he can check it."

I hesitated. The last thing I wanted was to speak to Derek again. "I don't think it would work from this distance, and I don't want to bother Derek. It's after eleven. He's probably asleep."

"I'm sure he wouldn't mind. He's probably wide awake thinking of you." A grin touched the sides of his mouth. A sudden memory returned of the first kiss I'd shared with him when I was ten.

"Sarah," he continued, snapping me back to the present. "Even if you don't want to call your husband, I think we should wake your aunt and tell her what's going on."

"She's picking my mother up early at the airport in the morning. I'd hate to upset her at this hour."

He gave me an exasperated look. "Okay. Let's do this. I'm in the Lighthouse Room. It's the first room on the opposite side of the hall."

"I remember the room, Russ." How could I forget it? It had been Michael's room. Glen, Wendy, and I had often been invited in there to talk with him, browse his history books about lighthouses and South Carolina, and look out his window at the lighthouse and the ships sailing across the water.

"Good. If anything else happens tonight, don't worry about waking me. I'll help you look for your phone tomorrow, but you need to tell your aunt everything you shared with me. If Wanda is up to this, she needs to be confronted."

"Yes," I agreed. "Thanks, Russ."

He gave me a wary look as he left the room. I worried he might wake Aunt Julie and tell her, but I hoped he'd wait for me to do it in the morning as he'd promised.

After I'd locked the door behind him, it was impossible to sleep. I kept thinking about Al rushing out of my room after he'd been closed in by whoever had taken my phone and removed the note from the drawer. I also thought of Derek. Was he sleeping alone or with his young mistress? I turned those painful thoughts away and walked to my bookshelf. I was relieved to find my diary still there. I knew reading another chapter probably wouldn't help me fall asleep, but I had to admit I was curious about how I'd described my first kiss with Russell all those years ago. I flipped open the pages to July 4th, two weeks before Michael allegedly threw himself off the lighthouse tower.

From the Notes of Michael Gamboski

Henry Wadsworth Longfellow (Wikimedia Commons)

Steadfast, serene, immovable, the same
Year after year, through all the silent night
Burns on forevermore, that quenchless flame,
Shines on that inextinguishable light!

(from "The Lighthouse" by Longfellow)

Chapter Nineteen

Sea Scope: Twenty years ago

Sarah and Wendy helped Aunt Julie pack snacks in a picnic basket for the viewing of the fireworks. She asked Glen and Russ to help carry fold-up chairs for the adults to sit on and a large blanket for the kids to share. Glen asked his father if he could bring his binoculars along, and his dad agreed. Ms. Wilson suggested they also bring sweaters in case it got chilly. She'd thrown a white lace wrap around her shoulders.

Mrs. Brewster stood in the door waving as the group departed. Russell's father and Aunt Julie walked in front leading the group toward the lighthouse. Michael was already there setting up the tripod Ms. Wilson gave him to take photos of the event.

As they joined him on the wide lawn in front of the lighthouse, Glen ran up to him and asked if he could help him take pictures when everything started. Michael smiled. "Sure. I can use a helper. I'll show you how to adjust the camera's light settings, so we can capture the fireworks in the night sky."

Glen's face lit up. For the last week, he'd been spending time at the library asking the librarian to find information for him about fireworks—not only what they were but how they were made and the science behind them. He could quote from the books and also the websites the librarian brought up on the library's reference PC in answer to his questions. He told Sarah fireworks were invented by the Chinese a long time ago and were used during festivals to scare away evil spirits and bring good luck. Fireworks were used early in America's history and were even part of the first Independence Day. Different color fireworks are made with different metals. Glen loved the red ones created by lithium, while Sarah liked the blue copper ones. Both of them enjoyed the sparkler effects made by aluminum. Sarah cautioned Glen that even though he now knew about the black powder, mortar, stars, shells, bursting charge, and fuses that were part of fireworks, he shouldn't think about making them because they were very dangerous. Glen promised he wouldn't do that, but he said he wished he had his own computer at home to look up other science facts. Their dad promised he'd get one for his ninth birthday.

Sarah and Wendy laid out the plaid picnic blanket. It was thin and not very soft, but it was wide enough for all four children. From past experience, Sarah knew Glen wouldn't be sitting there. He preferred to stand and drive the adults crazy repeating what he'd learned about fireworks. While she was sick of hearing Glen's science speeches, she found the opposite was true when Russ talked about history. He didn't show off his knowledge and brag about the facts he knew but threw in details she found interesting. He'd picked up things from his father who Michael idolized because he'd been so helpful with part of Michael's research.

While Glen boasted that the fireworks display was taking place at their lighthouse, Sarah corrected him by pointing out that the town owned the lighthouse. It was on a separate piece of land than the inn, and the show wasn't private to them as was clear by the growing crowd of townspeople and those who'd even travelled from other parts of South Carolina to view it. Sarah was happy her father had insisted they leave early because they were able to stake out a good view of the lighthouse and the fireworks that would soon fill the sky around it.

When the festivities finally began, the excitement as well as the noise level rose. Sarah watched her brother still standing by Michael in a small group that included her father and Wanda on one side and

Russell's dad and Aunt Julie on the other. She'd been lying on her back gazing up at the stars that Glen would've happily named if he wasn't too busy playing with Michael's camera. Wendy had been picking dandelions and other weeds from the grass. Sarah worried that their sleepover that night would be boring because Ms. Wilson's daughter wasn't much of a talker.

"We'd better get up," Sarah prompted her. "We won't see much lying on the blanket."

Wendy was preoccupied picking off and blowing the fuzzy petals of a weed as she whispered some words.

Sarah urged her again. "Hurry up. We'll miss the show."

Wendy finally stood up to join her in time for the first explosion of light, a burst of red streamer over the top of the lighthouse. "I was making a wish," she said.

"Shhh, it's starting," Sarah silenced her as everyone turned their eyes forward and Michael clicked the camera.

The rest of the night was full of color, sound, exclamations of awe, and laughter. Against the darkened sky, the fireworks shone in beautiful detail. The loud pops covered the accompanying music that was being played from a CD player. As Sarah kept her eyes on the sky, she also scanned the crowd, observing her family and the other inn guests who were watching the show. Michael had allowed Glen to take photos, and her brother's eyes were still wild with excitement. Ms. Wilson was dancing to the music as she stood by Michael and Sarah's father. At some point, she tried to persuade them to join her, but neither accepted. Sarah noticed that Aunt Julie eyed Ms. Wilson with displeasure even though she was sitting close to Russell's dad and had her hands interlocked with his.

Russell, who'd left the small inner group to join Sarah and Wanda, whispered in Sarah's ear, "That's why I'm staying with your brother tonight." He, too, was watching his father and Aunt Julie.

Sarah, having recalled her growing-up talk with Aunt Julie, nodded in understanding.

Wendy, who'd overheard Russell's words despite the fact her attention was focused on the fireworks, said, "I'm in Sarah's room because my mama will be with her boyfriend."

Sarah looked back at Ms. Wilson shimmying next to Michael and her dad, but both of them seemed immune to her charms.

"I didn't know your mom had a boyfriend," Russell said.

Wendy smiled knowingly and shook her braids giving an affirmative reply.

"Who is he?" Russell probed.

"I'm not telling."

"You're not telling because you don't know. If your mom had a boyfriend, why doesn't he ever come to the inn and take her out? It's like your imaginary father." As much as Sarah liked Russell, she knew he could be cruel at times like other boys in her classes at school.

"I'm not telling because it's a secret. Mama doesn't even know I know about him, but I saw them kissing. I hope she marries him, but I don't think she can."

Sarah's heart began to race as she looked over at Ms. Wilson smiling at her father and Michael, laughing at the things they were telling her but what she couldn't hear over the fireworks. Aunt Julie would call that flirting. Sarah wondered if the reason Wendy's mother couldn't marry her boyfriend was because he was already married to Sarah's mother.

As the fireworks show ended with a finale of multi-colored rockets that Glen and Michael rushed to film, Russell asked Wendy again, "So, who is your mother's boyfriend? If you don't tell me, I'll tickle you."

"Russell, no," Sarah said. "Leave her alone, or I'll tell my aunt." Wendy's mouth was pursed in a similar way as her mother's when she wanted to hold back her words.

Everyone started packing up. Glen folded the tripod following Michael's instructions after he handed him the camera. Sarah's father was helping Ms. Wilson put her lace wrap over her shoulders that she'd removed while dancing. Aunt Julie called over to Sarah and Wendy for them to help her clear the trash their group had made. Russell joined his father who was chatting with Michael. Sarah hoped he wouldn't bring up the conversation he'd had with Wendy.

As Sarah added the last piece of litter to a can one of the organizers had left on the grounds, Russell called to her, "Wait, Sarah."

Wendy eyed him cautiously, stepping back as he approached.

"If you're all done helping Ms. Brewster, I wanted to show you something before we go back to the inn. It's up by the lighthouse."

Ms. Wilson, Glen, Michael, and Russell's father were calling and waving to them to join them on the walk back. Without the firecrackers lighting the sky, the night had darkened. There weren't any stars out either, which Sarah was a bit thankful for because Glen would be reciting a bunch of astronomy facts all the way to Sea Scope's door if there had been.

Russell ran back to his father. "Dad, is it okay if I take Sarah back after you all go? We won't be long."

Mr. Donovan nodded. "That's fine with me, son, but check with Ms. Brewster, too."

Sarah's aunt was already at Mr. Donovan's side. "It's okay with me, Russell, but be careful. It's gotten very dark out here. And, remember, you're staying with Glen when you get back."

The others began walking down the hill. Russell returned to Sarah as Wendy ran to her mother and slipped behind her next to Glen. Ms. Wilson didn't notice. She was walking between Sarah's father and Michael, still smiling as she talked to them. As she walked, her hips wiggled. Was she still flirting?

Sarah also saw that her aunt and Mr. Donovan were holding hands as they followed the others. She and Russell wouldn't be missed even if they stayed out the whole night.

"What do you want to show me?" Sarah asked as Russell led her to the lighthouse. As they came closer, the smell of smoke left from the firecrackers grew stronger, and she began to cough. "I hope you make this quick. It smells around here."

They were alone except for two of the firecracker maintenance people who were still cleaning up, their orange jackets displaying "Town of Cape Bretton."

She was surprised neither of the men said a word to them as they cut through the bushes that grew along the path leading up to the stone structure. The gate in front of the lighthouse was locked because the lighthouse was only open during the day, although Michael had permission to visit it after hours with a special grounds pass and key.

"I guess we have to go back," Sarah told Russell.

She couldn't read his face in the darkness and wondered why he'd moved closer to her. "That's all right. We don't have to go any further."

Behind the bushes, they were hidden from the cleaning men, alone with only the glowing beacon of the lighthouse casting off and on flashes.

"I thought you wanted to show me something in the lighthouse."

Russ shrugged. "It's not necessary. I only wanted to talk to you away from everybody."

Sarah was curious. "What about?"

"Come here." Russ ambled down the sand toward the beach and went over to one of the large rocks scattered there. Sitting on one, he turned his back to her a minute to look out at the sea.

She followed him still wondering what he had to say. Was it about her father and Ms. Wilson?

"I know why Michael loves this place so much," he said as she joined him on the rock. "I think he comes here to be away from people even more than doing research."

It was growing chilly. Sarah didn't want to talk about Michael. She wanted to go home. Maybe she could get more out of Wendy about Ms. Wilson's boyfriend if she talked to the girl privately.

"Are you going to tell me already, Russ, or are we staying here until morning?"

Russ laughed, and there was a slight echo. She could still smell the fireworks, but the scent was lighter, overpowered by the salt air from the ocean.

"Sorry, Sarah, but this isn't easy." He gulped, and she realized he was shaking. She thought he was as cold as she was, but then realized it was because he was nervous.

"Is there anything wrong, Russ?" She knew her father asked that when her mother was in one of her non-sober moods.

Russell looked down at the ground and then met her eyes, his blue gaze serious. "No, Sarah. It's all this talk about boyfriends and girlfriends. I've never even kissed a girl, and I really want to find out what it's like." In the darkness, she could see the blush that colored his cheeks. "Would it be okay if I tried with you?"

Sarah recalled what her aunt said about what she should and shouldn't let boys do with her. Kissing was okay, but it often led to that other gross activity that could make a baby.

"I guess so." Her heart beat a little as Russell brought his face close to hers. She closed her eyes.

Their lips touched briefly. It was like the flutter of a moth's wings, the soft sweetness of peach skin.

"That was nice," Russell said as he moved away looking a little dazed.

Sarah nodded. She wished it had lasted longer.

The night sounds around them were deepening, and a mosquito buzzed nearby. "Yes, I liked it. It was my first one, too."

"The bugs are starting to come out. Let's go back to the house." She noticed he was still a bit red.

As they got off the rock, Sarah said, "I don't think we should tell anyone about this."

"No, please don't. Dad might punish me."

"I doubt he'd do that. Do you know if he's going to marry my aunt?"

They were standing in front of the rock facing the lighthouse.

"I'm not sure. I would love to have her as my new mother."

"Do you remember your old one?" Sarah knew Mr. Donovan's wife had died young.

"Not too well."

They started walking back. When they were within sight of the inn, Sarah stopped.

"What's the matter, Sarah?"

"Russ, do you have any idea who Ms. Wilson's boyfriend could be?"

"If I did, I wouldn't have asked Wendy." He grinned. "Besides, I'm not around here all that often."

Sarah considered. If her aunt and Russell's dad got married, Russ would live with them at the inn. The thought made butterflies jump in her stomach.

Chapter Twenty

Sea Scope: Present day

I woke to insistent tapping on my door. At first, I didn't realize where I was but quickly remembered I was in my old room at Sea Scope. My diary lay spread on the floor open to a page I'd been reading when I'd fallen asleep. I picked it up and went to answer the door.

Carolyn stood there completely dressed, her eyes wide. "What took you so long? I was rapping forever."

I doubted it had been more than five minutes, but my friend could be impatient when she had to wait for anything. "I was sleeping. Come on in."

Carolyn stepped into the room. "I never thought I'd be able to get to sleep, but that bed was very comfortable, and I must've been really tired from the drive."

"Then I guess you didn't hear anything out in the hall last night?"

Carolyn brushed her fingers through her hair and tugged at her light blue scarf that coordinated fashionably with her jeans and short sleeve sweater. "Did I miss anything? Did anything happen?" Her face was full of concern.

I walked back to the bookshelf and re-shelved the diary without answering.

"What's that?"

"My diary from when I lived at Sea Scope. I was reading some of it, and I guess it helped me fall asleep after someone stole my phone and that note I showed you."

"What? Oh, my God. Did they break in? How could you possibly sleep after that?"

"They didn't break in. The cat scratched at my door, so I opened it and he ran away down the hall. I went to follow him but then I heard a noise coming from the room where my mom will be staying. Russell came upstairs and checked it out, but no one was there." I left out the part of me and Russell sharing milk and cookies.

Carolyn raised her eyebrows. "Too bad I was sleeping. I would've loved to have spent time with Russell. But, go on, what happened to your phone and the note?"

I ignored the comment about Russell. It was obvious Carolyn was smitten with him, but most of her relationships started with a physical attraction that dissipated quickly. "I told Russell what I shared with you, and he wanted to see the text message and note, but when I got in the room, they were both gone."

"How strange." Carolyn walked to where the charging cord still lay unplugged. She pulled out the drawer and looked inside as Russell and I'd done and shook her head. "Do you have any idea who would've taken them? Did you see anyone in the hall?"

I realized I had to fill in the rest of the blanks of my story. "Actually, Russell and I had gone down to the kitchen. He thought milk and cookies would help us get to sleep. When I got to the room, I found Al trapped inside, so someone definitely broke in while I was downstairs."

Carolyn thought things over. "I'm surprised you didn't invite Russ to stay and protect you."

"We're just old friends, and I locked the door."

"What if whoever took your phone has a key?"

"Only my aunt has keys to the inn's rooms."

"Are you sure? What about her helper, Wanda?"

I thought about that. "It's possible, and I know you suspect Wanda, but it doesn't make sense to me."

"Well, there must be a reason. I assume you're talking to your aunt today." It wasn't a question.

"Yes. Russell advised me to do that." I glanced at the clock on the wall. It was almost eight, an hour later than my aunt had asked us to come down to breakfast, so I figured she was already gone. "Unfortunately, it's probably going to have to wait until she gets back from the airport."

"Another thing you have to consider is that Derek won't be able to reach you. How did your call go with him last night?"

"As I suspected. He pretended everything was normal. He said he might be able to join me here in two weeks."

"That's wonderful." Carolyn's eyes lit up, and I wondered briefly if it was because she was anticipating uninterrupted time with Russ if I was looking forward to my husband arriving soon.

"I don't know." I went to the closet to look for something to wear. I had managed to unpack some of my clothes. "I have a feeling the girl who answered our house phone was with him last night even though I didn't hear anything, and he can still reach me on the inn's phone. He has that number."

"Remember, I told you to keep an open mind." Carolyn turned away. "I'm going downstairs. If there's any breakfast left for us late risers, I'll try to save you something."

I pulled a pair of capris and a long red, white, and blue short-sleeved shirt I'd worn for the Fourth of July from the closet. "Thanks so much." Food was actually the last thing on my mind.

Carolyn nodded glancing at the clothes I'd laid on the bed. "You get dressed. Pretty soon you'll be shopping for maternity clothes."

I tapped her lightly on the arm. "I'll see you downstairs, Carolyn."

I dressed hurriedly, but as I suspected, by the time I got downstairs, Aunt Julie had already been long gone. As I entered the kitchen, Russell, Carolyn, and Wanda sat around the table chatting like old friends sipping coffee and biting into Southern biscuits and the leftover cookies from the night before.

"Good morning," Wanda said as I joined them. "Have a seat. Your aunt changed her mind and asked me to make breakfast this morning. She should be back soon with your mother, and I'll cook hot food then."

I sat next to Wanda noticing Carolyn had pushed her seat close to Russell. Both of them looked like they'd enjoyed conversation with one another that hadn't included Wanda. Carolyn read my mind as she said, her voice lilting a bit, "Russ and I have had a nice talk while waiting for you, Sarah. It's so enjoyable to chat with a fellow writer."

Russell smiled. "Yes, it's been quite interesting, but I think Sarah has something to ask Wanda."

Wanda raised her eyebrows as she passed the basket of biscuits toward me. "Have a biscuit, Sarah, and I can get you coffee if you'd like. I'll be happy to answer your question."

I didn't know how to begin. I looked to Russell and Carolyn for support and then retold the story from the start of all that had happened to me on my way to Sea Scope to the occurrences of the night before. Throughout my tale, Wanda was quiet, her lips pursed in that old way I remembered. I ended by asking, "Do you know anything about this, Wanda?" I couldn't outright accuse her, but I took a deep breath as I waited for her reply.

"You must talk to your aunt," she said after a pause. Her eyes never left mine, and she looked sincere, but I wasn't very good at identifying liars. My own husband had probably been sleeping with a woman for months before he stupidly allowed her to answer our phone and finally alerted me to the situation.

"So you don't know anything?" Russ asked as if he were a lawyer or policeman verifying a witness's account.

"No, of course not. Why would I take Sarah's phone or leave those crazy messages?"

Before anything else could be said on the matter, the front door opened, and I heard my mother and aunt's voices. I couldn't hear their exact words, but they were bickering. That would be par for the course, as Mom and Aunt Julie had never been the best of friends.

"Sounds like they're here," Russell said, standing. "I'll go help your mother with her bags. I can get the rest of the stuff out of your car, too, if you give me your keys."

I'd forgotten about the rainstorm in which we'd arrived. The day outside was already sunny and hot. The fans were blowing throughout the house.

Fearing that someone would enter my room again, I'd taken my purse down for breakfast, so I fished inside it and retrieved the keys. "Thanks, Russ," I said handing them to him.

"I can help," Carolyn offered quickly coming to Russ' side like his shadow. I followed them to the living room where Aunt Julie and my mother were still arguing.

When the three of us entered, they finally quieted.

"Sarah," my mother said. It was more of an acknowledgment than a greeting, with no opening of arms for a hug, but I embraced her, anyway. She pulled away stiffly. I noticed she wore sunglasses, a hint that she'd been on a bender, possibly from too many drinks on the flight. She'd gained a few pounds since I last saw her the previous month. Ever since I was young, she'd constantly battled with her weight and envied Aunt Julie who she said had a "fast metabolism."

"I didn't know you were coming," I said. "I drove down here with Carolyn."

Mother nodded. I couldn't see her eyes behind the glasses. "Hello, Carolyn," she said. "It's nice to see you again." She turned back to me after Carolyn returned her greeting. "I didn't know I was coming either until the last minute, and you know how I hate long drives, although flying isn't much better. I was supposed to be here last night, but the flight was delayed. It was such a hassle."

"That must've been frustrating," I said. "Do you remember Russell?"

Mother turned around to where Russ and Carolyn were now standing by the door about to bring in the suitcases. She lowered her glasses to the bridge of her nose as if it would help her see better, and I immediately recognized the redness of her eyes. I wondered if she'd packed anything alcoholic with her and, if she did, how the airlines had allowed it on the plane.

"Oh, my goodness. He looks so much like Bartholomew."

Aunt Julie grimaced. "Russell is Bart's son, so it only makes sense there would be a likeness."

I prayed they wouldn't start quibbling again after that remark, but Mother ignored it. "Well, he did grow up very handsome."

"Thank you, Mrs. Brewster."

"Please call me Jennifer."

Suddenly, my mother noticed Wanda standing in the corner.

"Wanda Wilson after all this time. Don't tell me my sister-in-law has recruited you to work here again?"

"I'm just helping out," Wanda explained. "If you're hungry from your flight, there are biscuits and cookies in the kitchen, and I promised to heat up eggs and grits later."

"I'm more tired than hungry but thank you."

"I have the Garden Room prepared for you, Jennifer," Aunt Julie said, looking toward the staircase. "Russell will bring up your bags if you want to get settled before coming down to chat with us."

Mother pushed back her glasses as if trying to hide her dislike of my aunt's words. "Seems like you've thought of everything, Julie." She walked past my aunt and, as she alighted, I heard her whisper to herself, "Why did I agree to come here?"

Russell and Carolyn saw that as a good time to go to the cars for the luggage. Wanda slipped quietly back into the kitchen. I was left alone in the living room with Aunt Julie.

When she was sure my mother was out of ear shot, she said, "Same old Jennifer. I have to learn to be more patient with her. She's suffering."

"That doesn't mean she has to be rude to you," I said. "Can we talk a minute, Aunt Julie?"

"In the kitchen?"

"No. There's something I have to discuss with you alone."

She nodded. "Of course. Let's sit on the patio. It's a beautiful day after yesterday's storm."

As we went outside, Al came from a hidden spot and joined us. He rubbed against my leg purring, and I reached down and mindlessly petted his head. My thoughts were on what I was about to tell my aunt.

We sat in rockers next to one another. The sun was shining on the oaks that lined the walk up to Sea Scope, and I could see the ocean and lighthouse in the distance. It would be a lovely place to work on the Kit Kat sketches, but my mind was elsewhere.

"I apologize for my secretiveness in inviting your mother, Sarah, but I hoped this visit would be cathartic for her."

"This isn't about my mother."

Al padded over to my aunt, and she scratched his head as he circled her chair. "Then what's troubling you, Sarah? I'll try to help if I can."

I suddenly realized she thought I was confiding in her about my marriage problems. I set her straight by telling her everything I'd shared with Carolyn, Russell, and Wanda and also how Wanda denied having any part in what had occurred. When I was done, concern crossed her face. "I wish you'd told me when you arrived. Wait here. There's something I need to show you."

She returned with a folded paper that she handed me. "I found this in my mailbox two days ago."

With shaky fingers, I unraveled the paper to reveal the message written in crayon. I gasped. "You got a crayon clue, too?"

My aunt nodded. "I was going to throw it out, but I thought I should keep it. I'm glad I did. I'll have to talk to Wanda privately. Even though she denied playing a part in this, I agree with Carolyn that she's the only one here who could've done it."

"Why?" I asked.

My aunt looked out toward the lighthouse. "I don't know, but I'm going to find out, and we'll get your phone back, Sarah. Don't worry. I was afraid this would happen. When you dig in old dirt, you're bound to uncover something that someone wants kept hidden."

I was shocked. "Aunt Julie, you don't think this is connected to what happened at the lighthouse twenty years ago?"

She kept staring ahead as she answered. "I'm afraid that's what I believe, Sarah. Let's go inside. I'm going to get to the bottom of this, so you can enjoy the rest of your stay here with your friend."

"Are you calling the police?"

"No." She turned toward me, her eyes dark. "I can handle this. If it's Wanda, I can deal with her on my own. Trust me, Sarah."

From the Notes of Michael Gamboski

Cape Haterras Lighthouse (Wikipedia)

Standing 193 feet (above ground), the Cape Hatteras Lighthouse in Buxton, NC is the tallest lighthouse in the United States. The National Park Service allows visitors to climb the Cape Hatteras Lighthouse from the third Friday in April to Columbus Day. The climb is strenuous, equivalent to walking the stairs of a twelve-story building.

Chapter Twenty-One

Sea Scope: Twenty years ago

When they got to Sarah's room, Wendy jumped on the cot Aunt Julie had put out earlier. She'd brought her sleepover bag. This wasn't the first time she'd stayed in Sarah's room. Sarah knew Wendy was accustomed to taking turns with her in the bathroom to brush her teeth and prepare for bed. Sarah let her go first and watched as she returned in her pink pajamas, combing out her braids so that her hair fell loose to her chest.

"Does your mom take out her hair at night, too?"

"Yes. We usually help one another do it."

"I always thought you two slept on them. How do you fix them in the morning?" Sarah had always had a hard time with braids, but her hair wasn't long enough. She could hardly get it in a ponytail without the short ends falling out.

"It isn't hard. I can teach you if you want."

"That's okay. Thanks, anyway."

Sarah was about to head to the bathroom for her own nightly routine when she heard her brother and Russ from the room next door jumping around laughing. She tapped on the wall that separated them. "Quiet down, you two."

The noise lessened, but she could still hear their voices, her brother's above Russell's. She doubted they'd sleep that night.

After Sarah used the bathroom and came back to join Wendy, she was already asleep hugging her favorite doll made of dried corn husks that had been packed in her overnight bag. She'd told Sarah she'd made it with her mother who'd taught her the craft. She never seemed to be without it.

Sarah was disappointed. She'd planned to ask her about her mother's boyfriend. She thought she'd open up to her when they were alone. Then Sarah had another idea. She might be able to find out herself if she did some detecting. A year ago, Glen had been into private eye books and TV shows, a departure from his science obsession. He'd recruited her to investigate things with him around the inn. That was how the crayon clues started.

Sarah remembered the way they'd gone about solving cases. Falling back on Glen's scientific method, they stated a hypothesis they thought they could prove. One day it had been the fact that Ms. Wilson wore black underwear. The reason they thought this was that when Aunt Julie sorted the family's laundry, Sarah had been given a pair of black lacy underwear. Sarah only wore white cotton briefs. The black panties might've gotten mixed up with hers, but Sarah wasn't about to give them back to Ms. Wilson until she knew they belonged to her. There were other guests staying at the inn, and although they did their own laundry, there was always a possibility an item of clothing would've been left in the washer or dryer downstairs and found its way into the family's load.

Glen had laughed when Sarah came up with the suggestion, but he dived in and created the investigation plan. He said she would be in charge of entering Ms. Wilson's room when she was out and checking her underwear drawer to see if the black panties matched any of the ones there. He would be on the lookout by her door and signal Sarah if he saw or heard Ms. Wilson returning to the room. Then he'd keep her occupied until his sister could escape unseen.

Sarah remembered how nervous she was as they tiptoed down the hall. It was a Saturday morning, and Ms. Wilson had taken Wendy to her Bible class. She usually dropped her off and then came back to the inn until it was time to pick her up. The class lasted only an hour and was five minutes away. As soon as she and Glen heard them leaving, they tiptoed to the Peach Room that was next to the Lighthouse Room. Glen guarded the door while Sarah crept inside. Ms. Wilson's double bed with its cream comforter was neatly made. Aunt Julie was always after Sarah to make her bed before she left her room in the morning, but Sarah usually left it unmade. A school photo of Wendy stood in a frame on the night stand next to the phone with a fresh vase of summer flowers from the Sea Scope garden. Otherwise, the room was pretty bare. Sarah heard Glen breathing outside the door. She knew he wouldn't want her to spend time looking through the room, but she'd never been in there before. Through the adjoining door, Sarah saw Wendy's room. It wasn't as neat as her mother's, but there were no toys or clothes scattered around like in Glen's room. Sarah also had a habit of leaving books and her art supplies everywhere.

"What are you doing in there?" Sarah heard her brother's whisper from out in the hall. She speeded up her search. She walked to Ms. Wilson's bureau, a light-colored pine featuring brass knobs that gleamed with a recent polish. There were three long drawers. Sarah pulled out each one until she found where Ms. Wilson stored her underwear. It was the middle drawer. Along with neatly folded panties, Ms. Wilson also stored her bras and nightgowns. Sarah noticed everything was lacy and there were, indeed, a few black panties. She added the one she'd brought along because it would be far too embarrassing to hand it back to Ms. Wilson. Sarah made sure she folded it neatly and placed it on the pile. She was afraid Ms. Wilson counted them, but she'd probably figure Sarah's aunt was the one who'd returned it. Sarah turned back and began to head for the door when she heard Glen whisper, "She's coming, Sarah. Give me a few minutes to get her attention and sneak out."

Sarah followed his instructions, opening the door a crack to make sure Ms. Wilson wasn't outside. Glen must've diverted her downstairs or to the West Wing.

Sarah slipped out and went to the dining room to see if breakfast was ready yet. She felt heady with the excitement of their completed mission.

Now, listening to Wendy's soft snores, Sarah decided to create her own case. She wanted to find out if her father was actually Ms. Wilson's boyfriend. As she'd done with Glen, Sarah mapped out her plan. Checking the time on her Barbie watch that she'd left on her night stand, Sarah saw it was nearly midnight, late enough that most of the adults would be asleep.

She tiptoed quietly from the room making sure Wendy was still sleeping. As she closed the door lightly behind her, there was a shuffle from the room next door, and Russell and Glen joined Sarah in the hall. Her brother jumped, surprised to see her. "What are you doing here, Sarah?" he whispered.

She should've known Glen would've recruited Russ into his nightly wanderings through the inn.

"I think you should answer the same question."

"You first."

Sarah looked at him in his blue sailor pajamas standing next to Russ in his green train ones. She had the urge to laugh but didn't want to wake anyone.

"If you must know, I'm on a case."

Glen smiled and called her by the nickname she hated but that was only to mask his interest. "Silly Sarah. Don't you know you need assistant detectives on cases? Luckily, Russ and I were about to embark on our own mission."

"We were? I thought we were only patrolling the hall," Russ said, matching their whispers.

Glen gave him a light punch on the arm. "Yes, we were, Detective Donovan. We were trying to find out how many new guests are at the inn tonight."

Sarah was aware a bunch of people had checked in for the Fourth of July fireworks show and that more would arrive the next day for the weekend, but she also knew most of them were in the rooms downstairs, although there were several guest rooms in the West Wing.

"And how do you intend to do that, Detective Brewster?" She humored him.

"I'm not going to tell you, Silly Sarah, unless you tell us what case you're working on."

They'd moved slightly away from the Violet Room as they spoke. Sarah was hesitant to reveal her idea and slightly embarrassed by its nature, but she felt she had no choice. "Well, detectives," she glanced at both boys, "I'm trying to determine who Ms. Wilson's boyfriend is. I was going to ask Wendy again, but she fell asleep, and I know how stubborn she can be about keeping secrets."

Glen nodded in agreement. "Okay, so how do you plan to uncover this information?"

Until then, Sarah had been sure of what to do but now she found it hard to explain. It wasn't because of Glen's beady eyes on hers but because of the way she felt shy around Russ after their earlier kiss.

"I was going to listen at Ms. Wilson's door," she finally explained. If their father was Ms. Wilson's boyfriend, he would have to go next door to her room without waking their mother which was usually easy because she was deaf in one ear and usually slept like a log, especially after one of her drinking binges which Sarah expected she'd had that night.

Glen laughed, and Russ put his finger to his lips. "Shhh. We'll wake the whole place if you don't keep quiet."

"Sorry, but I can't help it. Silly Sarah has a stupid plan. I think we should forget ours and help her out. Each one of us can listen at a different door. That's the only way to narrow down the suspects."

Sarah saw the reasoning in that. After all, it was possible Ms. Wilson's boyfriend wasn't her father. In that case, Ms. Wilson might be in another room altogether.

"Okay," she said, remembering to keep her voice low. "But I say we restrict the search to the top floor."

"Agreed." Glen took a breath and snuck closer to Sarah and Russell. "This is the plan. Sarah, you check Ms. Wilson's room as you originally wanted to do. Russ, you check the first guest room on the left side of the West Wing," he nodded down the opposite hall, "and I'll check the Lighthouse Room and the other guest room."

"That's not fair," Sarah said. "You get to check two rooms and Russ and I only get to check one."

"Also, no one is checking Ms. Brewster's room," Russ said.

Glen smiled his hand-in-the-cookie jar grin. "We all know what's going on in that room, Russ, but to make it fair, you can check the Garden Room where our parents stay while Sarah checks the Ocean View Room where you and your dad usually sleep. I'm sure it's empty tonight, but it makes her even with us at two rooms each. Is that good?"

Russell and Sarah nodded, obviously humoring the younger boy.

"Do we need a map?" Sarah noticed Glen was holding a pad and paper in his hand and three pencils."I don't think that's necessary, Glen."

He ripped off three sheets of paper and handed one to Sarah and Russell along with the pencils Sarah was glad were sharpened. "You can take notes if you want. I wish my tape recorder wasn't broken." Glen had dropped his special third-grade graduation gift a few days after receiving it, and their dad said he wouldn't replace it because Glen had to learn to be more careful with his things. He'd promised to have it repaired if Glen paid for it out of his allowance, but he hadn't gotten around to doing that yet.

"If we talk much longer, people will wake up," Russ pointed out.

"Then let's go," Glen said, adding, "We'll report back here. Remember the rules. Be as quiet as possible, don't go in any rooms, and, if you're caught, say you were going to the bathroom or were hungry and wanted to get something to eat."

Sarah found it funny how serious her brother took this and how he acted as their leader even though he was the youngest. After agreeing to the instructions, she and Glen headed to the West Wing while Russ walked across the hall to the Garden Room door.

Chapter Twenty-Two

Sea Scope: Present day

When we went back inside, Russell and Carolyn gave me questioning looks as if they wanted to know what Aunt Julie's response had been to what I'd told her. Wanda was in the kitchen.

"It's a beautiful morning," Aunt Julie said, "if any of you would like to take advantage of it. Sarah, feel free to put up your easel and work on the patio or in the garden. Russell, maybe you can show Carolyn around the grounds. I'm going to help Wanda in the kitchen. We'll have a hot breakfast for everyone in about a half hour. I'm sure Jennifer will be down by then and join us, too."

I couldn't get over my aunt's flippancy. She acted as if nothing was wrong.

"I'd love to see the grounds in nice weather," Carolyn commented, and I noticed the way she practically batted her eyelashes at Russ.

"Let's take a walk then," he said. "We can talk more about Kit Kat." As they passed me, he whispered, "I assume she's having a talk with Wanda." Aunt Julie had already gone into the kitchen.

I nodded.

Carolyn smiled. "See you later, Sarah." She wasn't interested in what was going on.

I debated whether I should sketch, as Aunt Julie suggested, or hide outside the kitchen door and listen in on her conversation with Wanda as I'd done with Glen and Russ as children with our ears to the guest room doors. I decided against that childish behavior and went upstairs to see if I could help my mother.

The Garden Room door was closed. I knocked on it gently. "Mom," I called. "Can I come in?"

A few minutes passed, and I wasn't sure she heard me. I knew her hearing in her good ear had deteriorated as she'd aged, so I spoke and rapped louder. "Mom. It's Sarah. Are you awake?"

I considered she'd taken a nap after the flight, but she finally answered, wide awake and soberer than I thought she would be. "I was hanging up my clothes." She opened the door for me to enter.

I stepped into the room. The curtains were open to allow in the sunshine, and the fresh flowers placed by Wanda stood on the white pedestal side table. The room was wall-papered in a creamy pattern with roses. It had always struck me as old-fashioned. My mother's suitcase stood open on the queen bed, clothing scattered atop the floral-printed bedspread. I had the thought that the room was appropriately decorated for its namesake, but I knew it was named after the garden over which it looked.

"Can I help?" I asked.

Mother shook her platinum blonde head. I noticed her gray roots needed a touch up. "I can't see how, Sarah. Why don't you have a seat? We can have a little chat as I finish unpacking."

I sat on the tapestry-brocaded chair near the window and looked out. I saw Russ and Carolyn walking among the flowers. They were deep in conversation. I heard snippets of their words floating on the light breeze that came through the screen.

"This garden is beautiful," Carolyn said. "I would love to sit here on one of those benches and write."

"You should do that," Russ said. "I remember, as a boy, I used to come here a lot and think about things. It's a great place to come up with ideas."

"What did you think about?"

"Sometimes I thought about my mom. I never really knew her. She died when I was three."

"I'm so sorry."

I watched them sit on a bench under the weeping willow and across from the small pond my aunt told me my grandfather had added to the garden before I was born.

"Sarah?" My mother was calling me back to her.

I turned around. "Sorry, Mom. My friend is in the garden with Russ, and I was listening to them."

"Don't you know it's rude to eavesdrop?" She smiled, and it made her face pretty as I remembered it years ago when she wasn't in one of her depressed moods. "Your friend is attractive. I think she and Russ would make a nice couple."

I wasn't sure how I felt about that. I didn't want either of them hurt.

"Can you hand me a few hangers from the closet, please?"

I stood up and slid the mirrored closet door open. As I did so, a piece of paper fell out. I gasped.

"What is it, Sarah? Did you get your finger caught?"

"No." I picked up the paper trying to figure out how to hide it from my mother, but it was too late.

"What is that, Sarah? Did Aunt Julie leave me a note? What a strange place to put it." She walked over to me before I could open it. "Let me see."

I had no choice but to hand it to her. I watched her face change as she read it. "What type of joke is this?" she asked angrily, but I knew it wasn't me at whom she was mad. "This is written in crayon like Glen used to do in his game."

My heart beat fast. I had a flashback to seeing the light under the Garden Room door the night before. "Mother, I've gotten two of them myself and Aunt Julie got one, too. We think Wanda's behind it. Julie's talking to her right now. What does that one say?"

Mom looked up at me, her dark eyes brimming with tears, her voice choking on the words, "Michael was murdered." Collapsing on the bed, she covered her eyes with her palms. "I never should have come," she murmured. "I knew it was a mistake."

From the Notes of Michael Gamboski

Hunting Island Lighthouse (Wikimedia Commons)
The Hunting Island Lighthouse in South Carolina was originally constructed between 1857 and 1859. It was built of brick and stood 95 feet tall. This structure replaced the lightship on the shoals of St. Helena Island. In 1861, the lighthouse was destroyed by Confederates so that the Union would not be able to use the light against them. In 1875, another lighthouse was erected on Hunting Island. Engineers designed the structure to be movable should the ocean encroach upon its territory. In 1889, the structure was dismantled and moved 1 ¼ miles southwest of its original location. It took four months from start to finish.
(Information supplied by South Carolina Parks)

Chapter Twenty-Three

Sea Scope: Twenty years ago

Sarah was excited when her father asked her and Glen to help the people arriving at the inn with their bags. Russell's dad had taken him fishing, and Wendy was in the garden with her mother cutting flowers for the guest rooms. Although guests weren't supposed to check in until 3:00, many of them arrived earlier. Aunt Julie was surprised that there hadn't been more newcomers the day before, but there was another lighthouse show scheduled that weekend that visitors were probably hoping to attend. While the guests waited for their rooms to be ready, Aunt Julie entertained them in the living room with tea, cookies, and fresh peaches.

As Glen was carting luggage upstairs, Sarah's dad gave her the cases to take to the guest rooms on the main floor. They were alone together for a few minutes and as Mr. Brewster slid three suitcases toward her, she said, "Can I ask you a question, Dad?"

"Sure thing, Sarah. You look a little tired, sweetie. Did you sleep okay last night?"

Sarah recalled the detecting she, Russ, and Glen had done but knew not to admit that was what had caused the dark circles under her eyes. "Well, it was a little hard getting to sleep after the fireworks," she replied instead.

Mr. Brewster smiled. "I imagine you and Wendy were up all night girl talking."

The truth was, when Sarah returned to the room after sharing her findings with the boys, Wendy had still been out like a light embracing her doll, but Sarah nodded as if to agree with her father.

"So, what would you like to ask me, honey?"

She edged closer to him in the confines of the expanded closet her aunt considered the luggage room, checking if anyone else could overhear. When she was sure no one was outside, she asked, "Do you love Mom?"

A strange look crossed her father's face. She wondered if it was guilt, but he quickly replaced it with one of curiosity. "Why do you ask that, Sarah?"

"I want to know."

"Of course I love her. I know we fight sometimes like you and Glen but that doesn't mean we don't love one another." He didn't look convincing with his reply.

"Can you love more than one person at a time?"

Her father wiped his brow with his hand. There were no fans in the luggage room, but she thought he was sweating for another reason. "Sure, Sarah. I love you, your mom, and Glen."

"I don't mean that." She looked down. "I was wondering if a man could love his wife and another woman at the same time."

"Why are you asking these questions, Sarah?"

She jumped at the harshness of her father's tone, but she needed to know the truth because last night hadn't proved anything.

"I just want to know." She looked up into his angry dark eyes.

"It's possible a married person, man or woman, could be attracted to someone else but if that person is in love with their husband or wife, it shouldn't matter," he muttered lowering his voice and looking out the door, checking if anyone was nearby. "Here, take these to the rooms on the tags. Aunt Julie will be angry if the guests don't have their bags on time." He was dismissing her.

"There's lots of time," she persisted, but her father had already rolled the three bags toward her and walked through the door. "Thanks for helping, Sarah. I'm going to see if my sister needs anything now." His voice had calmed, but she noticed the tone was still rough. She watched him walk away and thought about the saying that had something to do with "hitting a raw nerve" and nothing to do with the dentist.

Chapter Twenty-Four

Sea Scope: Present day

I felt anger rise in me. Clutching the note, I told my mother, "Come downstairs. I'm going to get to the bottom of this."

I headed for the kitchen, Mother trailing behind me sniffling.

As we entered the room, the smell of grits, bacon, and coffee awakened my hunger, but I wouldn't let it stop me in my mission.

Wanda stood over the stove humming as she stirred a frying pan. Aunt Julie was next to her placing slices of bread in the toaster.

"Oh, good. You're both here," Julie said. "Breakfast will be ready in a few minutes."

"What's going on?" I asked. "Didn't you speak with her?" My eyes focused on Wanda who kept mixing the concoction in the pan.

"I did, Sarah, and she has nothing to do with it. I know Wanda well enough to see she's telling the truth."

I ignored the fact we were talking about Wanda as though she wasn't in the room. "Well someone sure as hell isn't. Look at what was in Mom's closet." I handed her the paper. Wanda stopped stirring.

"Carolyn couldn't have done that, and I doubt Russell is responsible."

"Responsible for what?" Russ asked, walking through the patio door with Carolyn.

"Good. Everyone's here now," I said. "I hate to ruin your meals, but I found another note." I turned to Russ. "This one says Michael was murdered. My aunt refuses to acknowledge that Wanda has to be the one leaving these, and it isn't a joke."

Mother had collapsed into a chair and was sobbing into her hands again.

Russ left Carolyn's side to stand between me and my aunt. "Can I see the note?"

Aunt Julie passed it to him.

"We have to call the police. You haven't found your phone, have you, Sarah?"

I shook my head.

"Since we know it's one of us, there's no reason to call the police," my aunt said firmly. Wanda looked on quietly, her lips pursed. I wondered if her silence was evidence of guilt.

"There's been a robbery, and these notes might be construed as threats. If you don't call the cops, I will." Russ took his cell phone from his pocket.

"No, wait." Wanda finally spoke. "I think I know who's doing this."

She turned off the pan and faced us. "Please sit down, and I'll explain. It's a long story."

From the Notes of Michael Gamboski

McGulpin Lighthouse (Wikimedia Commons)

An early love come again, abides within
Uses every crevice of time long gone.
In memory still agile
For open, iron-tower steps.
Tower-wind certain as a song –
Once known and loved in decades past,
The memories are pure joy –
They last, and last…

(from Love Letter to a Light by Thelma Shaw—age 98—owner of the McGulpin Lighthouse from 1937 to mid-1970s. The McGulpin Lighthouse is located on upper Lake Michigan near Mackinaw City.)

Chapter Twenty-Five

Sea Scope: Twenty years ago

Sarah, Glen, Russ, and Wendy were in Michael's room. He'd checked into the inn the week before hefting a backpack filled with books, clothes, binoculars, and a camera. He'd told Aunt Julie he was studying history at Cape Bretton University and was doing research about lighthouses over the summer. He thought Sea Scope would be an ideal spot for him to spend a few weeks, so he could study the nearby lighthouse. He'd arrived a day after another college student had quit suddenly after working part-time as a bell hop at the inn all spring. Sarah's father had been angry about that, but it worked out for Sarah and Glen because they got their jobs back of bringing up suitcases to the guest rooms.

Glen took a special interest in Michael, and all of them were delighted when the young man invited them into his room. The Lighthouse Room was their favorite because it had a clear view of the lighthouse.

Glen, in true detective mode, was examining the objects Michael displayed on his bureau. There was a photo of him with his parents, a middle-aged couple standing next to him in his graduation robe; a large seashell Michael used as a paperweight; a table-sized, illustrated book of lighthouse photos, and a key on a red lanyard the town had given him to open the gate.

"My dad has written about lighthouses, too," Russ said, sitting on the nautical quilt on the bed. "It's part of the history books he writes about South Carolina." Russ was very proud of his father.

Michael smiled and pushed his glasses back up his nose. "Your dad offered to help me, and I'm very thankful about that, Russell. I'll probably interview him next week."

Sarah and Wendy were gazing out the window. "This view is the best in the whole inn," Sarah said.

"Yes, I couldn't have asked for a better room. How long has your family owned this place, Sarah?"

"Forever," she replied. "It used to be our grandparents' before they moved to that old person's place down in Florida."

"It's called assisted living," Glen corrected. He turned to Michael on the other side of the bed. "After our grandparents moved, Dad and Aunt Julie took over, but our mom doesn't like it here much."

"Really?" Michael quirked a light eyebrow. "Why is that?"

"Mom has these moods. I don't think she'd be happy anywhere."

"Glen," Sarah cautioned. "Don't talk about Mother like that."

"Well, it's true."

"How much of your report have you written?" Russell asked, changing the subject.

"I'm on a first draft, but it's slow going. I've already written about several other lighthouses along the East Coast, but this is the first one I have an opportunity to explore firsthand." Michael mentioned details about his work that everyone except Wendy was interested in. As the three children gathered around him on the bed, he opened the Eastern Seaboard lighthouse book he'd taken from his bureau and showed them the photos. Wendy stayed at the window holding her corn-husk doll and looking at the waves splashing over the rocks in front of the lighthouse. A few sailboats drifted by. She remembered her mother said her father had been a fisherman, or was it a sailor? The story changed each time she asked.

Chapter Twenty-Six

Sea Scope: Twenty years ago

After the whispering and questioning died down, Sea Scope fell silent, but it was a silence that echoed through the halls and out onto the grounds. Glen told Sarah that the scientific term for something under the surface ready to explode was dormant. That's how the inn felt to Sarah a week after Michael's death as she walked through the garden with Wendy. Ms. Wilson wasn't feeling well, so Aunt Julie asked the girls to pick fresh flowers to replace the dead ones in some of the rooms. It wouldn't be such a difficult task because most of the guests had already checked out after having been released from questioning by the police.

"When we're done, Sarah, can we head down to the lighthouse?" Wendy asked as she clipped marigolds with the clipper her mother had given her. Sarah only had a scissor and found it difficult to cut through the tough stems. She was surprised by Wendy's question. Everyone at Sea Scope avoided the lighthouse, and Detective Marshall told Aunt Julie they were keeping the gate locked and not allowing tours until further notice.

"Why do you want to go there? Did you ask your mother?"

Wendy shook her head, and the light wind tousled her braids. "No. She's sick in bed with a bad headache. She said it's a migraine. I'm not supposed to disturb her."

Sarah snipped a few petunias pressing hard on the scissor handles to snap them off their stems. "I don't think they'd let us go to the lighthouse without an adult anymore. I could ask my aunt or mother. Dad isn't home."

Wendy walked over to her, holding the flowers she'd gathered. "No," she whispered looking around behind her as if someone was listening. "I want to go with you alone."

"Why? What's the big secret?" Sarah didn't understand. Wendy was a quiet type who usually kept to herself even when she accompanied Sarah, Glen, and Russell. While they'd never been exactly friends, Wendy had started to hang around more with Sarah since the lighthouse incident. Sarah couldn't figure out why, but there were rumors that Ms. Wilson was looking for a place in town and that she and her daughter would be leaving Sea Scope by August.

"I want to go," Wendy implored, her brown eyes large and pleading. "Please, Sarah. You owe me. I mopped up the kitchen last night when Aunt Julie punished you for asking Detective Marshall if he was her new boyfriend."

Sarah recalled the incident with embarrassment. It was the first night the detective had come to the inn by personal invitation. Aunt Julie had worn a silky lilac dress with her hair pinned up. Even when Russell's dad had come to dinner, her aunt hadn't dressed so nicely. Mr. Donovan was no longer a regular visitor at the inn, and Sarah had to admit she missed Russell. While Wendy's new offer of friendship may not have been sincere and would probably be short-lived, Sarah wanted to consider it.

"Okay," she relented, "even though we won't be able to get very close to the lighthouse." She was curious to see the place again with the new signs and the added locks. It was a fearful kind of curiosity similar to those who stopped to stare at car accidents along the road.

Wendy gave Sarah her gap-toothed smile showing two missing teeth on the top row of her mouth. "Thanks. Let's go put these inside." She indicated the flowers and, taking short skips, she hopped to the back door, her braids swinging behind her.

"I don't understand why you want to go to the lighthouse and why you need me to come with you," Sarah said as they walked toward the beach. "You could've sneaked out on your own."

"I was afraid to go by myself. I've been having nightmares about the lighthouse."

"I don't blame you. It's spooky now. Michael died there."

They were at the gate, and Sarah saw the new padlock and the large sign that read, "No Trespassing. Lighthouse Closed to the Public Until Further Notice."

"We can't get in, anyway."

"Yes, we can."

Sarah watched in dismay as Wendy began to scale the fence.

"Wendy, no. Get down. We'll get in trouble." Sarah had seen the police patrolling the area throughout the past week. She was surprised no one was around, but she was sure one of Detective Marshall's men would be back on watch soon.

Wendy ignored her. "Follow me. Hurry. This won't take long. I need to look for something."

Against Sarah's better judgment, she put her sneakered feet through the notches in the fence and hoisted herself over, landing a few feet away from Wendy. Standing up and dusting grass mixed with sand from her jeans, she said, "Is that what this is all about? What did you lose?"

Wendy cleaned off her jumper and faced Sarah. "I want to find Dottie." Dottie was the name Wendy had given her corn-husk doll. Sarah noticed Wendy wasn't carrying the doll around lately, but she wasn't aware it was missing.

"When did you lose her?"

"I don't know. I don't remember."

"Why do you think she'd be *here*? You haven't been to the lighthouse in a long time." The last time Sarah had been to the lighthouse was with Glen when they'd found Michael. Wendy hadn't been with them that day. Sarah tried to recall when she'd last seen Wendy with

Dottie, but the past week had been so crazy her mind hadn't been on little things like dolls.

"I figured I had to check just in case. I've looked all over the inn and even asked at Bible school." Tears suddenly formed in Wendy's eyes. "Mama promised to get me another doll, but it won't be the same."

Sarah knew what it was like to be attached to a toy. Never one to fancy dolls, she had a stuffed Minnie Mouse she'd brought home from Disney World when she and her parents had vacationed there when she was six. She'd outgrown sleeping with and carrying Minnie around years ago, but the mouse still occupied a favorite spot atop her bedroom bureau.

"Okay. Let's take a look, but we need to do it fast."

Wendy wiped her eyes. "Thanks, Sarah."

The girls scanned the area around the lighthouse with no luck. Sarah gave up the search first. "I don't see your doll, Wendy, and one of the officers who keeps checking this place for trespassers might be here any minute, not to mention Aunt Julie, once she notices us missing."

Wendy was still walking in circles keeping her eyes on the ground for sight of the corn-husk doll with yarn braids. When Wendy headed back toward the fence, she stopped in her tracks. "Wait, Sarah. There's one more place we need to search."

Sarah sighed. "We've covered the whole area. Where else can we look?"

"The lighthouse." Wendy pointed to the looming structure. With gray clouds hovering around it on the muggy July day, it looked ominous to Sarah.

"I told you we can't get in there. The doors are locked."

"I think I know one that isn't," Wendy said. "It's the secret entrance Glen showed us. Remember?"

Sarah hesitated. When the four of them visited the lighthouse, they usually went in the main door, but Glen had once found a back door covered with rust and slightly hidden by overgrown bushes.

"Alright, Wendy. We'll check it, but if it's open, we just take a quick look."

Wendy nodded, running around to the back of the lighthouse, her braids bobbing as Sarah tried to catch up.

The interior of the lighthouse was dark and damp. Sarah felt a chill crawl up her spine despite the hot air that flattened her hair against her head. When they reached the staircase, she nearly chickened out, but she couldn't abandon Wendy who was already climbing up.

"Don't you want to look around down here first?" she asked.

"We can do that on the way out."

Sarah nearly fell over her own feet as she rushed after Wendy. She tried not to recall the last time she and Glen had followed this same path to the lighthouse tower.

When they were at the very top, Wendy stood looking down over the guardrail as Glen had the week before. Seven days had changed so much in their lives.

Sarah hesitated to join Wendy, afraid she might see another shattered body on the rocks below.

"Aren't you looking for Dottie?" Sarah reminded her friend.

"She's not here," Wendy said, her voice cracking as if she was about to burst into tears again.

"We haven't really checked." Sarah took a few steps forward.

"I looked around already." Wendy turned. Her face held a strange expression. A thin smile spread across her lips, but Sarah couldn't tell if she was happy or sad.

"Then let's get out of here," Sarah coaxed her. The last thing she wanted was to be in this place where tragedy had struck. "Aunt Julie may have already called the police to search for us."

Wendy laughed. "If she called Detective Marshall, she'll be having tea with him and flirting. He's all she thinks about now."

Sarah wanted to defend her aunt, but she knew what Wendy said was true. She was also aware that Aunt Julie's attraction to the detective was why Mr. Donovan and Russell were no longer visiting Sea Scope.

"We still need to go home."

"Your home, not mine." Wendy had her back to the guardrail, and Sarah had a fleeting image of her turning and jumping over as she had the fence a few minutes ago.

"Is it true you and your mom are moving into town?" It was the first time Sarah had asked for a direct answer regarding the rumor.

"Yes, by August I think, and your dad is talking about moving you all back to Long Island." There was a hitch in Wendy's voice, and the smile that had touched her face was now replaced by pursed lips.

Sarah suspected Wendy was right. The other night, Glen told her he'd overheard their parents talking. He told her their mother was asking their father to consider moving to Long Island where she'd lived before she met him. Glen added that their mother was asking for a new start, promising to lay off the bottle and enter an AA program. Their father was agreeing that he would work harder to keep the family together.

"Sarah, can I ask you something?" Wendy still hadn't moved from the guardrail.

"Sure, but we can talk outside." Sarah was beginning to feel light-headed. She felt dizzy in high spaces, and Aunt Julie said she might be acquiring a fear of heights.

Wendy paused, and Sarah worried that she would insist on staying, but she finally gave up her spot and walked next to Sarah to the staircase. "Okay. We'll go down. It's creepy up here. It's making me remember my dream."

Sarah was relieved that Wendy felt the same way she did. She followed her downstairs and out the back door. When they were in the fresh yet humid air, Sarah said, "What did you want to ask me?"

Wendy pushed back her damp braids. Sarah noticed one of the yellow ribbons tying them was coming loose. "Have you ever kept any secrets from your mom?" she asked.

Sarah thought it was an unusual question. She couldn't recall any particular secret she kept from her mother because they didn't talk often. Mostly, she kept secrets from Glen, but she knew he kept more from her. "Maybe, but I can't think of any. Why?"

"No reason. Just curious." Wendy was checking the ground as she walked away from the lighthouse.

Sarah, looking ahead toward the inn, spotted a police car parked out front. "Wendy, look over there. We need to get out of here fast."

Wendy raised her head and followed Sarah's waving hand. She ran to the gate and jumped over, Sarah at her heels. Running across the field toward Sea Scope, the girls breathed heavily. They needn't have rushed because as they entered the inn, they heard Aunt Julie speaking to Detective Marshall. They were seated at the kitchen table having tea and biscuits as Wendy had predicted.

From the Notes of Michael Gamboski

(photo courtesy of Wikimedia Commons)

At the foot of the bare brown cliffs,
Half hid in the drifted sand,
With the rack of the sea for a winding sheet
And the moan of the waves on the strand
Sobbing a dirge o'er the resting place
Of a secret of wreck and woe,
Lies a broken mast and a few poor timbers
By which like sentinels guarding a city
The sea gulls come and go.

(From the poem, "Secret of the Sea" by H.A.)

Chapter Twenty-Seven

Sea Scope: Present day

Even though Wanda had asked everyone to sit, the group, except for Mother who sat at the table, remained standing in a circle. Carolyn moved close to Russell. Aunt Julie stood next to Wanda as if to support her.

Wanda took a breath and began. "It's about my daughter Wendy."

The room was silent except for Mother's quiet sobs. She'd grabbed a napkin from one of the place settings and was dabbing at her eyes.

"What about Wendy?" Russ probed when the silence grew too long. "I haven't seen her in years. Even though I knew you two still lived in Cape Bretton, I never thought about dropping by to see you. I guess I wanted to erase the bad memories of that summer."

Wanda nodded. "We all wanted to do that. I thought Wendy had, but after Sarah and her folks moved away and Julie closed the inn, Wendy began having terrible nightmares. She woke up screaming but couldn't remember the dreams. I took her to several doctors including a psychiatrist, but they couldn't find anything wrong with her. They diagnosed it as growing pains, but I always believed it had to do with Michael's accident." She took another deep breath and tossed her long braid behind her back. "As she grew older, the dreams lessened, so I convinced myself the doctors may have had a point, but part of me still felt the problem came back to Sea Scope."

"What does this have to do with what's happening now?" Russell asked. I noticed Carolyn had inched even closer to him while I had moved nearer to my mother's chair. She was no longer crying but listening intently to Wanda's words.

"I'm getting to that. Sorry." Wanda leaned back against the counter. The bacon and eggs sat cooling in the pan. I'd lost my appetite completely despite the aroma that still filled the room, and I imagined the others had, too.

"Take your time," Aunt Julie said giving Russell a look that told him to wait for the rest of the story.

"There's not much more to say except that part of this is my fault because when Glen had his awful accident, I brought Wendy with me to his apartment to help clear it out for Julie. She offered to go, but I should've realized it might awaken memories."

I thought maybe that's how they'd come across Glen's phone, but I kept quiet.

"When we returned to Cape Bretton," Wanda continued, "Wendy was fine except the nightmares were starting again. She'd been married for a brief time to a man I'd hardly known. The divorce had gone through recently, and she was now living with me."

I heard Russell take a breath and knew he was getting impatient again. The tapping of his foot was another clue.

"It was right after we came back from Los Angeles that I started finding the clues."

I was the one who interrupted now. "Are you talking about the crayon clues?"

Wanda nodded. "Yes. Wendy started leaving them around our house."

"What did they say?" I asked.

"I can't remember now, but they were all related to the incident at Sea Scope that summer. I asked her about them, and she pretended she knew nothing. Then I caught her writing one, and she laughed. She replied in a boy's childlike voice that she was Glen and that's when

I insisted that she see another psychiatrist." Wanda inhaled deeply as Mother began crying again.

"They diagnosed her with a personality disorder."

"Like Sybil?" Carolyn finally spoke from next to Russell.

"No. It wasn't a multiple personality disorder or dissociative disorder—that is the correct technical term. The psychiatrist explained that Wendy would have different symptoms with that. She would develop another identity but not take on someone else's."

"I wanted to protect her," Wanda continued. "That's why I knew it would be a bad idea to bring her along to Sea Scope when Julie invited me. Maybe I shouldn't have even accepted, but I think part of me thought I'd find the answer here that would help her." She wiped her eyes, and I thought she'd begun to cry like my mother. I'd never seen Wanda cry except for the day they broke the news to her about Michael.

Aunt Julie tried to comfort her by putting her arms around her, but Wanda broke away. "No. This is my fault." She turned to me. "Sarah, I'll get you your phone back or replace it. I promise."

"Wait a minute," Russell said. "If what you're saying about Wendy is true, she has episodes where she believes she's Sarah's brother when he was young during the time she knew him. After these episodes, does she remember them?"

Wanda nodded her head, bobbing her braid. Her tears had dried. "No. I think that's part of the condition."

"How long do these spells generally last? An hour? A day? Longer than that?"

Before Wanda could answer, Aunt Julie said, "I think Wanda's had enough of an interrogation, Russell. Why don't we all settle down and have breakfast before it turns cold."

Russell caught my anger that had now dissipated into disbelief. "Is that it? Mystery solved. Let's go back to our vacation?" He waved his hands for emphasis and then turned to face my aunt. "You know what I think? I think you cooked up this little inn opening to get all of us here who were there that summer. You wanted to put us on a stage, so we could act out our stories. That party idea backfired, but you still don't want to take down the decorations. Well, I'm not sticking around for your fake reminiscences of the good old days." He turned to leave the kitchen, and Carolyn grabbed his arm.

"No, Russ, please. It's okay. Sarah's aunt didn't mean any harm, and neither did Wanda. I wasn't involved in what happened back then, but looking at it from an outsider's point of view, I'd say that there are things to be settled here."

Sarah didn't think that would calm Russell, but he made no move to pass around Carolyn.

Mother, who had stopped crying, looked around the room. "I agree with Sarah's friend," she said. "I think we should stay here and face the truth finally."

"Too bad you don't take your own advice, Jennifer," Aunt Julie responded.

Wanda was the one who broke the tension in the room. "I'm going to call Wendy and see if she's home. I thought she would be okay left alone. She's been fine for months now, although she lost her job. I lied about her secretarial position in Charleston as an excuse for her absence."

"Did she know you were coming to Sea Scope?" Russell asked. He'd turned back around. I noticed Carolyn's hand was still lightly on his arm as if holding him there.

"No. I didn't want to tell her. I said I was visiting friends, but it's possible she figured it out. Our home is not very far from here, and she doesn't drive, so I imagine she walked here last night, took Sarah's phone, and left the note."

"She has Glen's phone, too," I said. "I received a message from it before I arrived."

Wanda didn't look surprised to hear this. "I wondered what happened to it. When we were packing up his stuff, I came across it. I laid it on the bed and then went to get boxes to pack the rest of his things. When I returned, it was gone. I asked Wendy if she saw it, and she said she didn't know. I thought maybe it fell under the bed. I checked but couldn't see anything."

"Was she having a spell then?" Russ asked.

"Not that I can tell, but the episodes are usually very quick. Other times, they can last for a day or longer. She doesn't recall anything she's done during the episodes because she literally becomes young Glen."

"Why Glen instead of me?" I asked. "I don't think she and my brother were particularly close as children."

"Who knows?" Wanda shrugged. "The mind can be a strange tool indeed."

I knew Glen would agree with that, having dedicated years to the study of psychology.

"I'll call her now. Sit down, please." Wanda went to the phone on the kitchen wall and dialed. Everyone waited, standing, but I noticed Mother and Aunt Julie eyeing one another with animosity.

After ten rings, the answering machine kicked in.

"She's not answering," Wanda said, hanging up the phone.

"You could check on her," Aunt Julie said. "Go home and see if she's there."

"What if she's still here?" Russell interjected. "Does she ever do anything dangerous during these 'episodes?' " He used Wanda's term.

"No." Wanda shook her head vehemently. "She's not dangerous. She won't hurt anyone."

"But these messages must mean something," Carolyn added. "What if Michael really was murdered?"

Her question echoed through the room unanswered.

From the Notes of Michael Gamboski

(Michigan Lighthouse Conservancy, 2018)

If Lighthouses had a birthday, it would be August 7 when National Lighthouse Day is celebrated each year to commemorate the anniversary of the federal lighthouse establishment and the commitment and service of those who tended America's lights for generations.

For the bicentennial of the United States Lighthouse Service in 1989, the U. S. Lighthouse Society petitioned Congress to declare National Lighthouse Day on August 7—the date in 1789 that the Ninth Act of the First Congress, establishing federal control of lighthouses, was passed and signed by President George Washington. The measure was signed by President Ronald Reagan as Public Law on November 5, 1988 but only for that day in 1989. A similar declaration was won in 2013, but efforts to add the day to the official national calendar have not succeeded.

Lighthouse organizations across the country are still encouraged to celebrate August 7 as National Lighthouse Day and see it as a great opportunity for lighthouse tours, programs, and activities, and a fitting way to commemorate a vitally important part of America's rich maritime heritage.

Chapter Twenty-Eight

Cape Bretton, South Carolina: Twenty years ago

Detective Donald Marshall was having a bad morning. His alarm had malfunctioned, so he was officially a half hour late for work which meant he had no time for breakfast or even coffee until he got to the station. It was either skip the food and java or the shower. He couldn't do without a quick wash, spraying the hot water that took forever to warm and, when it did, became so burning hot that he had to turn it down, anyway.

Stepping out of the bath, he went about his normal morning routine at lightning speed or as fast as his tired body could move. He'd just turned fifty, and he was looking forward to retirement. His friends in the Charleston and Beaufort P.Ds were jealous of him for what they considered the quiet life in Cape Bretton. It was true the town saw hardly any crime except for an occasional stolen bicycle or a tourist from Up East going through one of the red lights on the main street. It often puzzled him why people on vacation were in such a hurry.

Shaving quickly, he checked his face in the mirror. His blue eyes were watery, his square jaw displayed razor stubble, and his summer crew cut was already growing out. He wasn't handsome, but he didn't consider himself homely either. He didn't have the best manner with women and that's why he was still single after the divorce from Judy ten years ago.

As he was pulling on his trousers and blue, open-collared polo, the phone rang. He should've been gone already, so he hesitated to answer it, but something made him pick it up.

"Marshall, where are you?"

It was his partner, Ted Loomis. "I know I'm late, Loom," he said, calling him by the nickname he'd given the younger man. "I'm on my way."

"Wait." Ted's voice held a note of urgency he seldom used. "Don't go to the station. Come directly to the lighthouse. We have an incident here."

"What's going on at the lighthouse?" Donald pictured teens loitering with beer bottles or maybe marijuana, but the town had cleaned most of that up for the fireworks celebrations two weeks ago. Then he remembered the student that had been hanging around since June working on a school report. What was his name, Mike?

"Just get your a-hole over here," Ted said and clicked off.

Grabbing his keys from the table by the door, Marshall glanced at his old Collie. The dog had lifted his head from sleep when he saw his owner, thinking it was time for a walk. Marshall felt a pang of guilt. He knew he wouldn't have Buddy much longer but also knew he'd get another dog to replace him, as he'd had them all his life. "Sorry, Buddy. You'll have to take a rain check this morning, but I managed to fill your food bowl."

I hope he doesn't pee all over the floor, he thought leaving the house as Buddy whined behind him. If the dog did, it would be his own fault for oversleeping. Not a good way to start the day, and he wasn't looking forward to what Loomis was hinting at either.

Chapter Twenty-Nine

Sea Scope: Present day

Aunt Julie was the one who broke the silence. "I believe the authorities determined the cause of death was that Michael jumped. He must've been a troubled young man, although he hid it well."

"How did they know he jumped and wasn't pushed?" Russell asked.

My aunt paused, trying to find the right words to reply. "Why would anyone have done that? Everyone liked Michael. Besides, there was no evidence of a struggle. Detective Marshall and his men ruled that out."

"Detective Marshall. Wasn't he the cop who you left my dad for, Ms. Brewster?"

Aunt Julie, usually so composed, turned away from Russ' gaze. "You were only a child. How can you remember that?"

"I remember my father being upset, waking in his sleep and crying. He'd finally accepted my mother's death and was ready to make a new life with someone else. He was going to ask you to marry him."

I was shocked. Even though Bart Donovan had been a frequent visitor at Sea Scope, I never knew he was that serious about my aunt. Maybe that explained why, in the days that followed Michael's death, Bart and Russ drifted away from the inn as Detective Marshall questioned my parents and Aunt Julie, in particular, way more times than seemed necessary. Dad said that he was only doing his job because police have to ask questions many times to be sure that people respond in the same way to verify that they're telling the truth. Glen joked that Detective Marshall was a funny name for a police officer. It was like a chiropractor with the name Dr. Bones or a lawyer called Sue Me. He thought it was even funnier that the detective's first name was Donald. When he came to the inn, Glen whispered, "Detective Donald Duck is here."

"Is Detective Marshall still around?" Carolyn inquired.

My aunt looked over Russell's head at her. "I have no idea. I'm sure he's retired by now."

"Maybe it wouldn't hurt to look him up. Someone should at least be consulted about this."

"I don't think that's a good idea," Wanda said, taking a seat at the table next to my mother who remained quiet as people talked around her. Wanda looked deflated after telling the story of Wendy, as if it had drained the strength from her.

"Why not?" Carolyn asked. "If all you guys were here that summer and this Detective Marshall investigated Michael's death, maybe he can shed more light on what happened. After all, I know Sarah and Russell were only kids, and Wendy, as well. If she isn't answering at home and she's hanging around Sea Scope, we should be looking for her."

"I think Carolyn's right," I said. "Even if she isn't dangerous, Wendy might end up hurting one of us or herself by accident. She needs professional help, and I know if Glen were still alive, he'd advise her to find the right doctor." I walked over to my aunt and spoke to her directly. "Aunt Julie, if you knew Detective Marshall well, he might be happy to help us. I understand you and Wanda not wanting to go to the police, but a retired cop might be useful in handling this type of situation."

Aunt Julie weighed her options. "I'll see what I can do, but it's possible he's moved away or even died." Watching her face as she spoke, I got the impression she knew exactly where to find Detective Donald Marshall.

From the Notes of Michael Gamboski

(Point No Point Vacation Rental)

Besides being wonderful places to visit, there are some lighthouses where you can actually stay during a vacation. These include Bed & Breakfasts, Vacation Rentals, Hostels, Lighthouse Keeper for a Fee, Volunteer Host Keeper, and Coast Guard Recreational Lodging for military families. Links to many U.S. accommodations can be found on the United States Lighthouse Society's website at
http://uslhs.org/fun/lighthouse-accommodations

Chapter Thirty

Sea Scope: Twenty years ago

When he arrived at the scene, Loomis and a few of the younger cops were there talking with a man and woman around Donald's age. A yellow tape cordoned off part of the area. Police vehicles and an ambulance were parked by the lighthouse.

"About time you got here," his partner said in way of greeting as Donald approached.

"What happened?"

"Looks like a suicide. This is Mr. and Ms. Brewster from the inn." Loomis introduced the man and woman standing next to him. "The vic was a guest. His name was Michael Gamboski. His parents have been contacted."

Donald looked up at the lighthouse tower and followed the path down to the area that surrounded the yellow tape. The body and a pair of broken glasses lay there. He turned his attention to Mr. and Ms. Brewster. He knew Ms. Brewster. He'd seen her in passing in town usually when grocery shopping, although he ran into her housekeeper in the supermarket more often. He'd also seen Ms. Brewster's paintings and attended one of the shows she gave at the gallery. She'd asked to do a portrait of him once, but he'd declined.

He walked over to the couple who he knew were brother and sister. When Martin Brewster wasn't helping his sister at the inn, he did construction and repair work around town.

Shaking Ms. Brewster's hand first and then her brother's, he said, "Good morning, folks, although I see it hasn't been a good one for you." Donald liked to interject a bit of humor into serious situations. He saw his attempt hadn't been received well and cut his smile.

"Hello, Detective Marshall," Ms. Brewster said. She was clearly shaken but trying hard not to show it. Her usual neat auburn hair was flung around her face, a result of standing against the wind that was whipping the coast that morning.

Mr. Brewster nodded, his dark eyes meeting Donald's for a moment and then looking away. Seeing them together, Donald realized they didn't look much like siblings. Ms. Brewster was fair, while her brother was dark of hair, eyes, and complexion. He knew that happened in families sometimes. His brother didn't look anything like him either.

"Again, my apologies," he offered, trying to make up from his previous attempt at humor.

He turned to Loomis. "Who found the body?"

"The boy and girl. His kids." He looked toward Mr. Brewster.

"Where are they?"

"Sarah and Glen are back at the inn with their mother," Mr. Brewster replied.

Donald recalled the children were in third and fifth grades in the same classes as his niece and nephew. They were old enough to be questioned. "We'll have to talk to them later. Where is Ms. Wilson?" He was proud he remembered the last name of the housekeeper. Lately, he'd been having those senior moments that weren't welcome in his profession.

"My housekeeper's picking up her daughter from summer Bible school," Ms. Brewster answered. She glanced at her watch. "They should be back at Sea Scope very soon."

"We'll need to talk to all of you since Mr. Gamboski had been a guest at your inn."

"I understand," Ms. Brewster said. "This was so unexpected. Michael was happy. He was very enthusiastic about his research."

"Julie, I told you before not to say anything yet. They need to read you your Miranda rights first."

"This isn't an interrogation, Mr. Brewster," Donald pointed out, but I'll be sure to read you all your rights when we talk back at the inn." He wondered, for a moment, if Mr. Brewster was afraid of what his sister might say.

Chapter Thirty-One

Sea Scope: Present day

I didn't see how the day could return to being normal after all the hidden accusations and animosity shared in the kitchen, but Aunt Julie, efficient as ever, instructed Wanda to reheat the breakfast while she went upstairs to call Detective Marshall if she could find his number.

Even though I'd thought I'd lost my appetite, I found myself hungry again and welcomed the food. Sitting next to Mother, I saw that she hardly touched a bite. Carolyn ate heartily, but Russell, at her side, only drank his coffee. Wanda didn't eat either.

"I'd like to see the rest of the garden," Carolyn said, buttering her toast and breaking the silence. "Would you mind showing it to me later, Russell?"

Putting down his coffee cup, he replied, "I'd be happy to do that, and I know you wanted to see the lighthouse, as well. It's a beautiful day, and I think we should take advantage by being out of this house." He looked across at me. "Would you like to join us, Sarah?"

I nearly choked on the piece of egg I'd bitten off my fork. Should I accept? I didn't think Carolyn would be happy sharing me with the only male guest at Sea Scope and one she'd zeroed in on, but I felt a need to escape the confines of the inn. "That would be nice. Thank you."

A shadow briefly passed over Carolyn's eyes, but then she smiled and said, "That's great. It'll be good to have two guides to show me around."

"I don't think you'll be able to get into the lighthouse," Wanda spoke from next to Carolyn. "The gate is locked. Tours are only given by appointment now."

I knew that policy had been enforced after Michael's death.

"We can still see it from the outside," Carolyn said. "It looked beautiful from the porch, but I'd love to see it up close."

Mother stood and emptied her plate. "I think I'll go back to my room now. I have more unpacking to do." I watched as she left the room. She was more composed, but I was sure she was still troubled by the note that was found in her closet. Not only would it have brought back memories of what happened to Michael and, shortly after, my father; but more recently, her own son's death.

Aunt Julie came back to the kitchen a short time after mother left. She looked brighter to me. A slight smile played at the corner of her lips as she announced, "I got through to Detective Marshall. He's still in Cape Bretton and even accepted an invitation to dinner here tonight. I thought that would be a good way to talk to him about our situation. I usually don't serve dinner to guests, but you're all family and friends, so I'm making an exception tonight."

"Do you need any groceries?" Wanda asked, offering to help with the preparations.

"I may," Aunt Julie replied. "I could use your help planning the menu. I assume you all don't have any food allergies or dietary restrictions?" She looked around the table.

Russell and I shook our heads, and Carolyn joked, "I wish I did. I eat everything, unfortunately." She smiled at Russell as he stood up from his seat.

"This might be a good time to continue our tour," he said. "Are you ladies ready?"

Carolyn and I nodded and followed him to the patio door leaving Aunt Julie and Wanda conferring over dinner as if this was a typical day at the inn.

From the Notes of Michael Gamboski

(Statue of Liberty and Montauk Lighthouse – Wikimedia Commons)

There are many interesting historical facts about lighthouses. Here are a few:

While most people don't realize the Statue of Liberty is also a lighthouse, it is also the first U.S. lighthouse to use electricity.

The Montauk Point Lighthouse on Long Island was the first built in New York State and was visited by both the slave ship "Amistad" and a pirate.

Chapter Thirty-Two

Long Island: Nineteen years ago

Sarah and her family had only been in the new house in Smithtown for a few months. Their mother had rushed their father into finding something not far from where she'd lived with her own parents before they all moved to South Carolina when she was accepted to Cape Bretton University. Jennifer's parents had relocated to a retirement complex in Florida. The same one, in fact, that her husband's parents had moved to a few years later.

Sarah's mother hadn't wanted to live Down South anymore. She hated the heat and humidity that lasted all year. She prompted her husband to contact Suffolk County real estate agents in search of a home and to look for work in one of the island's construction companies. He found both rather quickly. After the accident, she'd wanted nothing more than to leave Sea Scope. Sarah's father was reluctant to hand the inn over to his sister, even though he knew she was more than competent to run it. Wanda had given her resignation less than a week after Michael's death. She and her daughter moved to a small apartment in town while Wanda applied for jobs at other inns and bed and breakfasts in the area. Sarah's aunt had been understanding and provided excellent references for the housekeeper as well as a hefty bonus check to get Wanda started.

Sarah noticed her father was very quiet at breakfast that Tuesday morning. Her mother, pouring him coffee, said, "It's hard to believe it's been a year already."

"A year since when?" Glen asked, scooping a spoonful of Cap'n Crunch cereal from his bowl.

Mr. Brewster looked up from his paper. "Your mother was considerate enough to remind us that this was the day of Michael's accident."

Sarah's father insisted on referring to what happened to Michael as an accident and not the suicide the authorities labeled it after the investigation ended. The truth was nothing conclusive had been proven, and it wouldn't have been easy for Michael to have fallen, yet there were no signs of a struggle. The guardrails were high and had been checked for safety by the town the month before. Although Michael's parents denied that he was ever prone to depression, his mother, crying and clenching the gold cross at her throat, insisted he would never take his life because he was a devout Catholic.

Sarah's mother glared at her father. "Sorry, I didn't mean to upset you, Martin. I know how close you and Michael were." The last was said through clenched teeth as she turned and left the room.

"Why is Mom mad?" Sarah asked. She didn't understand what her mother meant about her father being close to Michael. She thought Mr. Donovan was close to Michael because they shared an interest in lighthouses and South Carolina history.

Her father didn't reply. Instead, he pushed his coffee mug aside and asked, "Do you two kids have any plans today?"

"Mother said she would take us to the beach," Glen said, "but I wanted to go to Brookhaven Labs. They have cool kid's science programs in the summer."

"She won't drive out there," Sarah said. "She promised we could all go on a weekend if Dad's not working." Most of their father's jobs were on the weekends, although he did work during the week, too.

"But Dad's off today," Glen pointed out. "Right, Dad?"

His father nodded. Sarah still saw the anger brewing behind his eyes and something else she couldn't identify.

"Yes, I'm off, but I have paperwork to take care of in my office. It also looks like rain, so I think the beach is off for you guys."

"What about after you're done with the paperwork?" Glen insisted. "The lab's activities are all inside."

"I'll think about it. Maybe you want to straighten your rooms or call friends for a playdate."

"We haven't made any friends yet," Sarah said. They'd arrived at the end of the school year and wouldn't meet many kids their own age until they started classes in the fall. Sarah would be going into Smithtown Middle School while Glen would be attending fourth grade at the local elementary school.

"Then go watch TV." Her father seemed to want to be rid of them. "I'll let you know about the lab later." He got up and headed toward his workroom in the garage that he'd converted to an office when Mother insisted on having her own bedroom and a separate playroom for Sarah and Glen.

"When will you tell us?" Glen asked, following his father to the door.

"Ask me after lunch," was the reply.

"Can I help you with your paperwork?" Sarah knew her brother was asking because he was hoping it would speed up his father's decision and also sway it in his direction.

"No. It'll be quicker if I do this alone." Their father's voice sounded strange, but Sarah understood that Glen would be in the way.

"Come on, Glen. Bill Nye, the Science Guy is on," Sarah said, helping her father make his getaway.

As they headed to the den where the large TV was kept, Sarah thought she heard crying from upstairs. The den was directly below her mother's bedroom. But before she could identify the sound for sure, Glen had turned on the TV full volume to listen to his favorite show.

They were in the middle of watching Bill do an experiment. Glen was transfixed, sitting Indian-style in front of the set next to Sarah. Suddenly, the concoction Bill was mixing exploded. At the same time, a loud bang echoed from the garage. Glen jumped up. "Did you hear that, Sarah? It sounded like something blew up."

"We should go check on Dad," Sarah said.

As they ran through the den door, their mother called from upstairs. "Sarah, can you come up here?"

Sarah hesitated.

"You go see what Mom wants," Glen told her. "I'll see if Dad is okay. I wanted to ask him if he's decided about the lab today, anyway."

Sarah nodded and headed upstairs as Glen raced outside to the garage.

Chapter Thirty-Three

Sea Scope: Present day

As the three of us walked to the lighthouse, Russell said, "When we get back, I need to apologize to your aunt for my outburst. It wasn't called for."

"But was it true? Was your father intending to marry Aunt Julie?"

"Yes. Dad was even shopping for the ring. He told me he was going to give it to her for her birthday in August. He'd even checked with me to ask if it was okay." He chuckled at the memory. "I guess he was worried I would be upset with him for replacing my mother. The truth was I really liked your aunt, and I loved Sea Scope. I imagined living in it with you, Glen, and Wendy. It made me feel like I had a family instead of just a father."

"That's sad," Carolyn said from Russell's other side. "It looks like Julie didn't last long with this detective we're meeting tonight. She gave your dad up for him, but they never married."

"Aunt Julie had many chances to marry," I explained. "I don't really know what held her back. I used to think it was her brother's marriage. Even before we moved to Sea Scope, my parents never had a good one."

"I wonder why," Carolyn said. "It always surprises me how people are so in love on their wedding day and then break up easily when the smallest things go wrong."

I wondered if Carolyn was talking about me. We'd approached the rocks fronting the gate that opened to the lighthouse. The gate was now padlocked with a large sign saying, "No Entry Without Appointment."

"It's a shame we can't go inside," Carolyn said, frowning in disappointment. Suddenly, her phone buzzed. "Who could that be? I hope it's not Jack or Samantha." Samantha was our agent.

Carolyn walked to the side by one of the bushes while Russell and I sat on one of the rocks to wait for her. It was coincidental that it was the same rock where he'd given me my first kiss twenty years ago. I wondered if he remembered. I debated asking him, but before I could, Carolyn came back holding out her phone to me. "Sarah, it's for you. It's Derek."

I got off the rock and took the phone with a shaky hand. I hardly noticed Carolyn taking my place next to Russell as I walked a few paces away from them. I faced the lighthouse as I spoke into Carolyn's phone. "Hi, Derek. Is everything okay?"

Derek's nervous voice came though the cell's speaker. "It's fine now, but I was so worried. I tried calling you and kept getting voice mail. Rather than bother your aunt, I figured I should try Carolyn's phone."

I hesitated to tell him my phone had likely been taken by Wanda's mentally disturbed daughter. "I'm sorry I had it off," I said instead. "How are your classes going?" I figured it was safer to change the subject.

Derek paused. "I wanted to keep it a surprise, but you know I don't like keeping anything from you."

No, I thought, *only your affair,* but his next words were unexpected.

"I gave Jerry the rest of my sessions and am driving down there. If I make good time, I should be there by Sunday morning."

I didn't know what to say. Should I tell him what was going on?

"Sarah, are you still there?"

"Yes. Sorry. I'm a little surprised."

"I thought you'd be pleased. I've really missed you, honey. Oh, and don't worry about Rosy. I arranged for my mother to come by to feed her. You know she loves cats." When I didn't reply, he continued. "I think this will be like a second honeymoon for us even if it's a few weeks short of our anniversary."

"Yes. That sounds great," I said, but I knew he could tell I wasn't excited about it.

"Sarah, what's wrong?"

"Nothing. I wasn't expecting you to come here so soon."

"Neither was I." He paused. "I know things haven't been the best between us lately, but I want to change that. There's something I want to tell you, but I'm saving it for when we're face to face."

My heartbeat began to quicken. Was he ready to ask me for a divorce? If that was the case, why was he acting as if he really missed me and even mentioned a second honeymoon? More importantly, where was his young fling? Had she tossed him aside, so he could come running back to his wife?

"Let me go, so I can get on the road, Sarah. I can't wait to see you. I love you. Bye."

I was glad he hung up before I could reply. Walking back to the rock, I handed Carolyn her phone.

"What was that all about? I saw your face change a few times. You looked puzzled at one point."

"He's coming to Sea Scope," I said. "He's planning to make it by Sunday."

"That's great." I could tell Carolyn was truly pleased as she crept closer to Russell on the rock.

"Did you tell him about what's happening here?" Russell asked.

"No. It was hard to talk about it on the phone."

"Wonderful news," Carolyn said, getting up. "I'm going to walk around a bit and check the lighthouse from different angles. I wish I could draw like you, Sarah. I would be sketching it right now."

I noticed she wasn't upset with giving up her seat next to Russell. She strutted away, flinging her scarf back over her shoulder.

"Have a seat," Russell said, patting the area on the rock Carolyn had vacated.

I did as he asked but kept my attention on the lighthouse and Carolyn circling the area around it.

"It's funny how our pasts affect our present," he said, when I'd joined him. "So many things come back to me now that I'm at Sea Scope again. For instance, I remember my first kiss with you on this very rock." He laughed lightly. "I was so curious about girls back then."

"What about Wendy?" I asked. "Why didn't you use her for your first kissing experiment?" I realized how that sounded and apologized. "Sorry. I mean, maybe she was your second. I wouldn't know."

He laughed. "That's certainly okay and, no, I never thought about kissing her. I had a bit of a crush on you then. I wonder what would've happened had my father really married your aunt. If Michael hadn't died that summer, we might even be married today."

I'd never considered that, but he had a point. "It's possible, I guess, but people take different paths."

"Yes, they do." He took a twig by the side of the rock and snapped it. "I'm glad you brought Carolyn along. I think she's smitten with me and, to tell the truth, I found her attractive from the moment you two arrived. I've had my share of girlfriends but no one serious. I'd like to change that. I think she and I have some things in common."

I hesitated on whether I should mention that Carolyn, like my aunt, wasn't the marrying type, but I knew meddling in peoples' relationships wasn't a good thing to do.

"I'm glad you two hit it off."

Russell smiled. "Tell me about your husband. How did you meet him? Are you planning to have kids? I know you always talked about having a family when the four of us played together. You were a great mother to us."

I turned away, afraid for him to see the pain that must show on my face. "Derek's a professor at a college on Long Island where my parents and I moved after we left Sea Scope. I was one of his students." I wasn't sure how much more I should tell him. Did he hear the slight cracking of my voice? I was about to add that we planned to have children, but Carolyn was calling to us from the far side of the hill that sloped down near the water.

We both jumped up and headed toward her. Russ got there first. When I arrived, he was standing next to Carolyn examining the item she held in her hand.

I edged closer. “What did you find, Carolyn?”

“I took a stumble over there.” She indicated a broken log that was partially hidden under some leaves. “When I got up, I found this under the log.”

The object she displayed was covered with dirt and hardly recognizable, but Russell and I knew what it was.

“Wendy’s corn-husk doll,” I said.

“Yes,” Russell agreed. “What’s it doing here?”

From the Notes of Michael Gamboski

(Book Cover, courtesy of Amazon.com)

Throughout history lighthouses have been administered by different groups and organizations. Below is a table representing the timeline of lighthouse administration:
1789 – 1844: Lighthouse Establishment under U.S. Treasury Department
1845 – 1902: Revenue Department, Marine Division; August 31, 1852, Light-House Board established by Congress
1903 – 1938: Department of Commerce; 1910, Lighthouse Service of Bureau of Lighthouses formed
1939 – present: U. S. Coast Guard

(from Lights & Legends: A Historical Guide to Lighthouses of Long Island Sound, Fishers Island Sound, and Block Island Sound by Harlan Hamilton, Westcott Cove Publishing Company: Westcott, CT, 1987).

Chapter Thirty-Four

Sea Scope: Twenty years ago

They were all seated in the parlor except for Aunt Julie who, ever the hostess, was handing out coffee and tea to whoever wanted any. Sarah's father stood next to Detective Marshall talking in a low, serious voice. Aunt Julie had also put out a platter of cookies that Glen kept helping himself to while Sarah warned him with a look that he'd had enough and passed him a napkin to clean his mouth.

They'd returned to the house with Detective Marshall accompanied by the shorter officer he called Loomis. Mother had taken the news better than Sarah expected. Instead of the reaction Wanda had when she and Wendy returned from Bible school, Mother was quite composed. Sarah suspected her calmness was due to the whiskey Sarah could still smell on her breath. Wanda, on the other hand, had collapsed on the sofa sobbing as Wendy sat next to her trying to console her. A few other guests were in the room, even those who didn't know Michael.

Detective Marshall, after thanking Aunt Julie for the coffee, addressed the group. "I know this a tough time for all of you," he began, glancing at Wanda who still sat silently crying into a lace handkerchief she'd taken from the pocket of her long dress. "I thought it would be easier if we spoke here than at the station. Please be aware that no one is under suspicion at this point. There are details we need to check, so we have to question all of you."

One of the newer guests, a man in a striped T-shirt and shorts, said, "I don't understand why you need to talk with me. I'm on vacation here. I don't even know this guy who jumped off the lighthouse."

Loomis responded to that. "Sir, we need to talk to anyone who might've been in the area or seen something today. We're not labeling this a crime yet."

From the window, Sarah saw several other policemen gathered by the lighthouse. She wondered if they were looking for evidence of foul play, as they termed it in the movies and on TV. Glen, next to her, was excited by the whole situation. Although he had been very close to Michael, Sarah thought the reality of what happened hadn't yet touched him. He was caught up in the mystery of the moment as if he were watching a detective show where the victim was fictional.

Marshall took command while his sidekick jotted the answers to the questions on a pad he retrieved from his uniform pocket. To satisfy her father, the officer read the group the Miranda Rights but explained that this was an inquiry and not an interrogation, although a thin line separated them.

Sarah listened as the detective went around the room repeating the same questions in different ways. Glen whispered to her that this was how they hoped to trip up a liar. The main focus of the questions was who was where during the time period that Michael was at the lighthouse. Sarah's aunt had confirmed that Michael left the inn at 7:30 a.m. She didn't ask him where he was going, but he'd told her the night before that he'd finished his school project and was leaving Sea Scope in the morning.

"He was very happy to be done with his paper," Aunt Julie said. "That's why this is so strange. I think you officers contended that he was stressed by the thesis, but he'd already finished it."

Loomis jotted down this information as Marshall said, "It's possible he lied about that, but chances are you're right. We can assume that he returned to the lighthouse one last time. Maybe he left something there. In any case, we can pursue our other line of thought." He turned to Aunt Julie, and Sarah noticed he looked her over in a way that was more appreciative than curious. "Ma'am, did Michael ever bring a girlfriend to the inn? Did he ever speak of one?"

Aunt Julie shook her head. "No. I often wondered why a nice looking young man like he was didn't have one. There are so many pretty girls at his college."

Loomis scribbled in his pad again. Sarah wished she had her diary with her because she had an urge to draw this scene—the police officers talking with her family and the inn guests. She saved mental images to use when she was back in her room.

"Do you know who may have given him the gold band he was wearing on his right ring finger?" Marshall continued. "It looks expensive, and although it's not on the wedding finger, it looks like it has a special meaning. What do they call them these days, a friendship ring or a pre-engagement ring?"

"We had a birthday party for him at the inn last week," Aunt Julie said. "He opened the gifts in front of us, and I didn't see any gold ring, although I have noticed him wearing it since then. I don't like to pry, so I didn't ask him about it. It's possible it was a gift from a family member. I know he visited his folks the next day."

Sarah recalled a small box that had been left on the gift table after Michael's party, but she didn't say anything.

The rest of the questioning went on forever. When was the last time anyone saw Michael? Who was away from the inn during the hours of 7:30 to 9 a.m.? They asked Wanda, who was finally composed, what time she took Wendy to Bible school. She said they were running a little late that morning. Wendy had to be there by 8, but Wanda woke up with a headache, so they didn't leave until 8:15.

When the questioning turned to Sarah and Glen, their mother warned Marshall that they were only kids and had been exploring by the lighthouse as they had all summer.

Marshall ignored her and asked them, "What were you two doing at the lighthouse this morning? Why did you go there?"

Glen answered. "It's fun. We hang out there a lot."

"Didn't you think you'd run into Michael?"

"That's a leading question," Loomis said, talking for the first time.

"This isn't a jury hearing," Marshall explained, but he reworded the question. "Were you going there looking for or meeting anyone?"

"No." Sarah answered this time. "We were only playing. Glen likes to race me up the stairs because he always wins."

Marshall smiled, and Sarah felt more at ease. He was a nice man, and he looked about her aunt's age, but it was hard to tell adults' ages. She knew Aunt Julie looked younger than her father but was five years older than him. Too bad her aunt was seeing Russell's father. He hadn't come around the last few days, and she remembered an argument between them the last time Bart Donovan was at the inn.

"I think you'd spend your time more efficiently questioning other folks here than my children," Sarah's father interrupted. Sarah noted his nervousness. He kept pacing around and his hands shook around his coffee cup. There was a tremor in his voice despite the fact the words themselves were controlled.

Marshall turned to him. If he was a good detective, Sarah was sure he'd picked up on her father's behavior. "Who do you suggest we question then, Mr. Brewster?"

Her father looked at Wanda, who was still dabbing her eyes, and on Wendy next to her. Both of them sat with lips pursed as if they had nothing more to say.

"I think you should've questioned Ms. Wilson and her daughter a bit more thoroughly. They were the only guests who knew Michael and weren't around the inn this morning."

Before Marshall could reply, Aunt Julie stepped forward. "Wanda is my housekeeper, not a guest. She's a trusted employee." She glanced at my father with an angry expression. "And, to be honest, I didn't see where you went after breakfast, Brother."

"I was trying to repair my car. I noticed the engine making an odd noise the night before and meant to check it in the morning. I already told the officers that."

"I doubt anyone can corroborate that story, Martin. In fact, it's quite common for you to jog around the lighthouse, isn't it?"

"Please, Ms. Brewster," Marshall said. "Let us handle the questioning." He looked over at Sarah's mother. "Do you know where your husband went after breakfast this morning, Mrs. Brewster?"

Sarah watched her mother's face whiten. "I tend to sleep late, and there wasn't much left of breakfast by the time I got there at 8:30. I went out to sit on the porch with a glass of orange juice and saw Martin in the parking lot. It's true he was working on his car."

Loomis turned to Sarah's father. "Did you see your wife on the porch? Did the two of you talk?"

"No, I didn't see Jennifer. She may have been there, but she wasn't when I went back to the inn."

"We'll have to check the parking area later," Marshall said. "See if the parking lot is visible from the porch. I believe I saw a tree that might obstruct the view. You'll have to show us where you were parked."

Sarah's father looked annoyed, but he nodded. "Sure. I have nothing to hide. However, you do know Ms. Wilson was out and about during that time, so you should stop hunting around for other suspects and focus on her."

"I'm warning you to leave the questioning to us," Marshall said in a voice tinged with anger.

"It's okay," Ms. Wilson said in a whisper choked by a sob. "I can understand Mr. Brewster's concern, but Bible school is in the opposite direction from the lighthouse. Mr. Gamboski most likely left while Wendy and I were getting ready upstairs."

Sarah looked over at Wendy, still clinging to her mother's side, and noticed that her corn- husk doll was missing. Wendy had it that morning. Sarah remembered her carrying it as she went to the car with her mother.

Chapter Thirty-Five

Sea Scope: Present day

"What should we do with it?" I asked. "Should we bring it back to the inn and show Wanda?"

Russell considered. "Do you think Wendy was carrying the doll around with her? If she believes she's your brother as a child, maybe the doll was her connection."

"No. That's not it, Russell. She lost the doll years ago. After the police found Michael's body and were questioning us all back at the inn, I saw that she didn't have it. She even looked for it with me afterwards."

"What are you talking about?" Carolyn asked, still holding the dirty and half-disintegrated corn husk doll.

"Wendy always carried around that doll," Russell explained. "If she lost it the day Michael died, you know what that must mean?"

"It means she was here at the lighthouse and not at Bible school as her mother contended."

"That's right, Sarah. Didn't anyone ever ask her about it?"

"During everything that was going on, I don't think people realized the doll was missing. Wendy and her mother left a few weeks later."

"But you remembered," Carolyn said. "Why didn't you ask her about it?"

"I had my mind on other things. I recall drawing the missing doll in my diary along with the sketches of the detectives and the people they questioned. My parents were at each other's throats during this whole time even more than usual. Mother finally convinced Dad to move to Long Island. It was a time of upheaval in my childhood. A doll didn't matter much."

Russell nodded. "Okay, so here's the thing. We have the doll, and it might be evidence against Wanda. Then again, it might not. However, I think we need to bring it to Detective Marshall's attention when he comes tonight."

"Should we show Wanda first?" Carolyn inquired.

"No." He turned toward me. "Sarah, you take it and put it somewhere safe. Lock it in your car's glove compartment. If Wendy's still around, she might find it if you hide it in the inn."

Carolyn handed me the doll and wiped off her hands. "It's muddy, but I think it's best you don't clean it. It's in such poor shape, it might fall apart completely."

I took the doll and stuffed it in my pants pocket. It was small and didn't make much of a bulge there.

When we returned to the inn, Aunt Julie was out on the porch with Al by her feet. "Did you have a nice tour?" she asked.

"I would've liked to have seen the interior of the lighthouse," Carolyn replied, "but the outside is beautiful."

"It's very old," my aunt said, "but it's in great condition." She stood, and Al jumped on the rocker.

"Smart cat," Carolyn commented.

Aunt Julie smiled. "What do you all want to do now? Wanda is shopping for dinner. We decided on the special South Carolina recipe Wanda brought with her for Frogmore Stew, also known as Beaufort Boil. It's a hearty shrimp and sausage dish. I hope you all enjoy it."

"I was hoping to write," Carolyn said. "I have my laptop with me. I can get it and bring it out here."

"I can join you if you don't mind," Russell offered. "I don't have my computer, but I usually handwrite my drafts. I'm sure there's a notebook around I can use."

"I need to get something in my car and then I'm going to my room," I said. "Do you need any help setting up for tonight, Aunt Julie?"

My aunt shook her head. "Wanda is taking care of most of it. I was planning to work in my art studio. I'd love you to come see my latest portraits if you have a minute, Sarah."

"I'll be up soon," I promised as I headed to my car. The light doll was beginning to feel heavy in my pocket.

"I'll see you upstairs," my aunt said, entering the inn.

After locking the doll in my glove compartment, I almost ran into Russell and Carolyn as they were descending the stairs. Russell was carrying Carolyn's laptop while she held a notebook and pen.

"Did everything go okay?" Russell asked.

"Yes, it's in my car. Thanks," I said, placing my keys back in my purse.

"We'll be on the patio if you need anything," he said.

Carolyn clutched the notebook to her chest. "This feels like a writing retreat. Maybe we can critique one another." Forgetting about the doll and that we needed to tell the detective about it that night, Carolyn's mind was already focused on working with Russell.

I remembered that my aunt's studio, like my garret at home, was in the attic. My aunt used it for her portrait drawings. When I entered the room, she was seated on a stool in front of an easel. "Come join me, Sarah, but look around first if you'd like. There are several pieces you probably haven't seen."

Because the roof sloped, my head just cleared the ceiling. I imagined a tall person like Russell would have difficulty standing upright. The overhead lighting was provided by a skylight that my aunt told me her mother, also an artist, had installed. A large number of canvases were stacked around the area. They brought back memories. There were several drawings of Glen and me as children and one each of Russell and Wendy. My mother had never allowed Julie to sketch her, but Aunt Julie had drawn my father the year we left Sea Scope. Since he died the following year, his portrait was how he appeared to me as a child. Viewing it now, I saw something sad in his face. My aunt was very good at depicting emotions with her sketches. She'd added the lines by his eyes that appeared questioning or, if I looked closely, might be seeking forgiveness.

"I'm almost done with this one," Aunt Julie called, pulling me from my reverie. "Come see, Sarah."

I made my way carefully around the brushes and other artist paraphernalia that lined the wood floor. My aunt didn't keep her studio as neat as the rest of the inn, but I knew Wanda never came up here, so the place hadn't seen her tidy touch.

At my aunt's side, I peered over her shoulder to see Glen's adult face gazing back at me. His crooked, sweet smile broke my heart. Aunt Julie told me she started painting Glen after his accident from some of the photos she'd kept when she'd cleared out his apartment.

I felt tears threaten. "It looks just like him, Aunt Julie."

I knew she heard the tremor in my voice. "Sorry it makes you sad, Sarah; but by recreating his face, I feel like I can give Glen life again. I've done a few others of him. They're in that pile over there, but I think this one is the best. I'd still like to paint you. You've grown into a beautiful woman."

"Thank you. I wish I could draw people instead of the cartoon-like characters I use for my children's books."

"It's a challenge, but what I like most about it is the way I can convey not only the exterior but the interior of the subject. For instance, what do you see in Glen's face besides handsome charm?"

I paused and, holding my tears in check, said, "I'm not sure. I see humor there. He always liked to joke and tease, but you've also done a good job showing his serious side. His eyes show his compassion, how his whole life revolved around wanting to help people."

"Yes. Glen was a very special man. You were lucky to have him as a brother even if it was for a short time."

I thought about my father and wanted to ask why she and her brother had never been close despite the fact they'd owned and run the inn together. Before I could, Aunt Julie got up. "I think I should go downstairs now. I'm really not in the mood to work. You can stay up here if you want. Maybe you'd like to do your own artwork. It's very quiet, and you won't be disturbed."

"Okay," I agreed. "if you don't mind my dabbling a bit here."

"Of course I don't." My aunt smiled. "Help yourself to anything. I have blank sketchpads on the table over there." She stood at the top of the stairway. "I'll call you when Wanda returns. I asked her to pick up food for lunch after she finishes shopping. I didn't think anyone would have plans to go anywhere today while we're waiting for Detective Marshall."

I noticed how her voice changed when she mentioned the detective. It sounded a bit like Carolyn's when she spoke about Russell. "That was a good idea," I agreed.

After Aunt Julie went downstairs, I walked around the studio remembering how Glen and I, and occasionally Wendy and Russell, used to come up here to play hide and seek behind some of the paintings or in the nook and crannies under the window where Aunt Julie always kept bins and boxes. I suddenly noticed a canvas, set apart from the others with its back facing the window. I turned it around to check it out and was surprised to see that it was a double portrait. On one side, my aunt had sketched Bart Donovan as he appeared when he visited the inn twenty years ago. The other side featured Detective Marshall's face. Had she been trying to decide between the two? She hadn't ended up with either man.

I turned the painting back and reached for the sketchpad my aunt had indicated. After a few futile attempts at outlining Kit Kat, I gave up and decided to head to my room. I had an urge to read more of my diary.

As I approached my room, the door across the hall opened. Mother waved. "Sarah, can you come here, please?"

I recognized the slur of her words and the sway of her body. She was drunk.

I hesitated a moment. Mother didn't get angry when she hit the bottle. She became sad, and I always thought there was a certain irony about that because the reason she drank in the first place was to ease her depression.

"I need to talk to you." She sounded as if she was pleading.

I followed her into the room, and she closed the door behind us. The smell of liquor permeated the interior and even seemed to soak the sheets, although they were dry to the touch. I took a seat on the bed where Mother indicated, and she sat in the tapestry rose chair next to it.

Empty whiskey bottles lined her bureau. I was surprised they were in full view, as she always took time to hide them when I was a child.

"Where did you get those?" I asked. Surely, she couldn't have brought them aboard the plane, and I knew she hadn't left Sea Scope since she arrived.

"As much as Julie and I have our differences, she knows how to treat a guest."

It disheartened me to hear that my aunt, knowing my mother was off the wagon, had enabled her addiction.

"This is very important, Sarah. Before that detective comes tonight, I have to tell you about your father."

"What about Dad?" In the nineteen years since he shot himself in the garage, Mother rarely talked about him. I never believed it was because it caused her pain. She was hardly what one would consider a grieving widow.

She looked down at her hands clasped in her lap. I noticed her unpainted nails were chipped and bitten. "I loved him, you know. It may not have appeared that way to you and Glen, but we were happy once. I still believe he loved me. He never meant to hurt me, but I should've let him go long before this all happened."

"What do you mean, Mother?"

She sighed deeply and blew out a breath of whiskey. "All these years, I've been trying to escape through the bottle. It wasn't fair to you kids, but it was my only way of coping with the truth. I remember when I first met Martin's family. I wondered why they all acted so cold toward me. I assumed Martin had a lot of girlfriends before me because he was a good-looking man and was already in his thirties when we met. He never spoke about his past, and I was too enthralled with him to ask. I can't believe I didn't recognize the signs. I was a social worker before you and Glen came along. I tried to help people like him." She swallowed and glanced at one of the empty bottles as if wishing for a refill.

The memories of Glen and I trying to solve the mystery of whom Wanda was sleeping with came back to me. We'd never determined it was Dad, so that's what I expected her revelation to be. But as I let her continue, her words drew a different picture.

"I should've told you many years ago. Not when you were a child but when you were old enough to understand. God, these days it's very common. Even then, it wasn't the sin the Church considered it in the past." She got up and began to pace the room. Her steps were so uneven I was afraid she would fall.

"Mother, I don't understand. Are you saying Wanda was Dad's lover?"

She stopped pacing and stood before me, her eyes red from drinking and crying. "Is that what you thought?" She laughed, but it ended on a sob. "Oh, my God!"

Dropping down next to me on the bed, she took another breath. "I don't know why I held this back so long. I'm sure Julie knew. The whole damn inn probably knew."

"What are you saying, Mother?" I kept my voice gentle, even though I was growing impatient with how much time it was taking her to tell me what she wanted to say.

"Sarah, do you remember that young bell hop who left so suddenly? I don't think you would recall the young man before him. There have always been college students at Sea Scope, mostly men your father hired without Julie's approval because Wanda did most of the work, even the heavy jobs. But when Julie put her foot down after Bud, I think that was the bell hop's name, luck was on Martin's side when Michael checked in."

"I don't understand." What was she getting at?

"I guess I need to say this bluntly, Sarah. Your father was gay."

I was shocked. I couldn't talk for a few minutes. "Are you saying Dad was having an affair with Michael?"

She nodded. "The little time he spent in this room with me was only to keep up appearances; but as I said, most people knew. I could see it in their eyes. They pitied me, but I pitied myself more. I should've asked for a divorce when I first discovered what was going on, but you and Glen were young. I'm different from Julie. I knew I couldn't survive on my own with two kids, so I put up with him. The liquor helped." She sounded quite sober now.

"What about Dad? Did he stay with you for the same reason? For us?"

"I assume so, but he asked me to cut him free the day before Michael died."

"What?"

She looked back down at her hands. "He gave Michael a ring for his birthday. No one knew about it. After the party, he must've presented it to him. It wasn't an engagement ring. Same sex marriage wasn't permitted in South Carolina at that time, but it was a token to show his feelings."

"Were you going to grant him the divorce?" I asked, still trying to picture my father, a part-time construction worker, and gentle Michael, so studious and kind, being together, being in love.

"Yes. I told him I would. Even though I'd been so afraid to ask him, I knew I had to finally face life's hard knocks. I had no choice."

"What about Michael?" I asked, my heart starting to beat again. "Mother, you weren't involved in his death, were you?"

I waited, holding my breath for her answer.

"No, Sarah." She reached out and took my hand. My mother had never been the demonstrative sort, but I could see the love in her eyes as she met mine. "The reason I had to tell you all this is because Detective Marshall is going to bring it all up again tonight, and I don't know what to do. You see, when your father shot himself a year after Michael's death, he left a note."

I could hardly believe what I was hearing. “Mother, you told the police that there were no signs that Father had planned to kill himself.” I recalled how she told the officers, through her tears, that her husband hadn’t left a suicide note.

Mother still held my hand. “It was my fault he put that gun to his head. I’d goaded him that morning, reminding him it was the anniversary of Michael’s death. I knew he wouldn’t have forgotten it.”

“What did the note say?”

She took a breath and let it out filling the air with the scent of alcohol. “That’s the problem, Sarah. I couldn’t show it to the police, and I can’t tell Detective Marshall about it.”

“What did it say?” I repeated.

She let my hand go, and it felt like the umbilical cord that had connected us thirty years ago was clipped again.

“ ‘I killed Michael.’ That’s what it said, Sarah.”

From the Notes of Michael Gamboski

Heceta Head Lighthouse (Pixabay) and New London Ledge Lighthouse (Wikimedia Commons)

There are legends attached to many lighthouses related to ghosts and the supernatural. The lighthouse at Heceta Head in Oregon is supposedly haunted by the ghost of a mother whose baby daughter fell to her death from the cliff upon which it stands. The apparition is dubbed "The Gray Lady," as she is reported to wear a long, gray skirt while floating around the attic of the lighthouse, which has been renovated into a guesthouse.

In 1929, the U.S. Coast Guard began taking shifts at the New London Ledge Lighthouse. Not long after, strange things began happening. Legend has it that a lighthouse keeper by the name of Ernie jumped from the roof of the lighthouse to the ocean below, where his body never resurfaced. Many people don't believe that he killed himself. After the lighthouse was automated in 1987, several reports filtered in from boat crews that a figure at the lighthouse had signaled to them or tried to lure them to the dock. However, whenever these reports were investigated, not a living soul was found at the lighthouse.

(from the article "10 Creepy Lighthouses Surrounded by Spooky Legends" by Estelle Thurtle, August 12, 2014).

Chapter Thirty-Six

Long Island: Nineteen years ago

Sarah entered her mother's bedroom. Her father had his own room down the hall. Glen had once asked his father why he no longer slept with his mother as most married couples did. He said he snored too loud at night and kept her up. Sarah knew that was an excuse.

"You wanted me, Mother?" she asked, noting the large box on the bed and several items of clothing and papers strewn across it.

"I was tidying up, and I came across a few of your sketches. I don't want to throw them out unless you approve." She held out two drawings Sarah recalled she'd done at Sea Scope the year before when Aunt Julie allowed her to work in her attic studio.

"Where did you find these?" Sarah took the sketches from her mother's outstretched hands. One was of Ms. Wilson; the other of Michael. Sarah had drawn them, her only attempt at penning portraits, right before moving to Long Island after the subjects were already gone—Ms. Wilson to her new home in town and Michael to heaven.

"I still have boxes from South Carolina that I haven't unpacked," her mother replied. "I took one down from the attic. It's about time we go through them and get on with our lives."

Sarah didn't quite understand what her mother meant, but she was glad to see her working and not lying in bed with a bottle as she expected. Unlike her father who was almost as neat as Ms. Wilson, her mother was as disorganized as Glen. She even hired a cleaning woman who came in once a week to tidy up their house.

"Do you want them or what?" her mother persisted.

Before Sarah could answer, Glen came running up the stairs. He was out of breath and choking on his words. "Dad," he cried. "Dad's dead."

"What?"

"In the garage, Mama."

Sarah's mother put the sketches down on the bed with the other items, color draining from her face. Sarah followed her brother downstairs, their mother a few feet behind. When they reached the open garage door, the two children stopped so their mother could catch up.

"We heard this loud noise," Glen said, gulping tears and air at the same time. "It was Daddy's gun. Go see." He covered his eyes with his hands and began to shake. Sarah went to comfort him even as she felt fear ride up her spine.

"We have to call the police," their mother said. "Sarah, you remember about dialing 911 in an emergency. Take Glen in the house and call."

Sarah was surprised how calm her mother sounded giving instructions. She usually was the first to fall apart, unlike Aunt Julie who knew exactly what to do in any situation.

When Sarah hesitated, her mother said, "Listen to me. Take your brother inside. Now." Her voice was firm.

As Sarah took Glen's hand, she glanced into the dark interior of the garage. Although her father had a lamp and an overhead light for his workspace, they weren't on. She was afraid to look further. She hated the sight of blood and could hardly tolerate it when the doctor took some from her arm. She was thankful for the poor lighting because all she could see was the shape of her father slumped across his desk.

"Come with me, Glen," she said gently. "We have to call for help."

"It's too late," Glen said, even as he followed her toward the house. "He's dead. The bullet went right through his head."

Chapter Thirty-Seven

Sea Scope: Present day

After I'd composed myself, I said, "Mother, you have to share this with Detective Marshall."

She looked down at her hands. "I realize that. I've hidden this way too long. I wanted to protect you and Glen. I didn't want you to know your father was a homosexual and a murderer, too."

"I don't understand. If he was in love with Michael, why would he kill him? You told me you'd already agreed to a divorce."

"Sarah, I don't have all the answers. I haven't been the best mother to you by hiding this and trying to drink it away. I'm ready to face whatever happens now."

"What did you do with the note?" I hoped she'd saved it, which might make things easier when she spoke with the detective.

"I tore it into tiny pieces and threw it in the trash. I wanted to burn it." Her voice, low until then, began to rise. "I was so stupid. I was in my late twenties when I met your father. I should've known better. I still wonder why his parents or sister didn't warn me, but I probably wouldn't have believed them. I was so in love." She started to cry, but I wasn't sure if they were tears of sadness or anger. Maybe both. "Why did Martin even bother to marry me and have children with me?" The tears were falling freely now.

"Mother. I'm so sorry."

She looked at me through eyes filled with tears that were nonetheless clearer than I'd seen them in years. "I'm the one who should be sorry, Sarah. I wish I could make it up to you. It's too late for me to make it up to Glen."

We sat there for a while lost in our memories. It was the closest we'd been in years.

Our silence was broken by a knock on the door. "Jennifer, Wanda's back with lunch. Are you coming down to join us?"

Mother wiped her eyes with the back of her sleeve. "Answer the door, Sarah. I need a few minutes."

I opened the door and told my aunt we would be down soon. She was surprised to see me in my mother's room. I think she expected to find me still drawing in her studio.

"That's fine. Carolyn and Russell are already at the table."

When we joined everyone eating sandwiches from a local deli, Wanda told us that while she was out, she'd checked her house to see if Wendy was there. "I thought she wasn't answering the phone, but the place was empty. I believe she even took clothes with her."

"Is that typical?" Russell asked. "I mean, has she done this before?"

Wanda sighed. "Yes. There were several times during her marriage that she disappeared. I didn't know about them until I called her one day, and her husband said she wasn't home. I finally got it out of him that she would leave without notice on a regular basis. He would come home from work and find her gone. After checking with the bank where she was working part time, he'd discover she'd called in sick. Wendy always had trouble keeping jobs, so he thought she was trying to get herself fired again." Wanda sighed. "What worried him was when he'd find her suitcase wasn't in the closet and her clothes and toiletries were missing. She'd also withdraw money from their account."

"Where did she go?" Carolyn asked, putting aside her ham and swiss sandwich.

"He never found out. Every time she returned several days later, her only explanation was that she needed to get away for a few days." Wanda placed a pitcher of lemonade on the table. "I wasn't surprised when Richmond finally began divorce proceedings. He thought she was cheating on him even though she swore she wasn't."

"But the notes came later?" Russell asked, signaling to Carolyn if she wanted him to pour her a glass of lemonade.

"That's right. They started when she moved back in with me after her divorce."

"I wonder where she is now," I said. "We would know if she was here at Sea Scope. There haven't been any further messages, and I haven't found my phone."

"You said she didn't have a car," Russell said, pouring Carolyn lemonade and asking if I wanted any. "She wouldn't be able to get far on foot, and she'd need a place to sleep."

"She has a few friends in the area, but I don't know if she'd stay with them. I don't think any of them know about her problem." Wanda sat next to Aunt Julie who said, "That's why it's a good thing we've called Donald."

I noticed how Julie referred to the detective by his first name, and I saw from my mother's glance in her direction that she was aware of it, too.

"Sarah's husband is arriving tomorrow," Russell said, and I remembered I'd forgotten to notify my aunt.

"Sorry, Aunt Julie. I forgot to tell you. Derek is on his way. He managed to get out of his summer class and wanted to join me. I hope you don't mind. I know it's a bad time."

"No, it's fine. There's plenty of room here. If you're too cramped in the Violet Room, I can move you to a larger one. I look forward to seeing him again."

"What exactly are we going to tell Detective Marshall?" Carolyn changed the subject.

"We have to tell him about Wendy, the notes, and Sarah's phone," Aunt Julie said.

"I don't mean that." Carolyn took a sip of her lemonade. "From what you've said, this man is retired. He'll probably tell us to file a missing person's report with the police."

"We think this is all tied up with what happened twenty years ago," Russell said. "Because Detective Marshall was the one in charge of Michael's case back then, he's the best one to consult on this matter."

I suddenly felt queasy. With everything going on, I wasn't thinking about the baby, but the nausea that threatened seemed to have more to do with what my mother had revealed and the corn-husk doll that I was hiding in my car.

Chapter Thirty-Eight

Sea Scope: Twenty years ago

Sarah wasn't asleep, but the knock at the door still startled her. It was late. She and Glen had gone to bed at eleven. Their father had tried to get them in their rooms earlier, but they were wound up from snacking on the candy they'd bought in town with Aunt Julie after they'd spent time at the beach. Mr. Donovan and Russell hadn't been around for a few days, so Aunt Julie had more time on her hands to take them places. Wanda didn't allow Wendy to go because she was being punished for talking back to her mother at breakfast. Wanda was very strict with her daughter, and Glen said it was because Wendy had no father to discipline her.

As she lay against her pillow writing and sketching in her diary that helped her relax more than reading or counting sheep, Sarah heard three taps, a pause, and then two more taps —the Morse code signal Glen had developed to let her know it was him.

She got out of bed and put on her slippers, glancing at the alarm clock on her nightstand, which she only set during school months. What could her brother want at midnight?

Answering the second set of light taps, she saw Glen standing there with his finger to his lips. "Be quiet, Sarah, and come with me. You have to hear this. Hurry."

Sarah followed him across the hall to their parents' room. "Glen, are you eavesdropping again? We'll get in trouble." Just a few days ago, one of the new guests found Glen listening outside her door and reported it to Aunt Julie, who told their father. He'd given Glen a warning that if it happened again, he wouldn't receive an allowance for a month. He also wouldn't be allowed to the beach or the science museum during that time.

"It's okay. They won't hear us. This is important, Sarah. Listen. Please."

She took a step toward the door and pressed her ear against the surface. It wasn't that necessary because her father's voice tended to drift even when he was speaking low.

"I'm so sorry, Jen. I know I'm the reason for your illness, but I really did love you. Please believe me. It's better this way, for you and the children. I thought our staying together would be best at one time, but now I see it's not possible."

"He's leaving her," Glen whispered. "He said before that he's found someone else."

Sarah's heart began to race. She'd known for a long time that her parents weren't in love anymore. They never kissed and hardly touched at all. She still suspected Wanda was the cause. It seemed to start when they'd moved to Sea Scope, but she was too young before then to remember if they'd ever been happy together.

"It's okay, Martin. Don't try to sugar coat this for me. I've been to the meetings and spoken to others with my problem. This is my fault as much as yours. I wanted to protect the children, too, but they're growing up fast. We can end this as friends. I don't hate you." Her mother's voice was cracking. Sarah could tell she was crying.

"I thought you'd put up a fight. I'm glad you understand my position. I'm not leaving immediately. I'm trying to find a place to live near the university. I haven't even spoken to Julie about this yet. I'm planning to do that tomorrow. I had to ask you first."

"He sounds so calm about this," Sarah whispered to Glen who had his ear against the opposite side of the door. "He doesn't even care that she's crying."

From the Garden Room, her mother asked in a voice still tight with tears, "Will we be able to stay here? Are you giving up the inn?"

"I have to see what Julie wants to do. Don't worry. No matter what happens, I'll provide for you, Glen, and Sarah."

Her mother replied in a more controlled voice. "I think I want to go back to Long Island."

"We can talk about that. One step at a time. I'm going now. Thank you again, dear. It means a lot that you understand."

"Hurry," Glen said as they heard their father's footsteps walk toward the door. They both tiptoed quickly across the hall and dived into their rooms.

Chapter Thirty-Nine

Sea Scope: Present day

After lunch, I excused myself, saying I had a headache and wanted to rest in my room. Carolyn looked a bit concerned, and as I got up from the table, she asked if everything was okay. I told her I was tired from traveling the day before and the events of the previous night. She nodded and said she would be working on the next Kit Kat book on the patio for a few hours. She was somewhat disappointed when Russell said he'd love to join her but had other plans for the day. For Carolyn's sake, I hoped those plans didn't include a girlfriend.

Russell promised to be back at the inn by dinnertime. Aunt Julie and Wanda discussed the cleaning and cooking schedule. They were excited to have the detective for a guest, and I wondered if my aunt's zealousness was due to her looking forward to seeing Donald Marshall again and whether Wanda's jitteriness was her fear of the same.

Back in my room, I had the chance to read my diary again. I lay down on the bed, my stomach finally settling a bit, and opened the book. It was odd reading those words written in my childish hand again. The drawings that illustrated the text were also unfamiliar to my older eyes. Memory is strange and unreliable. Like a dream, your mind often embellishes the realities of your experiences. It's similar to the way a witness identifies a suspect. The mental image often varies significantly from the actuality. What I perceived as a child was both clear and obtuse. I shouldn't have been surprised that the accounts I transcribed at the time varied so much from what I thought I remembered.

As I skimmed through the journal, I hesitated to read the last page. When I flipped to it, however, I was surprised that it wasn't the one I expected. I recalled ending the diary on the day Michael died, but there were several pages that followed. Not only had I covered the visits by Detective Marshall to Sea Scope afterwards, but I'd also included events that happened before Wanda and Wendy moved away.

Skipping my entry of that fateful day our lives changed, I randomly chose to view my description of what occurred a week later.

From the Notes of Michael Gamboski

A portable library from the Seaman's Bethel containing books from the American Seamen's Friend Society, found from the wreckage of a schooner that sank in 1914, similar to libraries circulated among lighthouses (Photo: Bonnie Sandy/Martha's Vineyard Museum)

Recognizing the loneliness of many of the light stations, and the fact that keepers engaged in "monotonous routine duties," the Lighthouse Board in 1876 began distributing small libraries to isolated light stations. These libraries consisted of about forty books which were enclosed in a case that folded open to display their contents. Each library was different, for the board envisioned transferring the boxes among the lighthouses, at first leaving a library at each station for about six months. Specifically, the Lighthouse Board wanted the libraries sent "to isolated lighthouses of the higher orders, where there are keepers with families, who will read and appreciate the books the libraries contain."

Each library contained a mixture of novels, histories, biographies, adventures, religious works, and magazines.

By 1885, there were 420 libraries in circulation. It is not known how long the circulating libraries remained in use, but as late as 1912, the Bureau of Lighthouses reported having 351 libraries.

(from America's Lighthouses: An Illustrated History by Francis Ross Holland, Jr., General Publishing Company: Toronto, Ontario, 1972.)

Chapter Forty

Sea Scope: Present day

After reading a few pages of my childhood diary, I fell asleep. I awoke to tapping at my door and Carolyn calling me. "Sarah, are you up? It's dinner time."

I got out of bed and answered the door. "I must've slept for hours, Carolyn. What's going on?"

My friend stepped into the room. She had a wide smile on her face. "Everyone's downstairs, and the detective has arrived. Russell's back, and he's asked me to a movie after we eat. Aunt Julie told me to come up and get you. I'm sure you needed the rest. Pregnancy does tire one."

"Shhh," I said, putting my finger to my lips. "Remember, I haven't told anyone about my situation."

"I understand, but Derek's coming tomorrow. I think everything will work out once he's here."

I wished I could've been as optimistic as Carolyn, but of course she was looking through rose-colored lenses after Russell asked her out on a date. "I hope you're right. Let me brush my hair and freshen up. I'll be down soon."

She nodded and went back out into the hall.

When I joined everyone in the kitchen, Detective Marshall, who I recognized but who'd aged as we all had after twenty years, stood up from his seat next to my aunt and extended his hand to me. "Nice to see you again, Sarah. You've grown into a lovely lady."

I shook his hand. "It's nice to see you again, too, Detective Marshall, although I'm sorry we're meeting under these circumstances."

He nodded. "Your aunt has filled me in on the current problems at Sea Scope." His smile left his face. "Please call me Donald. I'm not a detective anymore."

"Let's not talk about this right now," Aunt Julie said. "Have a seat, Sarah. Wanda has cooked us a delicious meal."

I sat in the empty seat next to my mother, who I was relieved to see was looking sober and not as nervous as I imagined she would be.

"I'm sorry if I kept you all waiting. I slept longer than I expected."

"No worries," Russell said from his seat next to Carolyn. "We were talking a bit before dinner was served."

"I told Donald about Wendy," Wanda said. She was on the other side of my aunt.

"We can discuss that later with everything else," Aunt Julie reiterated.

"Why wait?" my mother asked. "There might be more that some of us want to add." I knew then that she hadn't mentioned what she'd told me earlier.

"Very well, but I hate to ruin our dinner."

"The truth doesn't ruin anything. It clarifies things." I wasn't surprised at the verbal sparring between my mother and aunt. I watched Aunt Julie's face change. It had previously been bright and focused on Donald Marshall.

"What do you have to tell us, Jennifer?"

Mother was twisting her napkin in her lap. Otherwise, she still appeared outwardly calm.

"Go right ahead, Jennifer," Donald said. "Anything you can add to this information will be helpful, although I've already said I'm not in the capacity to officially investigate this matter. Wendy hasn't been missing very long but, due to her illness, I'd advise contacting the authorities. I can help with that if you'd like."

"I already explained that we want this kept private for now," Aunt Julie said.

Donald sighed. "Alright. Let's hear what Mrs. Brewster has to say first." He turned his gaze toward Mother.

"Thank you, Donald. Please call me Jennifer." She let her napkin rest in her lap. "I'm not sure you're aware that after Michael's death my husband committed suicide."

"I am, Jennifer. I was still visiting Sea Scope then, and Julie told me about it. I was very sorry to hear the news."

"Thank you." She took a breath and released it slowly. "I've already shared this with Sarah." Mother looked at me. I reached over and held her hand under the table. Aunt Julie and Wanda's faces were expressionless as they waited for the rest of the story. Carolyn and Russell seemed more interested in themselves and their movie plans.

"After we found Martin…" she began.

"After Glen found Martin," Aunt Julie corrected.

Mother nodded. If I were she, I'd be upset by the interruption, but I think she was relieved that it gave her more time to think through what she had to say.

"Go on," Russell prompted. He wanted to get it over with for another reason. I wondered if, like his father, he would be hurt if Carolyn went back to Jack when she finished her visit at Sea Scope.

Mother smiled briefly and squeezed my hand. "That's correct. Glen found his father in the garage where he did his paperwork. He'd shot himself in the head."

"We know that," Aunt Julie said, "or at least most of us do." She glanced at Russell and Carolyn as if to exclude them. "So, what do you have to add, Jennifer?"

I felt sorry for my mother in the face of Aunt Julie's rudeness, and I wondered what Donald Marshall thought as he sat at her other side quietly observing all of us.

"It's true Martin shot himself, but there's something I didn't tell the police when they arrived." She looked toward Donald as if for support.

"Seems like a long time to keep a secret," he said. "Are you sure you want to tell us now? Does it have any bearing on what's currently happening here?"

"I'm not sure. I want to tell everyone because I have to get this off my chest, finally, but who knows if it's important at this late date."

"Are you going to keep us in suspense any longer?" Carolyn asked. I noticed Wanda and I were the only ones at the table who hadn't said anything. Wanda was looking down at her plate. She was probably worried the food she'd so painstakingly prepared was growing cold and wouldn't be eaten after whatever my mother said.

With another deep exhalation, Mother let it all out. "I found a suicide note. Actually, it was a confession."

Wanda gasped, her dark face turning ashen, and spoke for the first time. "Where did you find it? What did it say?"

Mother looked down at her lap and our clasped hands. "It was on his desk. Glen was probably so scared he didn't see it. I told Sarah to take him inside and call 911. After the children were gone, I looked around. It wasn't hard to find."

Everyone took a collective breath waiting for her to finish. "Martin didn't address it to me, the police, or anyone in particular. It was very brief. All it said was, 'I killed Michael.' "

"No." Wanda's cry startled me.

"Are you okay, Wanda?" Aunt Julie asked.

Wanda got up and pushed back her chair. "I'm sorry. I'm not feeling well. I'd like to be excused."

"Not yet," Donald said.

"Surely, you can make an exception for Wanda," Aunt Julie implored. "She's probably got one of her migraines again. I know how awful they can be. She needs to go lie down in a dark room."

"Julie, please." Donald's voice was firm. Wanda sat back down, her face still pale, but I had the feeling it was from what my mother said and not from a migraine.

"I thought you weren't handling this in an official capacity." Russell directed the comment to the retired detective.

"I'm not, but I still have questions. I was called here to consult on this matter, and I need information to be able to do that." He looked toward my mother again. "Why didn't you show the note to the authorities, Jennifer?"

She swallowed and then answered, letting go of my hand as she did so. "I wanted to protect my husband's memory. My children were still young. It was bad enough people would talk about his killing himself, but I didn't want their father labeled a murderer."

"What if he was? Do you believe what he wrote? I take it you recognized the handwriting?"

Mother nodded. "I'm sure he wrote it. Why would he lie if it was his explanation for committing suicide?"

Donald Marshall didn't have an answer to that, and neither did anyone else in the room.

After what seemed like forever, Aunt Julie said, "The food is getting cold. I think we should eat before we discuss anything else."

Donald raised an eyebrow, and I thought he would insist on asking more questions. Instead, he said, "I'm sorry I took up so much time with questions, Julie. This food looks delicious, and I thank you again for inviting me to dinner." With a nod toward my mother, he added, "and, thank you, Jennifer, for sharing that information with us. I know how hard it must've been for you, but its relevance to this situation has yet to be determined."

"I think it has major relevance," Russell interjected. "Most of us here were around twenty years ago when Michael's body was found. My father and I weren't at the inn that day, nor were we here much during the period following, but Michael had been more than a Sea Scope guest to us. For years, we've all been wondering why someone so bright and full of enthusiasm would take his own life. Now we know what really happened."

Donald contemplated Russell's words before replying. He tapped the table lightly with his finger. "In my previous profession, Mr. Donovan—Russell, if I may—I learned about confessions. You can't always believe them. I know that Jennifer identified Martin's handwriting, but none of us have seen the note ourselves. I take it that you didn't keep the note, Jennifer?"

"Of course not, but I didn't make this up. I've kept this inside for years and it's eaten at me. Are you trying to say that I lied about it? Why would I do that now?"

"I'm not saying you lied," Donald corrected. "However, it's possible that after all this time, you don't recall the exact words of the note. Even if you do, it doesn't mean your husband pushed Michael off that lighthouse. He may have felt responsible for some reason and that's why, in his mind, he felt that he killed Michael. Can you understand that? Is there a reason that he may have felt that way, Jennifer?"

I saw my mother fidget in the chair. I could imagine what was running through her mind. Should she tell those present my father's deep dark secret about his attraction to young men? Before she could decide how to respond, Aunt Julie took command again.

"I think that's enough for now, Donald. Wanda helped me prepare this delicious meal, and we're making it go to waste. Even though Russell believes this is important, I would rather concentrate on finding Wendy and Sarah's missing phone."

"I apologize. We'll continue this discussion later, but I have one last question." Donald surveyed the room again. "Have there been any further messages? Those crayon clues you mentioned to me?"

"Not as far as I know," Aunt Julie replied.

"After dinner, we need to search the inn. I know you told me you only have a few rooms open right now and the others are locked, but we should check them. Wendy may still be on the premises since Wanda hasn't had any luck finding her at home."

Aunt Julie raised her fork. "I'll unlock the rooms for you later, Donald. Let's enjoy dinner first."

I wanted to mention that I'd heard something in the Garden Room before Mother arrived, and I also needed to tell Donald about the doll Carolyn found by the lighthouse. I knew it wasn't the right time, though. I planned to do it privately if I could get Donald away from my aunt's side. I didn't want to speak of it in front of Wanda. Had

Dottie actually been lost on the day Michael died and not recovered until now?

From the Notes of Michael Gamboski

(photo of Ida Lewis, female lighthouse keeper, Wikimedia Commons)

Lighthouse keeping was one of the first U.S. government jobs available to women in the 19th century. There were many female lighthouse keepers (80 are on file), but most obtained their position when their husband died or became incapacitated.

Lime Rock Light in Newport Harbor, RI was first lit in 1854. After the first keeper, James Lewis, suffered a stroke in 1858, his wife Ida tended the light assisted by her young daughter. In 1879, Lime Rock was renamed the Ida Lewis Lighthouse.

Robbins Reef, also known as Kate's Light, is named after the wife of a keeper who, after his death, tended the light from 1886 to 1919 and daily rowed her children to school in Staten Island.

(Information obtained from the U.S. Lighthouse Society)

Chapter Forty-One

Sea Scope: Twenty years ago

When Sarah woke, the memory of the night before and what she and Glen heard outside their parents' door came back to her, filling her with fear. Was it true her father was actually leaving her mother? Would they be moving away from Sea Scope? She hadn't slept well thinking about what it all meant and how it would affect her and her brother.

As Sarah dressed, she realized today was also the day Michael was checking out of the inn. He'd announced yesterday at breakfast that he'd finished his report and was going to spend the rest of the summer at home with his parents. She and Glen had helped him load his suitcases into his car because he wanted to get an early start in the morning. They were sad to see him go, but he promised to come back and visit.

When Sarah went downstairs, she noticed no one was around. Ms. Wilson hadn't even started breakfast, and she usually did that early on Saturdays before she took Wendy to Bible school. Glancing at the kitchen clock, she saw it was 7:30.

She jumped when she heard footsteps behind her, but it was only her aunt. "If you're looking for food, Sarah, it won't be out until later. You can have fruit now if you'd like. Ms. Wilson is not feeling well this morning, so I'll be making breakfast. Is Glen up, too?"

"No, Aunt Julie. I haven't seen him. Sorry about Ms. Wilson. Is Wendy still going to Bible school today?"

Aunt Julie walked into the kitchen. Opening the refrigerator, she scanned its contents. "I hope so, Sarah. Maybe you want to help me get eggs started. Most of the guests sleep late on Saturday mornings, anyway."

"Is Michael gone yet?"

Aunt Julie brought a dozen eggs to the table. "No. He's out on the patio with your father. Maybe you can take them this basket of muffins while I put on coffee. They're not freshly made, but Michael really should have something to eat before his drive home." She handed Sarah the basket, and Sarah's stomach growled reminding her it was empty.

"Thanks, Sarah. You can have one if you want."

As she headed toward the patio doors, Sarah heard two male voices drifting toward her. She recognized her father's low deep voice and Michael's higher one. As she listened, she realized they were arguing. Her father's voice was raised. She recognized the tone from when he became mad at her or Glen. Afraid to disturb them, she stood inside next to the doors. Her intent wasn't to snoop but to wait to enter until they quieted down. However, she couldn't avoid hearing their words.

"I'm giving this all up for you, and now you tell me it's over."

"Martin, calm down. Someone might hear us."

"I don't care anymore. I'm sick of hiding. I spoke to Jennifer last night. I told you she's agreeing to the divorce. I didn't expect that, but I'm relieved."

"I didn't ask you to do that. What about your kids? Your sister? I assume you're giving up the inn."

"I spoke to you about that, also. I'm starting my own construction company. It'll take time, but I won't be under Julie's command anymore."

"I wish you luck, Martin, but I have my own plans. I have one more year at the university and then I begin my own career. I enjoy research. I'm thinking of becoming of an archivist."

Sarah had to move closer to the door to hear her father's next words because he'd finally calmed down and was speaking lower.

"So that's it then?"

"I'm sorry if you misunderstood. I shouldn't have accepted the ring, but you said it was only a token of your friendship."

"I don't want it back."

In the silence that followed, Sarah took the opportunity to take out the muffins. When she slipped through the patio doors, her father and Michael were hugging. She found it strange because her father wasn't a demonstrative man and hardly ever hugged any of them or even their mother. They broke apart when she said, "Excuse me. Aunt Julie wanted me to bring food out to you. Ms. Wilson has a bad headache this morning."

Her father turned, and she thought she saw tears in his eyes when he looked at her. "Thanks, Sarah."

Sarah placed the basket on the small wicker table between the rocking chairs. "Are you leaving soon?" she asked Michael.

He smiled, although she noticed his eyes looked teary, too. "Yes, Sarah. We already said our goodbyes last night. I'm going to miss you and your brother, but I'll come by when I can."

Sarah knew that wasn't going to happen. Whenever friends at her school said they were moving but would keep in touch, they never did. It was what people said to lighten the blow when they exited from your life.

She was about to head back to the kitchen to help Aunt Julie start breakfast when Wendy skipped out on to the patio swinging her doll at her side. "Good morning, Mr. Brewster, Michael, Sarah."

"Is your mother feeling better?" Sarah's father asked.

"Yes. She's in the kitchen making breakfast with Ms. Brewster. She asked me to come out and call you all in."

"I'll take a muffin to go," Michael said. He turned to Sarah's father. "Thanks again for you and your sister's hospitality. I enjoyed my stay at Sea Scope." Choosing a chocolate chip muffin from the tray, he headed down the walk, disappearing into the shadows of the hanging moss that lined the path.

"We might as well go inside," Sarah's father said, his eyes still wet, a catch to his voice.

She and Wendy followed him into the house.

"Where's Mama?" Wendy asked Aunt Julie as she entered the kitchen. A few of the inn guests were there eating and talking among themselves at one of the back tables. Aunt Julie always reserved the front table for the family. The only one there was Glen, and Sarah's father took the seat next to him. Sarah still saw a sadness in his eyes and doubted he would eat much. Sarah's mother wasn't down yet. After what she and her brother heard exchanged between her parents last night, Sarah wouldn't be surprised if her mother stayed in her room all day.

"She's outside already, Wendy," Aunt Julie said. "She told me to have you grab a muffin and meet her out there. You're already running late for Bible school."

Wendy did as she was instructed, whispering to Sarah that she was hoping she wouldn't have to go this morning. Then she raced out the back door to meet her mother.

Glen and Sarah's father were immersed in a conversation about Glen's latest science project. Sarah was surprised Glen hadn't even asked about Michael because they'd been very close. The day before, when Michael brought them into his room one last time and said goodbye, he'd given Glen a copy of one of the lighthouse books he'd purchased that he no longer needed. Even though it wasn't particularly related to science, Glen appeared happy with it. Sarah received a lovely shell Michael had found on the beach that he'd cleaned and polished. He told her it would make a nice paperweight for her sketches. For Wendy, he had a box of her favorite fudge from the candy store, but he made her promise not to eat all of it at once or she would get a stomach ache and her mother would be mad at him. Sarah wondered if he'd given the adults gifts, but she didn't notice any. Everyone was sorry to see him leave, especially her father.

Chapter Forty-Two

Sea Scope: Present day

I hardly had an appetite for dinner and found the food cold and tasteless due to my mood and apprehension about what I needed to speak to Donald about. He and my aunt had left to check out the locked rooms while I helped clear the table. Wanda said her headache was worsening and she needed to lie down. Russell and Carolyn had gone to the movies, and Mother offered to help me clean up. I was glad of her company.

"You did great before, Mom," I said as we stood at the sink washing the dishes. "I know how hard it must've been for you to talk about all that."

Mother dried the plate I handed her. "Thank you, Sarah, but I should've done this years ago. I keep trying to protect people, but I can't continue to make that an excuse for hiding from the truth."

"Do you really think Dad killed Michael?"

Mother paused, the dish rag in her hand. "I don't know. After breakfast that morning, he left the inn. I never told Donald that when he questioned me. I said I was out on the porch reading and saw your father working on his car. He was actually taking his morning jog toward the lighthouse."

I hadn't realized Mother had lied about my father's whereabouts on the morning of Michael's death. "What did Father tell the detective that day?"

"He said he had engine issues with his car and was trying to fix it. Donald didn't question us separately, so he went along with the story I told."

"How about your alibi?" I asked. "Did Father provide one for you?"

She shook her head. "No. He said he wasn't aware I was on the porch."

"What about Aunt Julie? She usually sits outside in the morning."

"She said she was up in her studio painting." Mother pushed back a strand of blonde hair streaked with gray that had fallen over her left eye as she'd bent down to dry the plate I'd handed her.

"So no one but you corroborated anyone else's story?"

"That's right, but it didn't matter, Sarah. They ruled Michael's death a suicide. I never believed it. He was on his way home. He'd finished his paper. The authorities created a scenario where he had a broken romance and couldn't face life anymore. Donald Marshall said the goodbyes Michael gave us all the day before were intended as last goodbyes. He never got in his car that morning. It was found in the parking area reserved for guests. He'd walked to the lighthouse instead and jumped off the tower."

"Glen and I heard you and Dad talking the night before about breaking up," I said, handing her another dish to dry. I figured if we were having an honest conversation, she needed to know everything. "The next morning, Michael told Dad he was sorry if he'd given him the wrong impression but that he had plans for the future that didn't include him. I couldn't understand what he meant, but I knew Dad was very upset afterwards."

Mother sighed and looked down at the wet plate dripping into the sink. "I had a suspicion you and Glen knew something. I believe your father agreed to move to Long Island and stay in our sham of a marriage to escape his guilt. I know that never works. Running away, whether to a distant place or through a bottle, isn't a solution to any problem. I should've realized that years ago."

I laid the last dish down and placed my hand on my mother's arm. "It wasn't easy for you." Anger at my father boiled up in me. At that moment, I knew he was a murderer. If not of Michael, then at least of my mother's dreams. He'd married her knowing he couldn't fully love her the way she loved him.

When Donald and Aunt Julie finished searching the inn, they met us in the living room where Mother and I were having tea and talking. It was as if a barrier had been torn down between us, and I felt closer to her than I had in years.

"No luck," Donald said as he entered with my aunt at his side. "There's no sign of her. Given that Wanda's house is nearby, it's possible Wendy is returning there at night. There haven't been any further messages or thefts, so she may even be back to her old self at this point. I would advise Wanda to check at home tomorrow or call there. I'm not a psychiatrist, but I don't think this type of episode that was described to me would last more than a few hours."

"Even so," Aunt Julie said, "I think it's a good idea that you stay here tonight, Donald, as we discussed. I'll set up a guest room for you."

I watched their interplay and knew finding Wendy or providing protection from her wasn't behind my aunt's plan. It was apparent by the brightness of her eyes and the special smile she gave Donald Marshall that she was still infatuated with him. I doubted he'd actually be sleeping in a guest room that night.

Donald and Julie joined us for tea, but the conversation lulled. It was obvious Julie wanted to be alone with her old lover, and mother was tired from her confession. I still needed to talk to Donald about Wendy's doll, but it didn't look like I'd be able to get him. I decided to go to bed and maybe read more of my diary to see if anything I'd recorded might shed light on what really happened to Michael the day he attempted to leave Sea Scope.

While I was in my room, I heard Russell and Carolyn return from the movie. They were laughing and talking about the show. I closed my door as their footsteps headed to the East Wing. I had a feeling my friend would be spending the night in the Lighthouse Room and not next door to me. I was happy for her but wary for Russell. If Carolyn was a younger version of Aunt Julie, she might give him his walking papers before the end of the summer. I tried to control my cynicism. Just because the man I'd married was sleeping with his young student didn't mean everyone's love was ill-fated. I tossed my diary aside. I'd be facing Derek tomorrow when he arrived at the inn. Part of me was excited at this prospect, but another dreaded our confrontation. I sought strength from my mother's admission hoping it would give me confidence to approach Derek about the girl who'd answered our phone. Although our relationship had been strained in the months before my trip back to Sea Scope, I'd never had proof of Derek's dishonesty or disloyalty until now.

I punched my pillow in frustration. Wasn't it ironic that at almost the same moment I learned I was carrying his baby Derek was in our bed with a coed?

I closed my eyes and tried to block out the painful thoughts. I anticipated staying awake worrying about the next day, but Carolyn may have been right about how tiring the early stages of pregnancy were because I found myself drifting to sleep with images of Derek and me floating through my mind.

From the Notes of Michael Gamboski

(Eddystone Lighthouse in 1759, after the death of Henry Hall)

Probably the oldest lighthouse keeper was Henry Hall, a keeper on the famous Eddystone Lighthouse, who was 94. He met a remarkable death on duty in 1755. The lighthouse caught fire and, while he tried to put out the fire, he swallowed nearly half a pound of molten lead. He died from lead poisoning about two weeks later.

Chapter Forty-Three

Long Island: Two years ago

Sarah and Derek were having breakfast. Derek had made sunny-side up eggs with toast that Sarah barely tasted. She wasn't eating much these days. A week ago, her brother was thrown from his motorcycle on an L.A. highway and was pronounced dead at the scene. A few days prior to that, her husband of seven years asked her to accept the fact that they wouldn't be having children.

"If you don't eat that, it'll get cold and taste horrid," Derek said, dipping his toast into the yolk on his plate. "You have to eat, Sarah. Glen wouldn't want you to starve yourself in his memory."

She looked across at him through teary eyes and wanted to tell him that she wasn't just mourning her brother. She was also mourning the babies she would never have.

"What if I take a day off today? It's beautiful. We can spend time together at the beach. Would that perk you up a little?"

When they first married, they used to enjoy walking by the beach a few blocks from their home each night after dinner. Occasionally, they even found a private area to make love or saved the passion the waves and sunlight ignited in them for the second they walked through their door. Now, when Derek returned from work, he immersed himself in his study with papers to grade and a beer. She spent more time in her upstairs studio drawing animals for the children's books she illustrated. When they met in bed, there was no spark, and both of them were too tired to care.

"I don't know, Derek. Thanks for the offer, but I'm not ready to go out."

Derek put down his fork. "Sarah, I know you're depressed, but you can't hide from the world like this. I know you haven't even been drawing. Carolyn's called several times, but you refuse to see her. I want to help you." He put his hand out to cover hers across the table, but she pulled back.

"What's wrong? It's not only Glen, is it?"

Sarah lowered her eyes away from his dark gaze and nodded. "No, Derek. It's about us. I still want a baby."

Derek stood and pushed his chair back with a quick motion. "So that's what this is all about? You think I'll feel sorry for you having lost your brother and give in to fertility treatments? Our discussion about that was closed before Glen's accident. If we're meant to be parents, it'll happen, Sarah. I don't want us going through more tests and invasive procedures. I know couples who spent thousands with no results."

Sarah pushed her plate away and stood to face him, hot tears burning behind her eyes. "I also know couples who have healthy and adorable children thanks to today's technology. You can't put a price on a family, and I'd even be willing to adopt if you're really against in vitro. As far as our not needing assistance, I can't see it happening like the Immaculate Conception. We hardly make love anymore."

Derek sighed. "Sarah, I'm sorry. Come here." He opened his arms and walked around the table. She fell into them crying against his shoulder. "We'll work this out, honey. Believe me."

Chapter Forty-Four

Sea Scope: Present day

I woke with a start from a vague memory of the dream, or was it a dream memory? Derek and I had been discussing his decision for us not to proceed with fertility treatments. I had only learned of Glen's death the week before. Although Derek remained steadfast in his opinion that things would work out for us without intervention, I still prayed he would change his mind. We'd walked on the beach afterwards, but it hadn't been the same. Neither had it ended with a romantic encounter.

I got up and showered using one of the rose-scented soaps Wanda left in the guest bathrooms. It was a concoction she prepared from all-natural ingredients. I substituted it for my Dove body wash and indulged myself in the scent. Afterwards, I threw on a pair of jeans and a bright lemon t-shirt that Derek said brought out the honey color in my hair. Glancing in the vanity where I'd once tried on makeup that I'd sneaked out of Aunt Julie's room and been grounded for a week, I applied a quick touch of my own cosmetics. I noted that my normally pale skin had a slight glow to it. I wondered if it was the rumored effect of pregnancy. Since I'd come to Sea Scope, I had very little time to reflect on the baby or my relationship with its father. A part of me realized that, like the fetus in my uterus, a tiny seed of hope was growing inside me now that Derek was joining me at the inn.

As I began to leave the room, I suddenly stopped. A note had been slipped under the door. I held my breath as I picked it up. Unfolding the paper, I found it was another crayon clue. I read the message: "Check out the boxes in the studio."

I contemplated finding Donald and showing him the paper immediately or sharing it with Carolyn who'd probably advise me to do the same thing. Then I remembered my friend had likely spent the night with Russell and my aunt with Donald. The retired detective had advised Aunt Julie to lock the inn's doors at night, so I couldn't understand how Wendy had gotten in to leave the note. I considered that Carolyn and Russell, having been the last ones to return to Sea Scope after the movies, may have forgotten to lock the door behind them. The other alternative was, despite Donald and my aunt's search of the house, Wendy was on the premises somewhere they hadn't looked. A chill ran up my spine at the thought of Wanda's daughter lurking outside my room.

I glanced back down at the message. Like Glen's old scavenger hunt game, the note was a clue. Should I go up to the studio? Was Wendy hiding up there? The sensible part of me wanted to seek Donald's professional advice but, as I stepped out into the quiet of the hall, I decided to head upstairs. My feet led me to the stairway at the end of the corridor. It was then that I saw the cat. He was stalking imaginary prey, possibly a fly near the stairs.

"Al, do you want to come upstairs with me?" I whispered. He obeyed and followed me.

I switched on the light, although sunlight was already streaming through the skylight. *What a wonderful place to paint,* I thought again. Where to begin? I didn't want to spend much time up there, but there were quite a few boxes lined up against the far wall, and I didn't know what I was looking for. I started my search in the right corner. Al was sniffing, padding around on his velvet paws.

"Okay, I'll check that one first," I said as Al poked his head into an open box.

The box was heavy, but I managed to move it a few inches toward me, so I could reach in and pull out the contents lying on top. Al scooted away and jumped atop a stool, surveying me with his green eyes as I crouched on my knees laying the notebooks and file folders across the floor. I recognized Glen's handwriting immediately. These were his case files.

When Aunt Julie cleared out his apartment, she found the keys to his practice and went there to retrieve any personal items he may have kept in his office. She also contacted those who hadn't read of the accident in the paper or had seen it on the news. She'd never mentioned that she'd brought patient records back to Sea Scope. She told Mother she'd handed everything over to the state. As I looked through the files checking their labels, I realized that instead of the numerous names I expected to see, there was only one. The books and files dating back to 2012, two years before Glen's death, were all marked with one name. Wendy Wilson.

From the Notes of Michael Gamboski

(Angels Gate Lighthouse, Wikimedia Commons)

The Los Angeles Harbor Light, also known as The Angels Gate Lighthouse, has stood at the entrance of Los Angeles Harbor for nearly 100 years and has withstood numerous earthquakes, a tidal wave, and the impact of both curious visitors, and vandals. The original name as designated by the Lighthouse Service was "San Pedro Breakwater Light Station." In 1914, the name was changed to "Los Angeles Harbor Light." (from the article, "Los Angeles Harbor Light—The Angels Gate Lighthouse" by Marifrances Trivelli, Director, Los Angeles Maritime Museum

Chapter Forty-Five

Los Angeles: Two years ago

The Los Angeles International Airport was crowded with people. Sarah was happy she'd only brought along an overnight bag, so she wouldn't have to search for her luggage at baggage claim. Glen had tried to persuade her to stay longer than a weekend. He wanted to show her the sights of the city including Hollywood, but she said she couldn't do it this time and promised to be back for a longer visit in the future. If Derek had joined her, she might've extended her stay, but he'd asked her to take the trip alone. "I'd feel like a third wheel between you and your brother," he said. "You two have a lot to catch up on, and the spring semester is almost over. I have a ton of finals to grade."

Despite the large number of people swarming the arrival gate, Sarah spotted Glen immediately. He was leaning against an airport pole, a lazy smile on his face similar to the one he wore when he took a slice out of Ms. Wilson's peach pie behind her back. His hair had darkened and was longer than she remembered. He'd grown a thin moustache and wore sunglasses perched atop his head. As she recognized him, his eyes met hers and he waved. She excused herself as she weaved through the crowd bumping a few shoulders and apologizing as she headed toward him. When she reached him, he threw his arms around her and embraced her in a huge bear hug. "So glad you made it, Silly Sarah." The use of her childhood nickname put a smile on her face.

He eyed her bag still slung over her shoulder. "I'll take that. Do you have any cases?"

She shook her head. "I packed light. I'll only be staying until Sunday."

He looked disappointed for a moment as she handed him the bag. "Let's get out of here. My car isn't far."

She followed him to the parking lot as he jangled a bunch of keys and pressed a button on the chain that lit up the headlights of his red Mazda.

"Nice car," she said as he unlocked the passenger door.

"Thanks. It gets me around. Pardon the mess." A bunch of cigarette butts and empty beer cans lined the car's floor.

Glen started the car and reached into the dashboard drawer where he withdrew a pack of Marlboros. "Want one?" he offered.

"No, thanks. I don't smoke. When did you start?"

He lowered his window, lit one, and took a few quick puffs. "About the time I took up drinking again. Didn't you know that shrinks are the most addicted people around, Sis?"

Sarah changed the subject. "How is your office? I know you opened your own practice."

He shrugged and stubbed out his cigarette in the ashtray on the console and then tossed the remainder of the smoke under his feet. "I have a few clients. They're all crazy." He laughed at his own joke. "I'll show it to you. It's actually below my new apartment." He put on his sunglasses, reversed out of the parking spot, and tapped on his CD player. A loud '80s tune she didn't recognize blared from the speakers.

"Sorry." He adjusted the volume. "I like loud music when I drive."

Once they were clear of the cars exiting the airport and were on the open road, she noticed his driving speed matched the tempo of the song. It was faster than she was used to traveling in her car or as a passenger in Derek's.

"I can't believe it's been five years, Sarah. You look the same. Prettier, actually."

"Thank you, Glen. You haven't changed much yourself." She remembered when he left for college at UCLA after earning his Associates Degree in Psychology from Nassau Community College on Long Island. He'd saved money from part-time jobs and summer work, also earning a scholarship. When he turned twenty-one, Glen also came into possession of a trust fund his father had set up for him when he was born. Sarah received her money two years earlier and used it to pay off the balance of her student loan.

Their mother had been surprised at Glen's decision to move away, but she hadn't talked him out of it. Sarah secretly believed her brother's choice of relocating to the West Coast was to escape the memories of Sea Scope and their father's suicide. She sat next to him as he navigated the tangle of cars entering the freeway. As he honked his horn and occasionally swore at drivers, Sarah realized Glen hadn't been successful. The anger and frustration had followed him across the country.

As they pulled into the parking garage next to Glen's building, he warned Sarah to watch her back as she got out of the car. "This isn't the safest place to live," he explained. "In fact, it's one of L.A.'s highest-ranked crime areas, but I chose it for that reason. I get plenty of patients here." He winked as he grabbed her bag from the back seat and hoisted it over his shoulder.

Sarah couldn't help sticking to his side as they walked from the garage out into the bright, smarmy Los Angeles street. It was earlier than her body expected, and she wondered if jet lag was already setting in as a dizziness assaulted her. Glen noticed and interpreted it as fear. He took her hand. "Didn't mean to scare you. It's pretty safe in daylight most of the time." As they walked to the front of Glen's building, Sarah glanced across the street at the rundown stores, a few porn shops, and tattoo parlors. Motorcycles roared by. Rap music blared. She was aware of people passing on the sidewalk—young women in short tight skirts and low blouses who she thought might be prostitutes and men of all races sporting tattoos spread over their exposed bodies.

"L.A. isn't all glamour and riches," Glen said, watching her look around. "If you were spending more time here, I'd give you a tour of the other side. We could head out to Hollywood and do the sightseeing thing. For the weekend, I'm afraid you're stuck in L.A.'s version of Hell's Kitchen." He stopped in front of his building, a shabby multi-floored structure with graffiti etched across it proclaiming, "Jesus is Watching."

"Home sweet home. Watch yourself on the stairs, Sarah." She was amazed he used no key or intercom to enter. "Don't worry. I have keys to my room and office," he said, and led the way down a corridor that smelled of tobacco and sweat.

They ascended one flight of grimy stairs to a metal door that opened with a creak after Glen turned his key in the bolt. He switched on the lights, and she entered his office. It was disorganized but clean. Papers were piled on the makeshift desk—a table that had one shortened leg supported by the L.A. yellow pages. Behind it was a black leather chair, the only item worth more than fifty dollars in the room. The patient files stood in open-sided crates. The walls were a light brown covered with posters of famous psychologists. She recognized Freud and identified the others by their labels—B.F. Skinner, Ivan Pavlov, Carl Jung, and John B. Watson. Glen's diploma in psychology also hung there with a UCLA banner. There was a copy of the DSMV on a side table next to a Keurig coffee maker with a revolving holder of assorted K-Cups and Styrofoam cups instead of mugs. Lastly, Sarah noticed the obligatory couch against another wall and one lopsided lamp with a tall rusted base. A few psychology books were stacked by one end of the couch. There was only one window in the room, quite high, with a dirty white shade covering it.

"I got this stuff secondhand from garage sales," Glen said. "Have a seat on the couch, Sarah. There aren't bugs on it that I can tell."

He placed her overnight bag by the table/desk and went to the coffeemaker and plugged it in. "I need caffeine. What about you?"

Sarah smiled as she sat tentatively on the sagging couch. "Sure. I'll have a cup. Is coffee another of your addictions, Glen?"

"You bet. It'll help your jet lag, too." He made them both a cup and joined her on the couch. "Don't worry about spilling it. There are enough stains on this sofa already."

Sarah didn't ask him what he meant. She'd already avoided the areas with spots.

"I'm glad you could make it," Glen said, sipping his drink. "I don't have much space upstairs, but it's cleaner and more comfortable. I'll bed down here for the weekend. I don't mind."

Sarah had offered to stay at a hotel, but Glen insisted he had space for her. "Are you sure? I can still book a room somewhere."

He waved his free hand. "I promise you it's not too bad. There's a dead bolt up there, and I'll be right here below you. If you're really worried, I can sleep on the floor up there with you."

Sarah didn't think she'd sleep much at all. "I don't want to put you out."

"Silly Sarah, you're my sister for gosh sakes."

Sarah took a sip of coffee and felt less shaky. "Glen, if you need money…"

"Stop," he waved his hand again. "I'm fine. You and Derek need the money more."

She was afraid the conversation would turn to this. She'd spoken to Glen about their problems conceiving, but he didn't know Derek was against fertility treatments.

He must've noticed the change in her expression because he added, "You guys haven't had any luck yet, have you?"

She hid the tears that suddenly gathered behind her eyes and looked away.

"Sorry. I wish there was something I could do. I'd love to be an uncle. I might know a few people back in New York, or you could try resources from infertility associations."

"Glen, no. You don't understand." Sarah put her coffee cup down. "Derek doesn't want us to pursue treatments."

"What? How come? Is it the cost?"

"I don't know." She glanced at him and saw the sadness in his eyes. "Please let's talk about something else. How are you doing? Any special ladies in your life yet?"

Glen sighed, but she thought she saw a quick flicker in his eyes before the lashes she always envied came down to hood them. "Who would want to come back to a place like this?"

"You could always go to their place."

He chuckled. "I spend so much time working; it doesn't leave much opportunity to meet women."

"Do you see people on the weekends?"

"Yes, nights, too. That's when most of my clients can come. I've cleared my schedule for the next two days, though, to make time for your visit."

"Thanks."

"No problem. I'll take you upstairs now if you want to get settled and rest a bit. The fridge is stocked with food, but I usually eat out or order pizza from the local delivery service. We can have dinner out of town later. We still have a lot to talk about and this place is not the most conducive to pleasant conversation."

Chapter Forty-Six

Sea Scope: Present day

When I'd gotten over the shock of discovering that Wendy had been a patient of Glen's, I remembered visiting him in California a few months before his accident. We'd spoken of his patients, by first name only, but he'd never mentioned Wendy. Then I recalled what Wendy's mother said about Wendy disappearing for days at a time both during her marriage and when she moved back home with Wanda. I could understand Wendy feeling more comfortable seeing Glen than another therapist since they shared a childhood connection, but why the secrecy?

I picked up the most current notebook from the pile around me. They were all dated and arranged with the latest on top. My heart lurched at Glen's small, tight handwriting on the cover. It read, "May 2014 -." I had visited him that same month and year. I assumed the dates hadn't been completed because he died that July, ironically close to the time of Michael and our father's deaths.

As I opened the book, I jumped at the sound of a thump, but it was just Al abandoning his perch and heading back downstairs. The first page was dated the day after my visit with Glen. Unlike the clinical notes I expected, it was more of a diary. I crossed my legs and placed the notebook in my lap as I read my dead brother's words.

It was so good to see Sarah this weekend. I almost told her about Wendy. I think she would understand, but we need to be cautious. When Wendy contacted me last year, she begged me to keep our meetings secret. Her mother had sent her to other psychologists because of her continued nightmares, but she thought I could help. She said her marriage was in trouble, and I was her last hope. I explained that therapy required regular visits, which weren't possible with our being in different states. She insisted, so I agreed to talk with her and give her an initial consultation. I didn't expect her to keep coming, nor did I expect how beautiful a woman she'd grown into or my non-professional attraction to her.

I caught my breath and read on, a growing sense of disbelief working its way through me as I anticipated Glen's next words.

I don't think either one of us expected it to happen. I've had infatuations with my patients before, but this was different. Maybe it was our common background, those days as children playing in the South Carolina sand. Maybe I'm being romantic, but the fact is I fell in love with the grown-up Wendy despite the fact she was married. I continued to see her against my better judgment. I started paying her travel expenses because her husband began asking too many questions about the missing money from their account.

I began telling her I needed to see her more frequently for treatment when the truth was she was helping me more than I was helping her. The episodes she mentioned, the strange dreams about the lighthouse, they were occurring more often since our sessions. I considered it was because I reminded her of those days and out sessions were bringing more memories back to the surface.

The next entry was dated two months later a few days before Glen's accident.

Wendy told me she's now living with her mother, after her husband and she mutually agreed to a separation leading to divorce. She said she was sick of hiding our affair and wanted to tell Wanda about us. I cautioned her to wait a bit longer. I felt that the stress building up in her was increasing the dreams and thought it would be best for her to finish treatment before making any life-changing decisions. I know I risked losing her, but I'd anonymously consulted with a fellow psychologist about her case. He suggested I try hypnotizing her. I don't use hypnotism often on my patients so am not too experienced with it, but I asked her if she would agree to try it one time.

I flipped to the next page assuming it would continue Glen's account of the hypnotism if Wendy had actually gone through with it. However, the rest of the book was blank. When I looked closer between the last page of writing and the one that followed, I noticed a neat cut across the center binding, as if someone had taken a razor or other straight edge and had removed pages. I ran my finger over the almost unnoticeable tear. If these pages had included a report of the hypnotism session, there must've been a reason why they were cut out and the fact hidden so carefully. Questions rose in my mind. Why hadn't the person who removed the pages destroyed the book? What was the book doing here with the rest of Wendy's treatment records up in my aunt's art studio? I knew what I had to do to find out the answers to these questions. I needed to speak to my aunt, but I needed to do it privately without Donald Marshall lustily looking over her shoulder. I placed all the books back in their original box in the same order in which I'd taken them out and headed downstairs.

As I descended, I spotted Carolyn outside my room. She turned when she heard me on the stairs. "Sarah, I've been looking for you. Derek is here. He's downstairs. I told him I'd come get you, but you weren't answering my knocks. I was beginning to worry. What were you doing up there?"

I had to think of an excuse quickly. I didn't want to reveal what I'd found to anyone until I'd spoken to my aunt. "I thought I left something there yesterday when Aunt Julie showed me her studio, but I must've put it elsewhere."

I could tell Carolyn didn't believe me, but she shrugged. "I'm sure it mustn't be that important. Your talk with Derek is. Follow me."

As we headed for the stairs, I said, "How was the movie with Russell last night?"

Her voice lifted. "I had a wonderful time, Sarah. I'm breaking the news to Jack today. I hope it doesn't jeopardize my career, but there are lots of publicists out there and only one Mr. Right."

"You've had several Mr. Rights," I reminded her.

"I thought they were Mr. Right, but I was wrong. This is different. I know it." She stopped at the staircase, her hand on the bannister. "Look, honey, I see you're spiffed up for Derek. I hope it works out for you. You're a family now, remember."

I took a breath. "He said he had to say something to me when he arrived. I'm afraid he's planning to ask me for a divorce."

"Sarah, that's crazy. Why would he come all the way here to do that?"

"I hope you're right, but I have to be prepared. I can't get my hopes up."

"I understand, but I have a good feeling about his joining you. By the way, Donald Marshall left this morning. I think he and your aunt had a nice night together because she's all rosy and gushing. He had to get back to his dog, but it looks like he's going to be hanging around here checking things out including Julie." She laughed.

"What about Wanda? Has she tried to contact Wendy again?"

"Yes. Donald advised her to go home for a few days and see if Wendy turns up. Wanda promised she'd let us know if that happens."

"So it's the four of us here now plus Derek," I said as we walked downstairs.

"Right, unless Wendy is still hiding out here, too."

I thought of the crayon clue that had led me to the studio and Glen's files on Wendy. If Wanda's daughter was around, despite the retired detective's fruitless search of the inn, why would she want me to see Glen's records about her? The only explanation I could conceive was that if Wendy was experiencing one of the episodes her mother mentioned, she would be thinking and acting as my brother. What was Glen trying to tell me?

From the Notes of Michael Gamboski

(St. George Reef Lighthouse plans, Wikimedia Commons)
The most expensive lighthouse built in America is St. George Reef, near Crescent City, California. It took 10 years to construct and cost $715,000.

Chapter Forty-Seven

Los Angeles: Two years ago

Glen sat staring at the words he'd jotted in his notebook during the session. Then he took a paper cutter and tore them out. Wendy had already heard the recording he'd made using the app on his cell phone. He could delete that later. He was surprised when she agreed to the hypnotism. She was hesitant at first, but after he'd assured her of its safety and the importance of confronting whatever was causing her sleepless nights, she said she would try it. She wanted to tell her mother about him and, when the divorce was final, she wanted them to be together. She was prepared to move to California and find a job there. They could save money and move to a better area where they could raise children.

Glen felt tears gather behind his eyes. He wasn't the type of man who cried often at a sad movie or a touching book. Even after he'd found his father dead in the garage, he'd only had one big cry and gotten it out of his system. As a man of science, he'd always appreciated the freedom that knowledge gave, the power of truth. Tonight, he'd faced Wendy's demons and had to admit it put him in a quandary. He'd made her promises he wasn't sure he could keep.

He took the papers he'd cut from the book, crinkled them up into a ball, and threw them in the wastebasket by his desk. She'd left in tears. He urged her to stay, but she said she needed time alone. She had an early flight in the morning and had brought enough money with her to find a place for the night. He tried to kiss her, but she was so upset she wouldn't let him. He hoped she wasn't mad at him. He was angry enough with himself.

Glen closed his office and took the flight of stairs up to his apartment. He'd been sober these past few weeks, but the impulse for a drink now hit him hard. He went to his secret stash reminiscent of his mother's at Sea Scope and at the house on Long Island. The bottles and cans were hidden in the bottom of his wardrobe. Out of sight, out of mind, but he knew they were there when he needed them.

He needed more than beer tonight. He popped open a bottle of scotch and chugged some down, feeling the familiar warmth and burn. He brought the bottle to his bed and sat there admonishing himself for being weak and needing alcohol to douse his pain. He couldn't stop replaying Wendy's words in his mind. Based on what she'd shared with him previously, he'd had a feeling the hypnotism would uncover something that happened when they were kids. The nightmares she suffered involved the lighthouse and Sea Scope. Most of the therapists she'd already seen believed the dreams were connected with her hearing about Michael's death when she returned to the inn from Bible school that summer day. He had a different hypothesis. Hearing something wouldn't cause the same trauma as actually witnessing it. He'd kept that theory from Wendy, but he knew she must've considered it herself.

Before he hypnotized her, Wendy warned him that Wanda had become suspicious of the excuses she gave her for the weekends she spent away. Wendy planned to tell her about Glen when she returned home. Now he had no idea what she was going to do.

The thought crossed his mind that he was only harming himself by falling back on his drinking. He put the bottle down and decided to go for a ride on his motorcycle to clear his mind. He might even catch up with Wendy. He was worried about her walking alone in this neighborhood.

Before he could grab his motorcycle helmet, there was a knock at the door. He thought it was Wendy coming back so answered it without checking the peephole. He didn't expect to see the person who stood there.

Chapter Forty-Eight

Sea Scope: Present day

As I entered the living room with Carolyn, my heart fluttered at the sight of Derek despite the fact he looked exhausted from his long drive. His hair stood a bit on end as if he'd ruffled his fingers through it, an old habit he had yet to break, and there was a day's growth of stubble on his chin.

"Sarah," he said, standing. His eyes lit up as he walked toward me with open arms. I fell into them, smelling his manly scent mixed with sweat and clothes that likely had been worn through the night.

"Sorry. I need a shower badly. I didn't want to stop. I had this feeling I needed to get here right away."

I pulled away from him aware that the others were observing us, especially Carolyn who still stood at my side.

"I'm moving you to the largest guest room, Sarah," Aunt Julie said. "So you and Derek can be more comfortable. I'll leave you two to catch up. Derek's already had a cup of coffee and one of the muffins Wanda baked yesterday, but I'll make a larger breakfast for us all later."

"Thank you, Julie," Derek said. "I might go up, shower, and take a quick nap, but first I want to talk with Sarah."

"Of course." She nodded and left the room.

"I'll catch you later, Sarah," said Carolyn following my aunt. I thought I saw her wink. I noticed Russell and my mother weren't present, but I could hear their voices drifting in from the patio as Aunt Julie and Carolyn joined them.

When the room was empty, Derek took a breath and looked at me. I was suddenly conscious of us being alone and what we had to say to one another.

"I have so much to tell you, Sarah, but I really am beat. Would you mind if we go up to the room your aunt's prepared and I can freshen up before we talk?"

I felt relief and regret at the same time. "Of course not. You must be exhausted. I know what room Aunt Julie gave us. I'll show you. Did you bring in your bags?"

"They're already upstairs. Russell took them. He seems like a nice fellow. He says he knew you since you were a little girl when he and his father visited here."

Was there a hint of jealousy in his voice? I found that ironic when I still needed to confront him about the young woman who'd answered our phone.

"Yes. There were four of us back then—Wanda's daughter Wendy, Russell, me, and my brother Glen. We all hung out together."

"They told me about Wendy. I hope they find her. She needs help."

I nodded and turned away from his dark eyes. "Let's go upstairs. I don't think I have much to move from my room, but I'll check while you're getting settled."

"Thanks, Sarah. We really need to talk, but I have to get a little rest first."

"I understand," I said as I led him to the stairway. I considered that while Derek was resting, I could find a way to get Aunt Julie alone and talk to her about what I'd found in the attic.

I showed Derek to the larger guest room, the one known as the Ivory Room because it featured neutral tones of beige and white and featured framed photos of elephants. Luckily, there were no mounted tusks. My grandfather had spent time in Africa and had decorated the room with my grandmother. He was a wildlife photographer, and it was possible that's where Aunt Julie and I inherited our art talent.

Derek apologized again before I left him promising to talk after he'd gotten a few hours of sleep. I went downstairs looking for my aunt and found her alone drinking coffee.

"Where did Russell and Carolyn go?"

"I offered them breakfast, but Russ wanted to take Carolyn out. I think they're planning to head to the beach later. I'm glad they're getting along so well."

"I think it's more than that, Aunt Julie."

She smiled. "I agree. Would you like me to make you anything? The coffee's still on."

"I'm fine, but I would like to talk to you. Is Mother still in her room?"

"No. She went for a walk into town."

"How was she this morning?"

"Lighter." Aunt Julie put down her cup. "I think it did her good to get that weight off her chest."

I took a seat next to her on the couch. "Do you believe my father killed Michael?"

She shook her head. "I'm not sure. Is that what you wanted to talk to me about, Sarah?"

I noticed I was clutching my hands in my lap as I'd done the previous night with Mother's. "No. I wanted to ask you about your studio."

"Ah. You can use it any time. I already told you that."

"That's not what I want to discuss."

A curious look passed over my aunt's face. She lay her coffee cup down on the table beside the couch. "I'm listening. What do you want to know?"

I took a breath. "I was up there this morning. I found another crayon clue."

"What?" Aunt Julie exclaimed. "I don't understand. Donald and I checked the whole house last night, and there was no sign of Wendy."

"I'm thinking Carolyn and Russell may have left the door unlocked after they came back from the movies."

"We need to call Donald and tell him."

I could see she was eager to speak to her old lover. "You can do that if you want. The note directed me to your studio where I found a box that belonged to Glen."

I watched her face darken, but her reply surprised me. "Yes, I stored some of your brother's things up there. I thought you or your mother might want them one day."

"Did you go through them? Do you know what they contained?"

Aunt Julie waved her hand. "I don't recall. I may have, or maybe Wanda did. She and Wendy helped me go through Glen's apartment and office as you know. There were a lot of things. We got rid of most of them. That place was what you young people would call a 'dive.' " She shuddered at the memory.

I thought back to my visit with Glen two months before his accident. I could still see the graffiti on the building, the dark stairwell, smell the scent of sweat and vomit on the close air. I decided to be blunt. "Were you aware that Glen was treating Wendy? That they were having an affair?"

Aunt Julie's steady gaze didn't waver from my face. "Yes, Sarah. I won't lie to you. Wanda suspected what was going on and spoke to me about it. She was planning to confront Wendy when she returned. I have friends who live in L.A. in a better neighborhood than Glen. I flew out there when Wanda told me Wendy had left on one of her impromptu trips. I didn't tell Wanda I was going. I thought it might be best for me to check on things and maybe warn Wendy. I personally didn't think it was an issue that the two of them were seeing one another."

"Did you find them? When was this?" My heart was starting to pound.

"I arrived the day of Glen's accident. I borrowed a car and went to his apartment that night. Wendy had already left. As I drove toward Glen's place, I saw her on the street. I couldn't believe she was walking alone in that neighborhood. I stopped my car and called to her. When she came to the window, I saw that her face was red and streaked with tears. I figured she and Glen had an argument. I told her to get in the car. She hesitated, but she finally took a seat in the back. I asked her what was wrong. She wouldn't tell me. She didn't even want to know why I was there, but I told her that I was going to Glen's apartment. She said she didn't want to go back there. I offered to bring her to my friend's house to spend the night and we could fly home together the next day. She was relieved at the offer, but I still thought I should visit Glen while I was in the area. When I found his place," she shuddered again, "I asked Wendy if she was sure she didn't want to come inside. I thought maybe I could heal the rift between them. She was insistent that she wait in the car for me. I hated leaving her alone, but I locked the doors and planned only a quick visit."

When my aunt paused, I asked, "What time was this?"

"Around seven, I believe."

Glen's accident occurred at 8:30. "Go on, Aunt Julie. What happened when you saw Glen?"

"His office was locked, so I went up to his room. When he answered the door, he was surprised to see me. I guess it was a bit of a shock. I noticed there was a half empty bottle of scotch on the floor by his bed."

I shut my eyes for a second recalling that they'd found Glen's blood alcohol level elevated in the autopsy and claimed his intoxication was the cause of the motorcycle crash.

Aunt Julie continued. "I told him about Wendy and asked why she was so upset. I inquired about what they'd fought over. He told me he'd hypnotized her during a therapy session and that she'd found something out that deeply troubled her. He couldn't tell me what it was because of doctor/patient confidentiality."

"What happened then?"

"I told him she was in my car, and I was taking her to my friend's house where I was staying. I asked if he wanted to go out there to talk to her, but he said he thought it best they be apart for a while."

"And then?" I prompted.

Aunt Julie lowered her head and her voice. "And then I left, took Wendy to my friend's house, and heard the news about Glen after our flight home."

"Why didn't you say anything about all this before? Did you tell Wanda or Mother anything?"

"Wanda never knew I went."

"Did Wendy start leaving the crayon clues after that?"

"I assume so. Whatever she discovered under hypnosis coupled with Glen's death probably caused her to develop a personality disorder or whatever the psychiatrists she visited coined it."

"Did she ever try hypnotism again?"

"No. She refused."

"Do you know why the pages were cut out of Glen's record book about Wendy?"

"I have no idea. They were that way when I stored them."

"Why didn't you give them to Wanda?"

"I didn't think she'd want them. I felt they belonged more to you or your mother because they contained Glen's writing. I actually wanted to tell you about them during your visit here, but so many other things got in the way. I had no idea Wendy would be hiding out around the inn and leaving notes. I still don't know what that means or what she found out during her hypnotism session."

"I don't understand. What could be so terrible that Wendy wouldn't want people to know and would initiate her illness?"

"Sarah, I've spoken to Donald about this back then and more recently. I've always believed that Michael's death wasn't an accident. That morning when Wanda took Wendy to Bible school, I think she met up with Michael."

"How can that be? The police verified her story. Wendy was late for Bible school, but she attended. Her teacher confirmed that."

Julie picked up her coffee cup and took a sip before replying. "I don't have all the answers, Sarah, but I know that trauma can cause strange reactions in those that experience it. I believe Wendy's nightmares and later her condition was caused by a terrible experience that her conscious mind refuses to accept."

"And you think it has to do with Michael's death?"

She looked me straight in the eyes. "Yes, I do. I believe Wendy witnessed it."

"But if that's true and it came out in her hypnosis session and Glen recorded it, which he must've done, wouldn't she know?"

"Absolutely. She knows, but something is preventing her from telling."

"Instead she's leaving clues? That doesn't make sense."

"Glen is leaving clues," Aunt Julie corrected. "Wendy is unable to face the truth."

"Why?" I asked, already suspecting the answer.

"That's obvious, Sarah. If Wendy was at the lighthouse that morning, so was her mother."

Chapter Forty-Nine

Sea Scope: Twenty years ago

Since Wanda didn't own a car and Bible school was only a few blocks from the inn, she and Wendy walked there on Saturday mornings. Sometimes Wanda would return to Sea Scope and help start breakfast before returning to the school to pick up her daughter, but there were days she just felt like spending the hour on a bench outside the school waiting to walk Wendy back to the inn after class. Occasionally, she'd talk to one of the other moms who were also waiting, but she often felt uncomfortable with them. At twenty-six, she was the youngest, and a few of them mistook her for a babysitter before she'd introduced herself at the beginning of the summer.

That morning, she was in no mood to sit with the other mothers. Her heart was heavy. Michael hadn't even said goodbye to her.

As she walked with her daughter, Wendy asked her why she was so sad. She wiped the tears from her eyes with a tissue from her purse and said, "I'm going to miss Michael. That's all."

"I'll miss him, too. I thought he was going to be my new daddy."

Wendy hadn't referred to her real father since they came to live at Sea Scope. Even though she never knew the married man who impregnated her mother when Wanda was a sixteen-year-old naïve girl, Wendy used to question Wanda about him often.

"Why would you think that, honey?"

"I saw you kiss him once. I thought he was your boyfriend."

How could she explain to her daughter the complicated triangle in which she'd caught herself? "We were friends, Wendy. Friends kiss one another sometimes." She hoped Wendy would accept that answer. The girl simply tossed back her braids and clutched her doll tighter. Fortunately, they were already at the school.

"Wendy, I have something to do this morning that may take extra time. If I'm late, please wait for me by the door. Okay?"

"Yes, Mama."

Wanda watched her daughter join a few other late children rushing into the building. None of them greeted or talked with her as she skipped to her class.

Chapter Fifty

Sea Scope: Present day

"What are we going to do?" I asked my aunt. "I agree what you said is the most likely explanation, but how do we prove it?"

Aunt Julie got up. "Maybe we don't. Wanda has been more than a housekeeper to me all these years and better than a friend. I've felt she was the daughter I never had. I think I can trust Donald, but I have to be careful. The main thing is to find Wendy and get her the help she needs even if it means having her confront her memories of that day. Wanda said she'd let me know if she finds Wendy at home. She hasn't called yet, and since you discovered that note, Wendy may still be around here. Donald is on his way over, and we'll probably go through the inn again. I have a feeling we're going to find her soon."

While my aunt was talking, a thought occurred to me. Since Wendy hadn't turned up at her house or at the inn so far, was it possible she was hiding in the lighthouse? Although the place was still closed to visitors without an appointment, I recalled how years ago, Wendy had scaled the fence and taken me through the secret back entrance Glen had originally found. I didn't mention this idea to my aunt but decided to check it out on my own. Derek would likely sleep a few more hours, and Carolyn and Russ were enjoying each other's company away from the inn. I might run into my mother and, since we were now strengthening our relationship, I was sure she would be happy to help me look.

"Aunt Julie, I think I'll take a walk."

"That's a good idea, Sarah." I could tell she was pleased at the prospect of being alone with Donald when he arrived.

As I stepped out on the patio, Al came up behind me meowing. He gave me a slight scare because I hadn't expected him. I bent down and began petting him thinking of the old saying about the dangers of a black cat crossing one's path. Although I never believed in that superstition, I noticed dark clouds gathering in the sky. It looked like another heavy rain was headed our way, so I hurried down the path, the hanging moss brushing against me. Al remained on the patio regarding me with what I imagined was a warning in his yellow eyes.

The first raindrops began to fall as I made my way across the beach. It was empty today, and I assumed people had heard the forecast and were spending their Sunday indoors. I kept an eye out for my mother but didn't see her anywhere. When I got to the sign that warned about trespassers, I put the toe of my sneaker into the middle link of the fence and hoisted myself up. It was more difficult as an adult, and a pregnant one at that. I was careful to drop down lightly, so I wouldn't hit the ground on the other side too hard.

The lighthouse loomed liked a haunted house with the dark sky as a backdrop. Up close, I noticed the signs of age—the fading gray metal; the smell of decay and neglect from the untrimmed bushes that covered its base. The back door was harder to yank open, but it finally gave when I tugged.

As I stood on the threshold, peering into the darkness, I nearly changed my mind about entering. My idea about Wendy hiding out here was a good one but probably not true. Surely, Donald Marshall had considered it and checked earlier.

I nearly jumped at the sound of a low echo from within. I identified the noise as a sob. Someone was crying. The door swung shut with a creak followed by a thud. I tried to get my bearings relying on memory and an internal compass to guide me forward in the unlit chamber. The sound of thunder outside and the rain falling harder kept me on edge. I listened for the cry, but it was muffled by the storm.

I suddenly felt the walls closing in on me and began to sweat. The morning sickness I'd avoided the last few days hit me with a vengeance, and I leaned over and vomited by the stairwell. Feeling slightly better, I took a deep breath. Then I noticed a pack of crayons, paper, and a duffle bag lying against the wall behind the stairs. I heard the cry again. It was coming from above. I supported myself by grasping the right bannister and headed up the stairs. I knew there were several landings before I reached the tower, and I paused on each one to catch my breath, something I didn't need to do as a child chasing my brother. As I approached the top, I started feeling dizzy, but I kept from looking down and took more deep breaths to calm my reaction to the elevated height. The crying became louder and then I heard a voice, a young boy's voice. It sounded so much like Glen that I almost believed I'd gone back twenty years and he'd, once again, beaten me to the top of the lighthouse.

"Mother, don't cry. It will be over soon. You know I need to punish you for what you did to Ms. Wilson, and of course, Michael. They would've been happy together, but all you did was drink and try to hide your failure as a wife."

I was on the top step. Looking toward the far end of the tower, I saw my mother backed against the railing. She was covering her face with her hands so probably wasn't aware I was there. Wendy had her back to me and, although she might have heard me come up the stairs or noticed my ragged breathing, her attention was directed at my mother and the gun she pointed at her.

"Please, Wendy. I wish it had been different and that Michael cared for your mother, that my husband was in love with me, but life isn't always fair. Killing me won't make up for that."

"I'm not Wendy. I'm your son, Glen, and I won't kill you Mother unless you refuse to jump off the tower like Michael did."

"What are you saying? Do you know what really happened to Michael?" Mother had uncovered her eyes and seen me tiptoeing forward. She was playing along with Wendy, trying to stall for time, so I could disarm Wendy before she noticed I was there.

"I wish I could fill you in." Wendy's laugh was like Glen's childhood giggle. "I wasn't there that day, although Sarah and I found the body."

I urged Mother silently to keep Wendy talking. I was a few feet from her now.

"But Wendy was there, wasn't she?" Mother said. "For years, she had nightmares about it, and when she finally learned what really happened, she couldn't face it, like I couldn't face the knowledge of my husband's preference for young men. Instead of becoming addicted to alcohol, Wendy developed a second persona—you, Glen, whom she loved and tragically lost the night she discovered the truth about Michael's death."

"No," the scream that bellowed from Wendy's mouth was her own. A crash of thunder accompanied the yell, and she turned and saw me approaching. She backed away holding the gun, swinging it between me and my mother.

"Well, look who's here, Silly Sarah," Wendy said using her real voice. "And, yes, I know what happened that morning. I have the recording of my hypnotism session on Glen's phone, and I still have your cell. You won't be needing it, though."

"Why did you pretend to be Glen? Was it all part of an act?"

She pushed back one of her braids with her unarmed hand. "No, of course not. Your aunt had the right idea about inviting everyone back after all this time. Although I wasn't on the guest list, I decided to crash the party. It jogged my memory and gave me an opportunity to make amends with the past."

"You know everyone's out looking for you. It's a matter of time before Donald Marshall and others are here."

She laughed. "Give me a break, Sarah. Marshall is probably too busy screwing your aunt right now."

"Even if that's so, there's two of us against you," I said motioning my mother to my side.

"But I have the gun. Mama showed me how to use it when I was young. We lived alone for so many years that it came in handy to have protection."

"Why don't you tell us what you learned from the recording?" Mother prompted, and I was proud of how composed she sounded.

"Good idea. I'm not in a rush, and the recording actually isn't very long. Glen promised he'd erase it, but I'm glad he didn't." She reached into the pocket of her jeans with her free hand and removed two cell phones. I recognized mine as she tossed it toward me. She lay the other down on the ledge of the railing next to her and pressed a button. I winced as I heard Glen's voice through the speaker. My mother reached over and took my hand. Her eyes glistened with unshed tears as we listened to the playback.

"Relax, Wendy. Concentrate on the pointer and breathe deeply."

"I don't think this is going to work, Glen."

"Don't worry. If it doesn't, we'll try another time. Keep staring at the pointer. That's good. Now I want you to think back to when you were a young girl living with your mother at Sea Scope with me and my sister. Do you remember? Visualize it in your mind."

"I can, but I don't want to." Wendy's voice became fearful and young. She sounded the way she did at ten.

"Why not?" Glen probed gently. "What don't you want to remember?"

Wendy paused and then whispered the reply that I could barely hear above the thunder. "He raped me."

"Oh, Wendy. I'm so sorry. Was it one of the guests?"

From the Notes of Michael Gamboski

(Boston Light, Wikimedia Commons)

All lighthouses in America today are automated except Boston Light. Congress declared that this lighthouse, the oldest in the U.S., always be a staffed station making Boston Light the only official lighthouse with a keeper.

Chapter Fifty-One

Sea Scope: Twenty years ago

She heard her mother crying. It had been this way every night since the Fourth of July. Wendy would wake up late at night or early in the morning to her mother's sobs. She knew the cause of Wanda's sadness. Michael had rejected her, and he was planning to check out of the inn soon. She wished she could make her mother happy again.

As her mother's cries subsided into sniffs and then into the light snores of sleep, Wendy got out of bed. Glen wasn't the only one who liked to patrol the inn at night, but Wendy didn't snoop around the guest rooms. She slipped out the back door and into the woods behind the inn. The night air invigorated her and helped her think. It was a welcome relief from the hot day, and she felt akin to the animals and insects that were awake around her. Glen would call her "nocturnal," the scientific term for those who were active at night.

As she tramped through the woods, trying to avoid the twigs and other sharp objects that would cut her bare feet, she filled her nose and lungs with a deep breath of air. When she'd walked a bit farther, she found her special place. It was a log in a clearing where she could sit and think about life. She didn't keep a journal like Sarah, but her mind was full of her experiences. She remembered the first time she realized she didn't have a father, unlike most of the kids at school. A few of them made fun of her and called her mother a maid. They said she'd probably end up pregnant before she graduated high school, but her mother had taught her enough to stay away from boys. She didn't need to instill this lesson too deep, for Wendy saw the pain relationships caused. Even Sarah and Glen's parents, although they were still together, weren't happy. She heard them fighting often and knew Mrs. Brewster drank because her husband cheated on her.

As she sat there, thinking about how men and women could hurt one another, she heard footsteps behind her. She prepared to run from what she suspected might be a wild animal native to the South Carolina woods. But, as she stood, she saw Mr. Brewster walking toward her.

"What are you doing out here?" he asked, and she noticed his words sounded blurry, like his wife when she'd been on what Sarah called a bender.

She didn't want him to tell her mother, or she knew she'd be in big trouble. "Hello, Mr. Brewster. I wasn't feeling too well, so I came out to get some air."

"Does your mother know?"

She pursed her lips in reply because she'd be punished even more for lying.

"You know it's dangerous for a young girl to be out at night, don't you?" he asked.

She nodded.

He regarded her with a strange look. "Let me walk you back. Take my hand. It's safer that way."

She didn't understand what he meant. She was self-sufficient. She didn't need anyone to hold her hand, but she hoped if she agreed with his requests he wouldn't tell her mother. She let him take her hand, his large one covering it completely. There were hairs on back of it and even on the palm.

"That's better." He smiled. "Come with me."

"That's not the right way, Mr. Brewster."

"It's a shortcut, Wendy. You'll see."

She knew all the shortcuts in the area; but where he was leading her was deeper into the woods, not toward the inn. She went along, anyway, afraid to disagree with him.

When they came upon the small cottage that used to be where she and her mother stayed when they first came to the inn, Mr. Brewster said, "Let's stop here a minute, shall we? I'm a bit tired, and it looks like it may start raining."

It didn't feel or smell like rain to her, but she remained silent as he led her into the small house. She was surprised to see it was in such good condition. The double bed where she and her mother once slept was neatly made, and the floors had been recently swept. The inn hadn't been overbooked lately, nor had any honeymooners reserved the cottage as far as she knew.

"I come here once in a while," Mr. Brewster explained, "when I want to get away from things." She realized he was talking about his wife. "Why don't you have a seat? We can rest a minute before going back." He indicated the bed.

"Mother might be worried," she said, knowing that once Wanda fell asleep, there was no waking her for hours.

"Don't worry. We won't be here long." He staggered toward her, and she caught a whiff of whiskey on his breath. Her heart began to race as he approached.

"It's okay, sweetheart. I'm not going to bite." He smiled again. "Sit with me a minute." Her instincts told her to disobey him, to flee from the house and run back to the inn, but she did as she was told hoping he was just being friendly.

"There. Isn't that better?" He sat next to her. "You know, you're as pretty as your mom." She hated the way he was looking at her, studying her as Glen studied insects through his microscope.

"Thank you." Her voice cracked a bit.

"What's wrong? Are you afraid of me?"

"No." The word came out weak, too weak.

"Why don't we lie down a minute? I think I hear the rain. We're safe in here." He guided her down against the pillow.

"Mr. Brewster, I really should go back to Mama now."

"Shhhh." He put his rough finger to his lips as he lay down beside her.

"This won't take long and then I promise I'll take you right back."

Her heart started beating fast again. What did he want with her? Why was he looking at her that way?

"Make yourself comfortable, sweetie. No one needs to know you were out in the woods tonight."

Panic shot through her as she watched him remove his shirt, throw it to the floor and then lower the zipper of his pants. She tried to get up, but he restrained her. "Don't go anywhere. You'll enjoy this one day. Your mother does and so does Michael. Jennifer doesn't care for it much, but that's how it is when you're married."

She began to struggle as he pinned her down. She wanted to scream for help, but she knew no one would hear her this deep in the woods. As his body came down on hers, and she gagged on the alcohol on his breath, she tried to close her mind to the terror of what was happening. She knew she should never have left her mother's side.

"This is going to be our secret," he whispered as he panted. "If you tell your mother, you'll both be out in the street and she'll be forced to sell her body like she did before my sister gave her a job."

His chest covered hers and muffled her scream of pain as he entered her and the world went black.

Chapter Fifty-Two

Sea Scope: Present day

"No. It was … it was your father."

"Oh, my God!" Mother said.

Wendy turned off the recording. "That's right, Mrs. Brewster. Your husband had a fancy for little girls as well as young men. No need to listen to the rest, although there is a bit more that would interest both of you, particularly what happened to Michael. I can fill you in on that before I shoot you."

I felt the nausea rise up in me but fought to keep the bile down. I had to be strong for the sake of my mother and the baby I carried.

"Wendy, please put down the gun," Mother pleaded. "I was Martin's victim, too. Don't you see that? And, Sarah, she's innocent. She has nothing to do with any of this."

"Only that she snooped up here. I was saving the lighthouse crayon clue for last, the one that would lead her to your dead body. Now she's ruined the fun, so I might as well kill the two of you." She aimed the gun at us and cocked back the trigger.

"Wait! You promised you'd tell us about Michael." Mother still held my hand, and I could feel the sweat from our palms mingling with the rain washing over us.

For a moment, I thought Wendy would ignore the request. Her eyes were wary as if she realized we were stalling for time. The rain pounded down drenching us, but getting wet was the least of our problems.

"Alright. You deserve to know, but, after I tell you, there's no more avoiding your fates." It was so hard to believe that the vengeful woman threatening us was the shy girl with whom I'd shared part of my childhood and who'd claimed my brother's heart.

From the Notes of Michael Gamboski

(Argand Lamps, Wikimedia Commons)

Originally lighthouses were lit merely with open fires, only later progressing through candles, lanterns and electric lights. Whale oil was frequently used in lanterns as fuel.

The Argand lamp, invented in 1782 by the Swiss scientist, Aimé Argand, revolutionized lighthouse illumination with its steady smokeless flame. Early models used ground glass which was sometimes tinted around the wick.

Chapter Fifty-Three

Sea Scope: Twenty years ago

After her mother left, Wendy sat at the desk she'd occupied every Saturday since vacation Bible school began in June. The classroom was in her elementary school. There were ten children attending religious lessons with her. She recognized a few from her fifth-grade class last year, but no one ever spoke to her. She wished Glen and Sarah went to Bible school so at least she'd have someone to talk to.

Miss Taylor was already at the front of the room which meant Wendy had made it in time for the class to start. The teacher reminded her a bit of her mother. She was probably around the same age and had a lovely voice. On Sundays, she sang in the choir at their church.

"Good morning, children. Please take out your Bibles. Today's lesson is about sin and the value of telling the truth when we've done a wrong."

Wendy took the pocket-sized Bible from the drawer under her desk where Dottie sat on the edge and placed the book in front of her. Miss Taylor didn't mind that she kept the doll there, although she wasn't allowed to in regular school. Wendy was teased occasionally by the kids for still having a doll at ten years old.

As Miss Taylor began the lesson, Wendy became fidgety. She didn't want to hear the Bible stories about sin and truth. She'd lied about going out in the woods last week and had paid for it dearly. She hadn't told her mother what happened nor the terrible dreams she'd started to have since the incident. She avoided Mr. Brewster whenever he entered a room. Instead of leaving, she looked away, so he couldn't give her a false smile. Once, she ran into him in the hall, and he'd whispered to her, "You haven't said anything to your mother, have you?" Fear would rise in her stomach, but she'd gulp it down and shake her head. "Good girl," he replied, "that's our little secret. My sister would be quite upset to lose her best housekeeper."

Wendy tried to keep her attention on Miss Taylor, but she couldn't. There was no air conditioning in the school and it was already close to ninety degrees that morning. She began to feel the hot air in the small room close in on her and knew she had to escape. She raised her hand and asked to be excused to the bathroom. Out in the quiet hall, she took a deep breath and, instead of entering the girl's room, she slipped out the back door and gulped in the muggy air. She decided a short walk would help. There was still more than a half hour left to the class, and her mother said she might be late picking her up. Wendy could even make it to the lighthouse and back before the class ended. If Miss Taylor asked why she'd been away so long, Wendy could say she had a stomach ache.

Holding Dottie, she skipped across the field toward the beach. The farther she went, the freer she felt. She didn't know exactly what drew her to the lighthouse. Her steps led her there. She spent a few minutes down by the water where it was cooler. Looking out at the calm waves, she felt the stress of the last week ease away. She was going to be okay. Her life had changed dramatically, but she was strong like her mother. She promised herself she'd forget about what happened, lock it away in her mind, and pretend to be the innocent and happy girl she used to be.

Feeling confident in her decision, she was about to make her way back to school when she heard a scream and a loud noise as if something heavy hit the ground. Then she saw a figure emerge from the lighthouse. When she realized who it was, she hid herself behind a bush and waited until the person was gone in the direction of the inn.

She then raced away but stopped when she saw Michael's body on the ground below the lighthouse, his broken eyeglasses lying a few feet next to him. She considered going to get help, but she wasn't supposed to be away from school, and she knew no one could survive a fall from the tower's height.

It was only when she was back in her seat in the classroom that she realized she'd dropped Dottie.

Chapter Fifty-Four

Sea Scope: Present day

"Is that how you lost your doll?" I asked, hoping the question would slow Wendy down and give us more time to plan an escape. When she didn't answer, I said, "My friend, Carolyn found Dottie under a log when she, Russell, and I were out by the lighthouse recently. I have her in the glove box of my car. I can give her to you if you'd like." Maybe, if I spoke kindly to her, she'd reconsider killing us.

A boom of thunder signaled another wave of rain. My mother and I jumped back as it assaulted us, but Wendy stood there taking the onslaught. "What do I want with a doll now? Your father took my childhood away from me. He ruined my marriage. When I finally found a man who understood my fears, he took him away, too."

"Glen had an accident, Wendy. It wasn't anyone's fault."

"He was drinking. Aunt Julie told me she saw the bottles by the bed when she went up to talk to him. If only I'd stayed with him that night, but I couldn't face him after he'd heard what his father had done to me."

I'd thrown her off track which was good. I wiped the water from my eyes and moved closer to my mother. Maybe the two of us could jump her, but there was a chance the gun would go off and hit one of us. Our best bet was to keep her talking and pray someone would come to our rescue.

"Stay where you are." Wendy noticed we'd moved together closer to her. "I'm going to finish the story now, and I don't want any further interruptions. I'm not answering any questions. If either of you open your mouth, I'll shoot the other."

Mother gripped my hand like a lifeline. We were dripping wet, our hair flattened against our faces.

Wendy smiled, and I felt nausea build up in my stomach again, but I fought the impulse to retch. "You want to know who killed Michael? I think it's obvious. He even left a suicide note, didn't he?" She looked at my mother who'd let out a gasp. "I forgot you can't answer me. You didn't show it to anyone, did you? I suppose you wonder how I know about it? You can nod your head if you want."

Mother nodded, and I could see the fear building up in her. There was no bottle for her to grab up here, only my hand, and her grip became so fierce I was afraid she'd break it.

"I heard you tell the story at dinner. I was at the house that night but not hiding in one of the rooms that Donald Marshall checked. I dropped by to see what the topic of conversation would be and if it would include me. Anyway, I didn't stay for dessert. I went back to the lighthouse. Sarah," She turned to me. "did you happen to see the paper and crayons with my backpack downstairs? Sorry, don't answer. I'm almost done with my story. After the villain is uncovered, it's rather quick to the end, isn't it?"

While Wendy was rambling, I caught sight of something I could use as a weapon. It was folded up against the wall next to me. At first, I didn't realize what it was, but then it came to me. It was the tripod camera stand Wanda gave Michael all those years ago for his birthday. I let my mother's hand drop. In one motion, I grabbed the end of the tripod and ran toward Wendy fearing for my baby's life if my movement triggered a shot but knowing I had no choice. As I rammed into her, Wendy dropped the gun. It slid toward my mother who picked it up.

"No!" Wendy screamed as the tip of the tripod hit her arm. I heard a crack. It was either bone or the lightning that illuminated our struggle. We both went down, rolling across the slick floor.

"I have the gun!" Mother screamed above us.

Wendy kicked and scratched me. I barely avoided a kick in the stomach, but her long nails dug into my arms. I yelled in pain as my blood mingled with the rainwater.

"Let go of Sarah or I'll shoot," Mother commanded. I didn't think Wendy heard her. It felt like she was battling me to the death. Was she thinking of my father and how she hadn't been able to protect herself all those years ago?

It was obvious I was losing. Wendy was so quick I found it hard to get in even the lightest punches. I finally managed to grab hold of the end of her braid and yanked. She responded with a yowl and rolled off me. Mother had her in clear aim, but her hand shook around the gun. I knew she'd never fired one before.

I got to my feet and ran to her. "It's alright, Mom. We have her now."

"Sarah, are you okay?" I wondered if I looked as badly injured as I felt.

"Shoot me," Wendy dared standing up against the railing and facing us. "Go ahead. Shoot me or I'll jump. My life isn't worth anything anymore."

Mother lowered the gun. "Yes, it is, Wendy. Think of your mother. She loves you. There are people who can help you."

"Like Glen?" She started to cry. "I don't need to be hypnotized again. I remember it all. Every awful detail."

"There are other therapies. Other doctors." Mother was trying to reason with her, but I knew she wasn't listening.

As Wendy turned her back to us, I heard voices below shouting above the storm. "I think someone's upstairs. There are clothes and crayons over here." It was Derek. Relief flooded through me.

"We should've looked here earlier," Donald replied.

Wendy heard them, too, and it hastened her decision. "Tell Mama I loved her, and I'm sorry for all the lies."

Wendy was poised against the railing about to jump as Derek and Donald appeared at the top of the stairway.

There was a shot. I wasn't sure from where it came, but it hit Wendy in the leg and she fell backward screaming with pain and surprise.

Mother stood with the gun pointing downward. "I had to save her," she said. "I couldn't save Michael."

From the Notes of Michael Gamboski

(Nantucket Station, Wikimedia Commons)

Lightships were employed where the water was too deep to construct a lighthouse or it was impractical. The first lightships were located in the lower Chesapeake Bay (1820) and the most stations were in 1915 when there were 72 lightships manning 55 stations. The extra ships were used for relief. Lightships displayed lights at the tops of their mast(s) and in foggy areas sounded a bell or other fog signal such as a whistle, siren or horn. In 1921, lightships began being equipped with radio beacons. The last lightship was removed from the Nantucket Station in 1984.

Chapter Fifty-Five

Sea Scope: Twenty years ago

Jennifer dragged herself out of bed. Even though her body ached from the heavy crying she'd done the night before, she felt amazingly light, as if a weight had been lifted off her. It was over. The years of hiding, protecting Glen and Sarah, drowning herself in self-pity were gone. She showered and dressed quickly. She hoped she hadn't missed Michael. She wanted to say goodbye to him. He was the reason for her new freedom.

Breakfast was almost over by the time she arrived. Julie was at the sink doing dishes. She wondered where Wanda was and then remembered the housekeeper must've taken her daughter to Bible school.

"Good morning, Julie. Is everyone gone? Did Michael leave already?"

"Hi, Jennifer." Her sister-in-law looked surprised to see her. She normally didn't make it down to breakfast on weekends. "There's still hot food and coffee on if you'd like. Michael left about a half hour ago. Glen and Sarah went back to Glen's room. I think Glen wanted to show Sarah a new science experiment. They mentioned wanting to go to the beach later. Wanda and Wendy should be back from Bible school soon. I'm going up to paint in the studio now."

"I'm not that hungry. I'll take a glass of orange juice out to the patio. I'm sorry I missed Michael. I didn't have a chance to say goodbye to him."

Jennifer went out on the porch with her juice. Before she could sit down to drink it, she saw Michael and Martin talking by Michael's old blue Dodge and strained her good ear to hear what they were saying. She left her drink and quietly walked toward the parking lot where she waited behind an oak, listening before she made her appearance.

"Thanks for helping me load my car, Martin. I'm heading up to the lighthouse to check if I left anything there. I think my tripod might be up in the tower."

"Can I come along and give you a hand?"

"I don't want to drag this out, Martin. I already told you it's over. I'm going back to my parents and then the university. If I were you, I would patch things up with your wife. Your kids are growing up fast. They're bright and sweet."

"I love my kids, but my leaving might be the best thing that could happen to them. Let me come with you to the lighthouse."

Jennifer had to suppress her laugh at his pleading tone. She agreed that Martin's going would benefit them all, but now it looked like Michael was turning Martin down. She hated the part of her that felt happy to hear this news. She decided to follow them to the lighthouse to see what would transpire there.

Jennifer watched Martin and Michael enter the lighthouse. Michael used his key to open the door, and she assumed he wouldn't lock it behind him. Since they were headed for the tower, she realized she couldn't wait outside. She gave them a few minutes to walk up the stairs and then made her way inside. She didn't visit the lighthouse often. She recalled with a jolt to her heart the first time she'd been there with Martin when he first brought her to Sea Scope. He'd led her upstairs where they'd looked out over the town. She was able to see the inn to the south and the beach to the east. As they gazed below, he'd put his arm around her. She'd turned to him, and they'd kissed.

If only she knew the changes in him that were about to occur. If only he'd moved with her to Long Island in their own home away from bell boys, housekeepers, and young male guests of questionable sexual orientation. She closed her eyes to listen, but the men were speaking too low. She climbed higher pausing at each landing, quiet on her padded moccasins.

When she was on the final landing, she began to hear their words.

"Michael, are you sure about this? I have money saved. I'm planning to make a new life. I'd like you in it."

"I gave you my answer, Marty. Please accept it, so we can remain friends. I never wanted to disrupt your family."

Martin gave a wry laugh. "My family was disrupted way before we met. You don't know what it's like having an alcoholic for a wife."

"I imagine that's hard but having an adulterer for a husband must be worse. Did you ever wonder what caused Jennifer's addiction?"

"I guess it's better to be single, carefree, and gay. How many other older guys have you lured away from their wives?" She recognized the angry tone in Martin's voice and was now able to hear the conversation without straining.

"Don't blame it on me, sir. I heard about the bell boy before me, and what of Wanda and her little daughter?"

"How do you know about that?"

"I'm not blind. I see how the girl avoids you. You could get in deep trouble for that, you know. At least Bud and I were over eighteen."

"Stop!"

"What's wrong? Hit a nerve. Let me go, Marty. I'll stay quiet. I wouldn't want my family to know either. I'm not out of the closet yet."

There was silence and then Martin replied in a more controlled voice. "Okay. Can I have one last kiss?"

Jennifer imagined them locking lips, Martin's tongue probing Michael's mouth. She almost gagged on the image. But then she heard Michael say something that alarmed her. "Martin, what are you doing? Where did you get that gun? Please put it down."

"You son of a bitch," Martin exclaimed. "You think I can let you go that easily. I already confronted Jennifer. I was prepared to break the news to Julie. I couldn't wait to get out of her life. That cold and calculating whore sister of mine. Just because Dad fucked her, she blames me for not coming to her aid. I don't owe her anything. She can have the damn inn as payment for her damage, and you can go to hell. Jump, or I'll shoot you."

"No, Martin, please don't."

Jennifer couldn't listen anymore. She was so afraid of hearing a shot. Instead, she heard only a scream. What had Martin done? She quickly but noiselessly descended the stairs. As she reached the bottom, she hid behind a pillar and watched her husband run down the stairs huffing, his face red. After he left the lighthouse, she went back upstairs to see if Michael was injured. She hoped Martin wouldn't return, but through the porthole-shaped window, she saw him race across the lawn back to the inn.

When she got to the tower, she was surprised to see it empty. Where was Michael? He couldn't have gotten downstairs without her seeing him, especially if he was hurt. The scream she'd heard had been intense.

A terrible fear gripped her as she considered another possibility. She approached the guardrail and peered down. "Oh, my God!" she exclaimed seeing the broken body lying below. She took a breath to steady herself. She wished for the first time that she'd woken up with a drink of her morning scotch. What should she do? She stood there a few minutes considering her options. Because she was sober, she realized if she called the police, it wouldn't look good for her. She'd agreed to a divorce from Martin the night before. Even though no one knew yet, she was sure people were aware of what was going on between her husband and the inn's young male guest. If not, then they would still believe Martin over her. He was the charming host with the phony smile. She was the alcoholic wife with whom he was burdened. A part of her still loved him and that's what hurt the most.

While these thoughts ran through her mind, she caught sight of someone crossing the field in the opposite direction of the inn. From this distance, she couldn't tell for sure who it was, but it looked a bit like Wendy Wilson. She knew that couldn't be because Wendy was in Bible school. She waited a few more minutes and then went downstairs. She decided to return to the inn and have a few drinks before she told anyone anything.

Chapter Fifty-Six

Sea Scope: Present day

The paramedics who arrived on the scene after Donald called them from his cell had no easy task transporting Wendy to the hospital. Even though the bullet had grazed her leg, she still needed medical attention, but more importantly, psychiatric treatment. They had to sedate her to get her on the gurney. Then they had to carry her down the winding lighthouse stairs. Donald contacted Wanda and gave her the information about the hospital where they were taking her daughter. He told her he'd meet her there to fill her in on what happened.

Derek wanted me to go to the hospital, too, but a paramedic had checked my arm and said it didn't need stitches. He'd applied antibiotic and wrapped my wounds while Derek looked on, a worried expression on his face. When I assured him I was fine, he helped me down the stairs. My mother followed behind. The rain had finally subsided, and a bit of sun shone through the clouds.

The moments after Derek and Donald arrived were a bit of a blur to me. I remembered Donald making calls to the EMTs, Wanda, and Aunt Julie. He also said he had to call the Gamboskis to finally set their minds at peace about their son. I recalled Derek's arms around me, and his voice nervous with concern asking if I was hurt. I even remembered my mother handing the gun to Donald, but the scenes were hazy in my mind. Nothing was clear until I was back at the inn with Derek at my side. Wrapped in Aunt Julie's afghan and wearing dry clothes, I held a cup of steaming tea in my hand. I realized that even in ninety-degree temperatures, soaking rainwater could chill you. Mother had also changed her clothes and sat next to Aunt Julie on the couch across from Derek and me.

Carolyn and Russell were at the inn with Aunt Julie when we returned. They already knew most of what happened, and Carolyn hugged me with an apology that she wasn't around to help. She and Russell had spent the morning at his house collaborating on a book that she was hopeful they'd publish together. It would be her first venture into adult fiction writing. She was thinking of moving to South Carolina after she settled things at home. I knew she was referring to Jack and her contract with our publisher. Even though I was sorry it meant we might not be working together anymore, I was happy for her. I was also happy for Russell. You never forget the boy who gave you your first kiss, and even after you move on to other relationships, there's still a special memory and a place in your heart for that first love.

"Are you sure you wouldn't be more comfortable in bed?" Aunt Julie asked as I sipped my tea. "You've had such a fright, Sarah. You should rest." Although I hadn't yet told her, I had my suspicions she knew about the baby.

"I'm okay, Aunt Julie. Thank you."

She smiled and turned to my mother. "What about you, Jennifer?"

"I'm fine as well, but I have a favor to ask."

"Of course. What do you need?"

"Please remove all the bottles from my room. I'm going to enter an AA program again and this time, I'm sticking with it. I also have one more request."

Aunt Julie raised her eyebrows in question. I was happy to hear my mother sounding so confident and wondered what else she had in mind.

"If you'll have me, I'd like to help you reopen Sea Scope this fall. I'm not sure Wanda will return, and I know you'll need someone to assist you. Although this place doesn't hold the best memories for me, I think I'd like to make new ones here."

A light appeared in Aunt Julie's eyes. "I was actually hoping Sarah would consider moving back here to manage the place with me, but I know she has other commitments. I think this would work much better, Jen. I would love to have you. We share some bad memories, but maybe we can turn them into something positive. I've managed to eradicate some of mine with my painting, and I'd like to start showing the portraits in galleries again. Maybe you can find a creative outlet, too. I also hope that Donald and I can have a future. It's taken me many years to learn to fully trust a man who is nothing like my father or brother."

Derek spoke then. "If you're up to it, Sarah, the rain's stopped. Can we take a walk? I still want to tell you the things I came here to discuss."

My heart beat faster. I'd begun to feel hopeful that Derek and I could make a new start, but now I wasn't sure. His concern for me might've been a temporary reaction to the traumatic circumstances. Now that he knew I was safe, it might be easier for him to break the news to me about wanting a divorce.

I took a breath and got up. I could put off the walk and say I was too tired, but I knew I had to face the truth eventually. "I'm ready," I said. "Let's go."

There were still a few puddles in the path through the trees heavy with hanging moss. Occasionally a few drops spattered off the leaves on to us as we passed, but they felt good, refreshing in the afternoon heat.

"So, what did you want to say, Derek?" I asked, my heart still pounding.

"Sarah, I know you've been through a lot. I'm sorry about all that happened. I'm even sorrier that I didn't get here sooner or go with you in the first place."

"You had your classes," I reminded him, taking a breath of the scented air. Honeysuckle mixed with wet moss.

"I could've cancelled them or assigned them to somebody else sooner. I was selfish. I knew we were drifting apart, and I did nothing to pull us back together." He stopped and turned to me. I could see the sadness in his eyes. "I want a family as much as you do. That's what I came back to tell you. I'm willing to go through with any treatments you want to try. I want to make you happy. I love you so much."

I was still in shock from his words as he bent down to kiss me. I tried not to think about the woman who'd answered our phone, but I knew I wouldn't be able to rest until I knew the truth.

"Does that mean your affair is over?" I asked as I pulled away.

"Affair? What do you mean, Sarah?"

I faced him, my heart hammering in my chest. "I called you from the road one morning when Carolyn and I were on the way to Sea Scope. A young woman answered the house phone."

I watched the expression on his face change. I was expecting to see guilt. Instead, awareness dawned on him. "Oh, Sarah. I'm so sorry. I didn't tell you. You may not remember my niece Lainey. You met her years ago when she was a kid. She's been at college upstate and decided to come home for the summer. She and my brother Paul dropped by unexpectedly. They didn't know you were away. Lainey had questions for me about the thesis she's working on, and Paul thought I could be of help. While I was showing Paul your wonderful sketches up in the garret, Lainey took it upon herself to make us breakfast in the kitchen. I didn't hear the phone ring, and she didn't mention picking it up. I guess she assumed it was a wrong number. She should've told me, especially since I was worried about you on the road."

I couldn't believe how stupid I'd been. "Derek, I'm the one who should be sorry for not trusting you. All this time I imagined you were coming to see me to ask for a divorce."

"Silly Sarah," he said. "Don't you know how much you mean to me?"

As we kissed under the oak trees, I could only imagine how surprised and happy Derek would be when it was my turn to tell him what I had to say.

-The End-

Acknowledgements

I want to thank fellow Creativia author James J. Cudney, IV, for sharing information about his publisher with me and Miika Hannila for accepting my manuscript for *Sea Scope* and offering me a publishing contract for it.

I'd also like to thank Colleen O'Felein for helping me edit the prologue for this book, and beta readers Judy Ratto, Cherrie Forrest, and Christopher Merlino for their suggestions on improving the manuscript. Judy Ratto, author of the excellent Lucas Holt mystery series and a fellow cat lover, gave great feedback about *Sea Scope* and the cat character, Al, who was originally named Alabaster but who reads better with a shortened moniker. Erin L. George, MA MFT, family systemic therapist writing under Erin Lee, USA Today bestselling author, helped with my research of mental conditions and how they manifest.

Jeff Gales, of the U.S. Lighthouse Society (www.uslhs.org) and Megan Stegmeir, Interpretive Park Ranger at Hunting Island State Park in South Carolina, provided important information for the book's research, and I'm grateful to both of them for their assistance with this project.

My thanks also to Ed Escoffier, my co-worker and fellow librarian, who suggested South Carolina as the setting for my novel.

Lastly, I want to thank the readers who purchase this book and those who have enjoyed my Cobble Cove cozy mysteries and other novels. I appreciate all reviews, feedback, and comments. I hope my words have meaning for you and that you find entertainment, education, and some surprises in my books.

About the Author

Debbie De Louise is an award-winning author and a reference librarian at a public library on Long Island. She is a member of Sisters-in-Crime, International Thriller Writers, the Long Island Authors Group, and the Cat Writer's Association. She has a BA in English and an MLS in Library Science from Long Island University. Her novels include the four books of the Cobble Cove cozy mystery series: *A Stone's Throw*, *Between a Rock and a Hard Place*, *Written in Stone*, and *Love on the Rocks*. Debbie has also written a romantic comedy novella, *When Jack Trumps Ace*, a paranormal romance, *Cloudy Rainbow*, and the standalone mystery, *Reason to Die*. She lives on Long Island with her husband, Anthony; daughter, Holly; and three cats, Stripey, Harry, and Hermione.

You can connect with Debbie on the following sites:

Facebook: https://www.facebook.com/debbie.delouise.author/
Twitter: https://twitter.com/Deblibrarian
Goodreads:
https://www.goodreads.com/author/show/
2750133.Debbie_De_Louise
Amazon Author Page: http://amzn.to/2bIHdaQ
Bookbub: https://www.bookbub.com/profile/debbie-de-louise
Website/Blog/Newsletter Sign-Up: https://debbiedelouise.com/

Printed in Great Britain
by Amazon

49346130R00166